Rhea set down her mug. "So roll up your sleeve."

"Actually, I was thinking of the Midgard Serpent."

Rhea laughed nervously. "Right. Because that wasn't at all awkward the last time."

"I wasn't present the last time," he reminded her. "At least not mentally. And you said you could focus on an event from the past."

She looked suspicious. "Why does it have to be the serpent?"

"Because the question I want answered— Do I tell you beforehand?"

"It's not a parlor trick, so, yeah, that information would be useful."

"Right. Sorry. I want to find out exactly when and where I got the tattoo."

"And you don't want to know where you got the others?"

Leo gave her an apologetic smile. "Not from you."

Jane Kindred is the author of the Demons of Elysium series of M/M erotic fantasy romance, the Looking Glass Gods dark fantasy tetralogy and the gothic paranormal romance *The Lost Coast*. Jane spent her formative years ruining her eyes reading romance novels in the Tucson sun and watching *Star Trek* marathons in the dark. She now writes to the sound of San Francisco foghorns while two cats slowly but surely edge her off the side of the bed.

Books by Jane Kindred

Harlequin Nocturne

Sisters in Sin

Waking the Serpent
Bewitching the Dragon
The Dragon's Hunt

THE DRAGON'S HUNT

JANE KINDRED

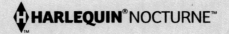

Recycling programs
for this product may
not exist in your area.

ISBN-13: 978-0-373-14054-1

The Dragon's Hunt

Copyright © 2017 by Jane Kindred

HARLEQUIN®
www.Harlequin.com

Printed in U.S.A.

Dear Reader,

Ever since reading C. S. Lewis's *The Silver Chair* at age seven, I've had a soft spot for enchanted princes—especially enchanted princes tied up in chairs. Not that I quite understood why that particular concept interested me at age seven. But I digress.

Now, my hero in *The Dragon's Hunt* isn't exactly a prince. But what could possibly be better than an enchanted prince tied up in a chair? Why, an enchanted thousand-year-old Viking chieftain tied up in a chair, of course.

Like the prince in *The Silver Chair*, Leo Ström is only aware of his true self during those brief hours when he's bound. But he happens to be bound in the chair of tattoo artist Rhea Carlisle, who has the ability to read the tapestry of fate through the ink on his skin. The ink can't tell her whether Leo bound or unbound—or leading the Wild Hunt as a disembodied soul—is the true Leo Ström. But that doesn't mean she can't have fun trying to find out.

Wishing you unexpected magic,

Jane Kindred

Prologue

Blood ran into his eyes as he struggled to his feet. The groans of the maimed and the dying around him were eclipsed by the battle cries of his comrades who remained, and by the crack of iron against leather and wood—and against flesh and bone. They never should have followed their enemy into the woods. They'd been set upon by forces they couldn't count, swarming out from behind every tree and every rock like a band of brigands, surrounding them with no room to maneuver, no way to stand in shield formation. It quickly became every man for himself.

Through the blood and mud caking his vision, he caught sight of the sudden arc of a battle-axe swinging down on him from his left. He'd lost his shield, and he turned and parried with his sword, but he'd taken a fierce blow to his sword arm from the last man he'd killed, and he stumbled back under the force, pain radiating like fire through his arm to the shoulder. The next swing from his opponent's axe he couldn't evade, and the blade caught him under the ribs, hooking in the links of his hauberk. He prayed to the Allfather as he went down that he might take one more enemy with him as he died. Let him die an honorable death. The axe descended, and he summoned all his strength, thrusting his sword to meet the bastard's gut as his enemy fell on him.

The blade should have split his skull. He thought he'd felt the blow. But he was blind as a newborn kitten in the muck and mud. And then he realized he must have gone deaf as well. Silence fell over him like an oncoming bank of fog, muting the clangs and cries, engulfing him in an utter lack of sensation. Perhaps he'd died. But this was no Valhalla. This was...nothing. Had Odin not chosen him after all? Could this be Fólkvangr, the field of the slain in Freyja's domain? Or was he in cold and empty Helheim? Surely he'd not been consigned to the Shore of Corpses. He was no oath-breaker; and murder—it didn't count in war.

A hand, cool and feminine, touched his forehead. Perhaps this was only the in-between place where warriors waited for the Valkyries to come for them. He tried to clasp the hand but found he couldn't make his limbs work. A cool kiss now brushed his forehead.

"Beautiful one." The whisper at his ear was a soothing breeze, quieting the fire in his veins with the beauty of its cadence. "You shall not die."

Was he to go back out to the battle? He must be in the tent being tended by his father's slave girl. He'd lost consciousness.

"Did I kill him?" His voice came out in not much more of a whisper than his benefactor's, though much rougher. His throat still felt the fire that had eased from the rest of him. A fever, no doubt, had taken him. He'd lain delirious and was only now coming around. Yes, this made sense. "Did I send my foe to Hel?"

"You were victorious. And I have claimed you."

Before he could ask her to repeat the odd phrase, a searing pain encircled his heart, not fire this time, but the burn of ice, accompanied by the sensation of pins and needles in the flesh of his forearms. He could neither move nor speak, and the pain was becoming intense.

"Hush, beautiful one. Now they cannot have you."

"They?" He managed to croak out the single word, though his tongue felt like wool batting.

Soft lips breathed against his. "That Which Became, That Which is Happening, That Which Must Become."

Chapter 1

Summoning a demon probably wasn't the smartest thing Rhea Carlisle had ever done. But the Carlisle sisters weren't exactly known for doing the smart thing. Phoebe let dead people step into her, and Ione had picked up a dude in a bar and boinked him until he turned into a dragon, so, really, anything Rhea did after that was fair game.

Technically, though, it wasn't her fault. The ink was to blame.

Rhea had picked it up at a body art convention in Flagstaff from a guy who sold his own custom blends—pigments supposedly mixed with the ash of Mount Eyjafjallajökull and consecrated under the full moon. All that mattered to her was the exceptionally rich color. It was the perfect deep poppy red with just the slightest whisper of blue. It made her think of a dark chocolate cherry cordial spilling open. Or pools of fresh blood. Maybe pools of blood oozing out of a dark chocolate cherry cordial. It was just the thing to fill in the crescent moon and descending cross she'd outlined on her calf—a symbol representing the "Black Moon Lilith," the geometric position of the moon at the apogee of its elliptical orbit.

It was Rhea's way of claiming her heritage as a descendent of the goddess. Demoness. Whatever. Whether a real "Lilith" had ever existed, Rhea's great-great-great-grand-whatever, Madeleine Marchant, had believed she was her direct descendent. It had been enough to get Madeleine kicked out of her coven in fifteenth-century France and burned at the stake. It seemed the decent thing to do to claim Madeleine's blood. Not to mention defiant. Ione was a high priestess in that same coven today, which made things a little awkward for everyone involved.

Before she'd even finished inking the tattoo, Rhea felt the tremors of a vision moving in the pigment. Reading the ink was her gift—she'd dubbed it "pictomancy"—and one that had been growing with her skill as a tattoo artist, but the visions were becoming increasingly intrusive, and she'd been actively trying to avoid them. They came now without conscious effort, giving her glimpses into minds she'd rather not have access to. But she hadn't yet been able to read a tattoo on her own skin. Maybe this was her opportunity to get some answers about her own fate for once. She smoothed her thumb along the edge of the fresh pigment and concentrated on what she wanted to know: *What does my future hold? Will my business be a success?*

The room around her winked out, replaced with the image of a snow-covered hill and a frigid sky blazing with stars.

Rhea leaped to her feet as thunder rumbled over the hill, a froth of dark snow clouds swiftly gathering as though in time-lapse. From within them, what could only be a Viking horde emerged on horseback, wolflike hounds howling as they charged through a bank of snow that billowed and roiled like an ocean of thunderheads beneath the horses' hooves. The leader of the hunt, ruddy-blond hair wild about his head, and eyes the pale, bleached cornflower blue of the Sedona winter sky, was close enough to touch as the horses rumbled right through Rhea like spectral apparitions. Or maybe she was the apparition.

Either way, the hunters vanished as swiftly as they'd come, leaving her standing in the living room of her one-bedroom apartment—with the fully solid figure of a demon. At least, she thought it must be a demon. Standing on its hind legs, the creature was the size of a human with the appearance of a fox, green eyes fixed on Rhea. It was a weirdly attractive fox, red fur flowing down its back in feminine waves, piercing eyes rimmed in black that rose to a charming point at the outside corners, putting Rhea's cosmetic attempts at the effect to shame.

"Why have you summoned me?"

She hadn't expected the fox to speak. Which, given that it was standing on its hind legs in her living room giving her its foxy resting bitch face, seemed a little obvious now that she thought about it. The voice was decidedly female.

"I didn't. Summon you. At least, I wasn't aware I was summoning…anyone."

"But you're a sorceress."

Rhea laughed. "Sorceress? You've got the wrong sister. I'm just a college graduate with a useless degree and a crap-ton of student loan debt trying to make a living as a tattoo artist."

The fox narrowed her eyes and gave Rhea an up-and-down look, taking in the slightly overgrown shock of unnaturally blond hair streaked with rainbow pastel hues, the oversize flannel shirt, and Rhea's bare legs. Because who didn't tattoo herself in her underwear?

Being made to feel self-conscious made her testy. "Just who are you, if you don't mind me asking?"

One tuft of russet fur rose over an outlined eye. "I am Vixen, the Guardian of the Hunt. You have spilled blood upon the pristine snowbanks and summoned me."

"Well, I didn't mean to summon you. I was just inking a tattoo." Rhea pointed her toes and indicated the crescent moon on her left calf still seeping blood in little dots against the fresh ink. "I guess that's the blood you meant? But I don't know anything about pristine snowbanks or hunts. I think there's been some kind of mix-up."

Vixen looked offended and crossed her downy little paws in front of her chest. "There is no mix-up. I come when I am summoned. Whom do you wish to have hunted?"

"Hunted? This is getting a little out of hand. I don't want anyone hunted."

Vixen was looking decidedly more human as she observed Rhea with a slightly suspicious—and more than slightly irritated—expression. "If you did not summon me, how were you privy to the Hunt?"

"What hunt are you even talking about?"

"That which rides in Odin's name to claim the souls of murderers, adulterers and oath-breakers. Odin's Hunt. The Wild Hunt."

"The Wild...?" Rhea felt light-headed. Maybe she was hallucinating from low blood sugar. "Okay, I'm done with this. This isn't happening. You're not real. Go away." She headed into the kitchen. There was orange juice in the fridge. Rhea grabbed it and drank straight from the carton.

When she set the empty carton down, Vixen was gone. Maybe it was time to wrap this up for the night. She'd finished the fill on the calf piece, anyway; she could do the shading another time. And maybe it was time to quit this pictomancy crap once and for all. Rhea cleaned up and bandaged the tattoo before putting her kit away and heading off to bed.

The peculiar incident continued to nag at her as she tried to fall asleep. It *had* been her imagination, hadn't it? The whole thing was probably the result of the blood sugar drop. She always told her clients to be careful to eat something before she worked on them, and she'd ignored her own advice. It made more sense than having conjured some kind of vulpine Guardian of the Hunt with her own blood. And why a fox, anyway? As a symbol, those were always trouble. Maybe Theia would know.

Her hand was on her phone on the nightstand, ready to dial her twin out of habit, when she remembered. She wasn't speaking to Theia. They hadn't talked since Theia had revealed the bombshell she'd been withholding about their father's infidelity and his double life with a second family. How could Theia have kept that from her? They'd never had secrets from each other. Even when Rhea had gone off to college at Arizona State in Tempe, and Theia had gone in the opposite direction to Northern Arizona University, it was always "Rhe" and "Thei" against the world. Until now.

Rhea turned and punched her pillow a few times—fluffing it and getting out her frustrations at the same time—before giving up. She sat up and thumbed through her social media news feed, trying to quiet her mind, unabashedly cyberstalking her own twin sister to see what she was up to. Nothing much, it turned out. In the past week, she'd posted a couple of kitten memes, reposted some inspirational platitudes, and posted a status update consisting of a picture of the Flagstaff sunset over the snow-covered San Francisco Peaks from her back deck, with the caption, "Snowbowl is open. It's officially assclown season at NAU."

By the following morning, Rhea was convinced it had been a dream after all, and by noon, she'd forgotten all about the talking fox in her living room. But the images of the Hunt itself still lingered. She sketched out a quick drawing of the riders before heading into Sedona for the day.

She'd spent her whole life in the town that was part pro-

vincial charm, part metaphysical tourist trap—with a dash
of Western mystique thrown in for good measure—but now
she was a commuter.

The first half of the drive was dusty high desert dotted
with snakeweed and desert broom and scrubby piñon pines
until the bluish-gray shades and shadows in the distance
differentiated into striations of burnt orange and creamy
café au lait and succulent green. But from the moment the
pale sandstone dome of Thunder Mountain came fully into
view amid the red cliffs and mesas, it was like driving into
a secret world. Being away at college had given her a new
appreciation for its visual magic.

Although she'd forgotten just how crazy Uptown could
get at Christmastime. Just south of the strip where she'd
rented her shop, the Tlaquepaque Arts & Crafts Village was
in the grips of a full-on holiday orgy of decorated trees—
and decorated saguaros—complete with strolling midday
carolers in Dickensian garb.

The galleries would be stunning at night with the glow
of the six thousand luminarias now lining the walkways
and walls. Rhea allowed herself a quick drive around the
circle to admire the artful kitsch before heading back up
the hill to deal with the mundane aspects of starting a business. Pretty much all she'd done so far was hang the sign
out front, and there were barely two weeks before her official opening.

In between setting up her accounting software, filling
out DBA forms and scrubbing graffiti off the stairwell,
she couldn't help returning obsessively to the drawing of
the Wild Hunt. In the back of her mind, she knew this was
classic avoidance—a habit that had plagued her all through
school—but the central figure in particular was compelling,
as if he demanded to be drawn. She labored over the details of the wild hair and leather armor, trying to remember

whether it had been trimmed with fur or whether the fur had been underneath—

"I have to say, I did *not* expect to see someone like you sitting behind the counter."

Rhea jumped at the warm, rough-edged voice and glanced up, surprised by the intrusion and trying not to show her irritation at having been dragged out of the mental world of the drawing. She hadn't even heard the bell on the door. She opened her mouth to say she wasn't open yet, but the scruffy, muscle-bound dudebro didn't give her a chance.

"Is this your side project?" A pair of bespectacled blue eyes twinkled at her beneath a somewhat careless mop of blond hair with a hint of strawberry in a face framed by stubble with a more decidedly red hue. Something about those eyes gave her a little shock. A warning premonition? Déjà vu? His smile was amused, one well-developed arm in a snug, black Henley resting on the counter as he leaned against it. She realized she was staring.

"I beg your pardon?"

The smile faded. "Ouch." He straightened and scrubbed his fingers absently over his scalp in the hair at his crown, making it clear how his hair had gotten that way. "I guess I kind of ghosted on you. Not cool. Sorry." He had a slight accent she couldn't place.

Rhea blinked at him, trying not to physically squirm at the little frisson of unease tickling her spine. "Ghosted?" Did he have something to do with last night's visitation? The possibility that he'd been a part of that intrusion into her mental peace made her testy. "Who are you supposed to be, Christmas Past?"

"I…" Rando-guy looked startled—and a little hurt, as though no one had ever spoken to him in such an unfriendly manner before. Maybe he expected women to be dazzled at the sight of his muscular Nordic perfection and quirky little smile. And those sky blue eyes. And his ginger beard and tousled bedhead. "Sorry, I didn't mean to bother you. I just saw the sign..." He messed up his hair again, distractedly, like he was *trying* to be that freaking adorable. "Never mind." He turned and headed for the door, and Rhea had an attack of conscience (because it certainly wasn't the firm ass in those jeans affecting her); he was here about the Help-Wanted sign.

"Sorry, wait." She closed her drawing pad and set down the pen. "I didn't mean to bite your head off. I'm a little cranky this afternoon and you kinda caught me off guard. We're not officially open yet, and I wasn't expecting anyone to wander in. You're here about the job?"

He turned, tucking his hands into his jean pockets, looking like a damn little lost lamb. A two-hundred-and-twenty-pound lost lamb. In cowboy boots.

"Uh, yeah. Is the position still open?"

"Do you have any retail experience?"

"Not...as such."

"Been around tattooing much?"

"Um, no."

"Are you inked?"

One hand slid out of its pocket, going for the forelock once more. "This was a bad idea."

"Why don't you let me be the judge?" Rhea handed him her tablet and switched over to the job application. "It doesn't have to be super detailed. I'm just looking for someone with a demonstrated ability to hold down a job. And someone who's personable." She gave him a pointed look to let him know that so far he hadn't passed the test for the latter.

His sky blues lit up with an engaging smile. "I can be personable."

"We'll see." Rhea turned her stool toward the credenza

behind her, making a point of going back to her drawing and paying him no attention. The rider on the most prominent horse took shape under her pen, the wild hair and eyes she remembered from her vision—eyes that bore a striking resemblance to her applicant's—the rugged furs, the upraised sword—

"All done."

She started at the second interruption. She hadn't expected to get drawn so deeply into the image so quickly.

Her determined would-be employee slid the tablet across the counter toward her when she looked up. "There wasn't that much to fill in, to be honest. I just moved here, so none of it's local—I don't have a permanent address yet. But I'm dependable." He gave Rhea that amiable smile once more. A little too amiable for her taste. It gave the impression he wasn't too bright.

She took the tablet and looked it over. Leo Ström had waited tables at a family restaurant chain in Flagstaff for a few months, bagged groceries in Tucson over the summer, worked as a lab assistant at the University of Arizona for a semester. He also had a degree in biology from Stockholm University.

Rhea glanced up. "You studied in Sweden?"

Leo shrugged. "I've lived all over the place."

"And what made you come here?"

"Ley lines."

He said it with a grin, but Rhea couldn't help rolling her eyes. It was bad enough when tourists treated the town like a wacky sideshow, but people who moved here strictly for the metaphysical ambiance could be even worse.

"Kidding." Leo smiled. "When I dropped out of the grad program at NAU, I decided I wanted to regroup in a place that spoke to me. And Sedona…" He shrugged. "Spoke to me."

It was still kinda ley lines. "What were you studying in grad school?"

Leo gave her a peculiar look. Had she already asked that question?

"Molecular biology."

"No kidding? My sister's in the molecular biology grad program at NAU."

Leo laughed awkwardly. Maybe he thought she was making fun of him somehow.

"Seriously. She's studying autosomal recessive neuro-degenerative disorders in rats or something."

"Are you…?" Leo's hand was in his hair again. He looked completely flustered. "I thought…" He shook his head, the flustered expression turning to a look of understanding as his pale skin went pink. "You're not Theia, are you?"

Chapter 2

Now it all made sense. She wasn't usually this slow on the uptake, but over the last four years of living more than a hundred and fifty miles apart, she'd become less accustomed to being mistaken for her twin.

"You know Theia."

Leo nodded, combing his fingers through his hair. "This is embarrassing."

"When you said 'ghosted'…"

"We met on Tinder. We went out a couple of times, but I kind of stopped answering her texts because things got weird. I mean, not *weird*. We just weren't hitting it off." He exhaled deeply. "Oh, boy."

All the times some guy had mistaken her for Theia in high school came crashing back. Theia was the "sweet" one, the normal one who didn't dress weird or act like a clown, and guys were always falling for her. And more often than Rhea cared to recall, they had run into her somewhere and taken her for Theia, treating her the way guys usually *didn't* treat Rhea. Then they'd realize they were talking to the "other one" and the disappointment would be palpable and awkward.

"I made this weird, didn't I?" Leo tucked his hands back into his pockets. "Sorry. I hope you find someone to fill the position. Take care." He was walking away again.

Anger flared inside her, irrational and childish but impossible to suppress. "So Theia was good enough to bang for a while, but I'm chopped liver." Damn. Why did she have to say that out loud?

Leo's shoulders stiffened as he reached the door, and he turned back with a miserable look of discomfort. "Look, I didn't mean to—"

"No, it's me. Sorry. I'm totally overreacting." Rhea sighed, setting the tablet on the counter. "You just triggered some stupid childhood drama." She tried to laugh it off. "Should we try this again? Rhea Carlisle." She held out her hand.

Leo squared his shoulders and came back to the counter. "Nice to meet you, Rhea Carlisle." He smiled as he shook her hand. "I'm Leo Ström."

"Yeah, I know." Rhea indicated the tablet with a nod of her head when Leo looked suspicious. "It's on the application."

"Right." He laughed, still a bit awkward but more at ease.

"So what's your availability?"

"My availability?"

"For the job. What hours would you be available to work? I'm open seven days."

Leo's eyes widened within the wire frames. "You'd actually hire me after this disaster?"

"It's hardly your fault someone Xeroxed your exgirlfriend." *Without telling you, apparently.* Which was a new low for Theia.

"Whoa. Wait. She's not my ex-girlfriend."

"Oh, so you're still seeing her." Rhea laughed at the look of mortification on his face as he stuttered, trying to answer. "I'm just giving you crap. I need someone to work about twenty hours a week to help get the place in shape and book appointments, mostly mornings, occasionally closing if you prove trustworthy." She winked at his expression. "Sound okay to you?"

"Uh, yeah." Slightly bemused, he took her outstretched hand once more and shook on it. "Yeah, sounds great. Thanks."

"You didn't ask what it pays."

"At this point, I'm thinking maybe I shouldn't press my luck." Leo grinned as he pushed up his glasses on the bridge of his nose. "Tomorrow morning, then?"

She was probably going to regret this. Honestly, she was already regretting it. Why hadn't she just let him walk away? An entanglement of Theia's was the last thing she needed.

Rhea put on a professional smile. "Morning is a relative term. Eleven o'clock sharp. We open at noon."

The temperature, mild when she'd set out this morning, had dropped precipitously by the time she headed home, and the first snow of the season was falling. Not heavy enough to cover the ground yet, but if it kept up, it might have some staying power by morning. She wasn't looking forward to snow driving after spending the last five years in Tempe. Especially now that she'd chosen to live in Cottonwood, half an hour from her shop. Not that *choosing* was precisely the word for it. The tiny apartment was all she could afford, especially without a roommate. And she'd only been able to swing the one-bedroom because the manager had offered to give her the studio price for the first three months.

For a while, she'd thought she might move up to Flagstaff with Theia, but that was out of the question now. Unbelievable that Theia wouldn't even have mentioned having a twin to someone she was dating. Was she ashamed of everyone in the family now? It was bad enough that she'd officially changed her name, taking her middle name, "Dawn," as her last name because she didn't want to acknowledge the father who'd lied to them all their lives. Rhea wondered if Theia recognized the irony of her secret keeping.

The wipers swished across the windshield, set to intermittent, and as they slid back into place against the hood, something else whooshed past in their path. Something large and white and moving fast. Rhea slammed on the brakes—and, of course, began to hydroplane on the freshly wet road. The back end of the car whipped about and Rhea was in free-spin. Luckily, no one else was on the road. She managed to get the car under control and pull onto the opposite shoulder, although she was now facing the wrong way.

Shaken, she watched the wipers snap up and fall back a few times, trying to put together what could have whizzed past her window. A bird? Its wingspan, if it was one, must have been wider than her windshield. While she contemplated it, a loud horn split the air, making her heart pound.

That wasn't a car horn. It was some kind of literal *horn*, with someone blowing into it, the notes of a herald or a mounted charge. Rhea braced herself, gripping the wheel as the ground rumbled with the impact of something heavy— or many somethings. It was like the vision in her living room, only this was right out in the open and there was no tattoo to read. But the riders were here.

This time, they'd taken on a more spectral appearance, the horses looking almost skeletal and the riders gaunt and wraithlike, dressed in contemporary clothing. The wet road was visible through their translucent forms as they thundered across the highway toward her. Rhea shrieked and ducked against the seat with her arms over her head as the riders began to leap across her MINI. She was sure they were going to trample the roof and crush her inside, but they somehow all managed to clear the top of the car—though some just barely, as hooves rattled and scraped across it.

As the last horse thundered onto the ground on the passenger side, the gaunt-faced horseman paused and turned, spectral gaze fixed on her as she sat up. Oddly, he was wearing a cowboy hat. He tipped it at her, sunken orbs in the hollowed spectral flesh flashing a vivid aquamarine, before turning and galloping away.

She'd finally started to exhale when something jumped onto the hood of the car and scrambled over it, making her heart leap into her throat. A wolflike hound trailed the hunt. Like the rider, the hound turned and fixed its wolfy eyes on her—pale blue and disturbingly sentient—before tearing off into the brush. They were all swallowed up—the vision and the thunder, the horns and baying alike—into the billowing, unearthly fog that traveled with them.

In their wake, the snow became a sudden, violent hail, with large marble-sized pellets hammering her roof and windows. She waited it out, making sure the worst of it was over before putting the car in Drive and turning around on the slick road to head home.

Delayed shock hit her once she was inside her apartment. Rhea collapsed onto the couch in the dark, shuddering and trying to catch her breath. She hadn't had an asthma attack since she was a kid, but her chest was tight and her airway felt like it was closing.

She sat up and deliberately slowed her breathing, listening to her lungs make a peculiar wheezing rattle as she breathed in deeply, and finally got herself under control. Maybe it was time to get some expert advice, because this was getting too weird. Not from Theia, of course. And lone would freak out and go into "mom" mode. It was hard for her oldest sister not to slip back into the role their parents' deaths had forced her into—a teenager herself at the time—whenever anything threatened one of her siblings. But Phoebe, the middle child of the family, was used to dealing with weird.

Phoebe answered on the first ring. "Hey, kiddo. What's up?"

"When you have shades stepping into you...do you ever see anything ghostly or is it just their presence you feel?"

"Well, hello to you, too. And, no, I don't perceive the shades visually. Rafe sees them, of course. Dating someone who commands the dead has its perks." Phoebe's boyfriend happened to be the last scion of Quetzalcoatl. Because of course he was. "Why, did you need me to contact someone for you?"

"No." Realizing she was scratching at her jeans over the healing tattoo, Rhea snatched her hand away. "No, it's... never mind. I think I'm overtired."

"Rhe. Come on, this is me. What's going on?"

Her hand slid under the jeans, but Rhea curled her fingers and managed to stop herself. *Damn this stupid tattoo.*

"I thought I saw something a little...weird."

"How weird?"

Rhea hesitated.

"Rhe? How weird?"

"Johnny Cash 'Ghost Riders in the Sky' weird. Only on Highway 89A and not in the sky."

"Okay. That's decidedly in the weird column."

"And it's not the first time I saw them. I had a vision while working on one of my tattoos. And then there was a fox in my living room, and she said I'd summoned her from the Wild Hunt."

Phoebe was quiet for a moment. "Honey…are you still taking those antidepressants?"

Rhea let out an exasperated sigh. "I wasn't hallucinating."

"Sorry, but it's a little hard to process. A talking fox?"

"And *who* has a boyfriend that turns into a feathered snake god, can shift into crow form and talks to coyotes? Jesus, Phoebes. Talking to a fox in my living room is hardly the weirdest thing anyone in this family does. Ione has sex with a goddamn dragon."

"She doesn't actually have sex with the dragon. Dev and his dragon demon are two separate entities who happen to share the same corporeal form."

"Right. Okay. You're absolutely right. I am being completely ridiculous with this fox-spirit thing. That's way more normal. Good night." Her thumb was poised to end the call.

"Rhea, wait." Phoebe made a noise suggesting she was blowing her bangs out of her face. "I'm sorry. I didn't mean to be a jerk. After everything that's happened lately, I guess I owe you the benefit of the doubt."

"Yeah, I guess you do."

"What does Theia think?"

It was Rhea's turn to blow at imaginary hair—or not so imaginary, as her spikes were getting way too long these days, and one in particular kept flopping over and hanging in her eyes. "I don't know what Theia thinks."

"You didn't call her first?"

"I'm not really talking to Theia."

"You're what? Rhe, what's going on with you?"

"Besides talking fox hallucinations? Just trying to deal with the fact that Theia kept Dad's second family a secret for months."

"I thought you two found the genealogical information together."

"That part was all Theia. She knew we had three other

sisters, and she knew one of them was living a few miles away from her. And she never said a word to me. Maybe if she had, Laurel wouldn't have apprenticed herself to a psycho necromancer and tried to kill you."

"Nobody's to blame for that but Laurel herself—and that bag of dicks who took advantage of her vulnerability, Carter Hanson Hamilton." Phoebe delivered the name of Ione's ex with all due mocking disgust. Though "bag of dicks" was being kind, as far as Rhea was concerned. "You can't let that come between you and Theia. Does she even know how you feel about it?"

Rhea sighed. "She knows. Anyway, I don't want to talk about it. I just want to know if there's any kind of precedent for seeing a ghostly hunting party. Can you check with Rafe to see if he knows anything about the Wild Hunt or if he's seen anything out of the ordinary in the spirit world lately?"

"Of course."

"And Phoebes? Don't mention any of this to Ione or Theia."

She lay awake later, unable to stop thinking about the haunting eyes of the straggling rider—and his straggling hound—as they'd paused to acknowledge her. The hound had lacked the skeletal appearance, but it certainly possessed the same unnerving gaze. Had all of the hunting party seen her? Or just those two? And why her?

According to Vixen, Rhea's blood had summoned the Hunt. Of course, the name of the custom ink was Bloodbath. A bit macabre, maybe, but the color really was lovely. And unusual in its intensity. As was the damn itching. The healing skin was driving her mad again as she thought about it.

Rhea drew her leg from the covers. It could do with a little moisturizer. As she stroked the lotion over the Lilith mark, her fingers tingled with the precursor to a vision.

Rhea pulled her hand away. She was so not in the mood for another vision.

But the pictomancy had a mind of its own.

This time it was an image of blood pooling onto a pristine field of snow. Something dark and hulking stood in the periphery, casting its shadow on the blood under a stark full moon. And then the darkness seemed to swallow the vision entirely.

There was no clear distinction between when the vision ended and when sleep and dreaming began.

Chapter 3

Leo climbed back into bed after dashing from the bathroom over the cold tile floor, folding his arms behind his head on the pillow as he stared up at the ceiling. The vague stuff of dreams fluttered at the edges of his consciousness, but he could never quite recall his. What he remembered, though, was Rhea Carlisle. He had the feeling she'd traipsed through his dreamscape. He'd never met anyone like her. An absurd assertion since he'd dated her twin, but indisputably true.

Her eyes, like Theia's, were a true gray, made more striking by the dark limbal rings encircling the irises. But Rhea's gaze seemed to lay him bare. Theia, even after they'd hung out several times, had remained somewhere on the surface with him, never allowing him deeper, her eyes warm but guarded. Rhea's eyes challenged the one gazing upon them to see her, to be drawn into her. Within moments of meeting her, he'd felt the challenge: *I dare you to know me.* And he wanted to. Intensely.

But taking the job at Demoness Ink was a bad idea. Because being around someone who wanted to be known, whom he wanted to know, meant risking being known. And, frankly, he wasn't sure he wanted to know himself. His nightly ritual kept whatever darkness was inside him from coming out, but it was a constant discipline. And the foolishness of romantic entanglements in the workplace aside, that discipline made dating difficult and awkward. Claiming he was busy whenever a potential partner suggested an evening date became quickly suspect, and he couldn't blame Theia for having gotten weird about it.

And, anyway, what if she came into the shop to visit her sister? She'd never believe he'd just happened into the obscure tattoo parlor in Sedona where her twin worked by chance. She'd think he was crazy. Of course, he *was* a little crazy. And it didn't matter what Theia thought of him. What mattered was Rhea. Which was why he was absolutely not going to show up to the job. It was out of the question.

He arrived at the little upstairs hole-in-the-wall that was Demoness Ink at five minutes to eleven and stood waiting in the lightly spitting snow until he realized, at five after, that Rhea was watching him calmly from behind the counter inside. The corner of her mouth turned up as he met her eyes, and Leo lowered his gaze, shaking his head with a laugh as he pushed open the door.

He brushed the soles of his boots against the sisal mat inside, hands in his coat pockets, before glancing up with a sheepish smile. "How long did you know I was out there?"

"Saw you come up the stairs." Rhea's heathery eyes were bright with amusement. "I thought I'd see how long it took you to try the door."

"Employee intelligence test?"

Rhea laughed. "The opposite of what you're thinking, though. I like mine a little bit stupid." She meant her employees, of course, but for a split second he heard it as how she liked her men.

Before the heat in his cheeks at his foolishness could give him away, he took his hands from his pockets and blew on them, rubbing them together. "Well, you're in luck, then,

because I'm an idiot. I didn't even think to put gloves on.
Guess the joke's on me."

"The joke was already on you." Rhea grinned at him,
those starkly outlined irises merciless. "There's a coatrack
in the back if you want to hang your jacket up."

"Thanks." Leo headed past the counter to the back room,
pulling off his hat as he went. At least he'd had the sense
to wear it. Both the hat and coat were already significantly
damp from standing in the snowfall. He found the rack and
hung them on it, noting the sturdy, adjustable dentist's-style
tattoo chair. It might work in a pinch if he had to close some
night and didn't want to chance being late. Of course, he'd
have to bring his own restraints, though he always carried
them out of sheer necessity.

"Did you get lost back there?" Rhea's perpetually
amused voice carried from the front.

Leo tried to ruffle his hair back into place as he returned to the reception area. It was usually a losing battle,
hat or no hat.

Rhea was eyeing his marks. He'd worn a T-shirt despite
the cold, and the fading ink of his gauntlets and the band
around his upper arm peeking out under the sleeve seemed
more visible than usual under the fluorescent light.

"I thought you didn't have any ink."

He thought about saying he wasn't sure it even was ink.
How crazy would he sound if he said he didn't remember
getting tattooed?

"I didn't say I didn't have any ink. I said I didn't have
any experience with tattooing." He glanced at his arm. "I
got these done ages ago, so I'm not sure they even count
anymore."

Rhea came out from around the counter to look them
over. "You must have been underage when you got them
to have that much fading. Are they home jobs?"

"You could say that." Let her think they were prison tattoos if that's what she meant. Gang tattoos he'd gotten in juvie. Hell, maybe they were.

Rhea took his arm to inspect one of the marks more closely, and his skin rippled along his spine. "It's nice work for a home job." Her palm moved up his arm, warm and soft, and he flinched involuntarily. Rhea let go and took a step back. "Sorry. I should have asked first. I hate it when people touch my skin without asking just because it's decorated."

"No, it's fine." He couldn't help wondering where she was decorated, since nothing was visible. "It's just goose bumps. Feels like the temperature's dropped a bit."

Rhea tucked her hands into her back pockets, looking up at him. "Can I ask what they mean?" He hadn't realized how stark the difference was in their heights until now, despite having dated her twin. But she seemed somehow smaller, more petite than he'd expected. He had a good six or seven inches on her.

She was still waiting for his answer.

Leo held out his right forearm. "This one is the allrune." Two sets of three parallel lines crossed each other diagonally over three vertical lines. "It symbolizes the Web of Wyrd."

Rhea's eyes crinkled. "The web of what, now?"

"Wyrd." He spelled it out to clarify. "One of the Norse fates. It's supposed to symbolize the tapestry fate weaves."

"Oh, *Urd*, sister of Skuld and Verdande."

Leo smiled. "You know your Norns."

"Actually, I know manga and anime." Rhea laughed. "The series *Oh My Goddess!* The third Norn is called Belldandy in the series, which always made me giggle, so I do know a little bit about Norns, but only enough to know the names."

Leo was intrigued. It was the first he'd heard of Norn manga. "I'll have to check it out." He held up his other arm, turning his wrist to reveal the knotted designs of the wraparound. "This one's Mjölnir—"

"Thor's hammer."

Leo cocked his head. "You're sure you don't know Norse mythology?"

Rhea grinned. "Marvel Comics. And the other?"

One of Jörmungandr's coils was visible under his sleeve at his right biceps. Leo pushed the sleeve up to reveal the coiling solid cuff. "The Midgard Serpent." A look of apprehension and surprise flashed in Rhea's eyes. "I know what you're thinking. I have all these Nordic tattoos. I promise I'm not a Nazi skinhead. I'm just proud of my Swedish heritage. And apparently, as you've already noted, fairly stupid." He smiled wryly. "I never realized most of these symbols had been co-opted by white nationalists. I tend to keep them covered most of the time."

"I wasn't thinking that." Rhea's look was guarded. She was so thinking that. "But now that you mention it, I can see where someone might make that mistake." *Uh-huh.* "I have to say, though, that scruffy puppy-dog hair pretty much ruins the skinhead look for you. If that's what you were going for, it's another big fail." Her laugh, letting him know she was cutting him slack, was infectious, and he found himself smiling at the warmth in her eyes. A smile he realized was probably only adding to the impression he wasn't the brightest bulb in the pack.

But Rhea had switched into business mode. "Before I put you to work, we should probably talk pay."

Leo rolled down his sleeve over Jörmungandr. "I was thinking maybe we could work out a deal. I'd be happy to exchange some work for touch-ups. Maybe some new ink, too." Why had he added that? He didn't want new ink. He didn't even want the ink he had. But it did need touching up. In fact, it was what had brought him to the shop in the first place. Before he'd seen the Help-Wanted sign, the name of the place had caught his eye, and he'd figured it would be as good a place as any to get the work done. It wouldn't be wise to put it off any longer. Like the nightly ritual, he knew the marks helped him keep his equilibrium, though he wasn't sure why. It was a stupid idea, anyway. She'd probably think he was some kind of scam artist.

But Rhea cocked her head, considering. "The first gauntlet would probably take less than an hour, maybe two for the second, and the cuff might run a little longer. Let's give it a conservative estimate of six hours for the three. Anything else you want, we'd have to negotiate based on the size and complexity and whether you want original artwork or have something of your own in mind. Normally, I charge one fifty an hour, with a one-hour minimum. So let's say ten hours of work equals one hour of tattoo work. That would take you through the end of the year and my official opening. We can decide on any additional commitment after that."

Leo's eyes widened at the dollar figure. "Fifteen dollars an hour? That seems awfully generous."

Rhea shrugged. "To be perfectly honest, there's no way I could pay you in cash right now, so let's just say I'd be giving you a good deal on the ink. Besides…" That devilish half grin she'd given him through the window earlier turned up the side of her mouth. "You don't know what I'm going to have you doing."

What she had him doing, it turned out, at least for that first day, was little more than counting inventory and learning her booking system. When she ran out of things for him to do, Rhea offered to start working on his touch-ups while he was still on the clock. He hadn't expected her to start right away, but he certainly had no objection. It wasn't like he had anywhere to be. As long as he was back at the motel before nightfall, everything would be fine.

As soon as Rhea's fingers brushed his ink, there were whispers of visions. Her gift had initially manifested as shared visions with her clients, a kind of psychic reading, and she'd done a few for family and friends. But her skills had recently expanded to include the delivery of more immediate images that popped into her head without the client even being aware of it—and without her wanting to see them. Ever since she'd gotten images from some creep thinking about pushing her head into his lap, she'd been very careful not to indulge in the latter type.

She tried to keep her mind occupied by focusing on the physical anchors of the here and now—the sharp scent of the alcohol as she swabbed Leo's skin, the soft snick of the razor as it traveled over the blond hairs on his arm, the warmth of Leo's body heat as she leaned in close to examine the lines she'd be tracing. And the scent of his skin, like amber-resin oil and pumpkin spice and— *Wow.*

Rhea got up and busied herself readying supplies to get herself under control. What the heck was that about? He was kinda hot, sure, but not so-hot-that-smelling-him-makes-you-wet hot. Except, clearly, he was.

She worked to keep from blushing as she gave him a smile after setting up the machine and ink caps. "Okay, ready?"

Leo smiled back, and it nearly melted her. "Ready as I'll ever be."

She managed to act like a normal person as she sat and got to work on the outline. When the needles made contact with Leo's skin, the image bombarded her psyche: blood spattered across a dazzling field of snow, like a giant cherry slush spilled on a white rug.

Leo was looking at her funny. "Are you okay?"

She'd taken her foot off the pedal. "Hmm? Yep, sorry, just thinking for a sec. I might want to use round needles for the line work instead of flat. Give it some more depth, since some of these strokes are really fine." She hoped she wasn't babbling nonsense. She could barely remember the words as they left her mouth. Rhea took a breath and went back to work. "I'll start on the thicker lines on the three parallel columns."

"Staves."

"What's that?"

"The columns are called staves, like in the tarot."

"Oh, that makes sense." And like the tarot, they were drawing pictures she couldn't unsee. *Running through thick overgrowth in an ancient wood, tree branches scoring limbs and face. After someone. On the hunt.* A pause in the here and now to wipe the blood. *The enemy emerges from the darkness. Now the hunted. Swinging the blade to block the blow and missing. Stumbling headlong into the snow as the light grows dim.*

Somehow, she got through it without botching the original work and actually managed to make the tattoo sharper and bolder while giving the lines a bit more definition and character—a subtle woodiness to the staves, with ridges and bumps of texture in the outlines if you looked closely.

"This looks fantastic." Leo studied his tattoo in the light, obviously pleased, as Rhea cleaned up.

"I hope you don't mind the little extras I added. If you prefer the lines smooth, I can go over it again."

"No, it's great." Leo looked up, his eyes shining behind his glasses. "I hope I can earn it."

"It took me a little longer than I expected, but I'll honor the estimate. So ten hours of work should do it."

Leo shook his head. "Nope. I'll pay for the time it took. Plus, there's the tip, which you've totally earned. This is excellent work."

Rhea felt her cheeks warm, as if he'd complimented her on her body instead of praising her skill. "Well, thanks. But you don't have to tip." *Yes, he does, Rhea. Shut up and take the money.* Even if the money was paid in labor, she *had* earned it, and she needed to stop devaluing herself if she wanted to make a living as an artist.

"But I want to. So what would twenty percent bring it to?"

"An hour and a half at one fifty an hour would be two twenty-five—"

"An hour and a half?" Leo's brows drew together as he drew his phone from his pocket.

"Yeah, I know. Really, I'm absolutely cool with charging what I originally estimated. It's not your fault I got fancy. Let's make it one fifty plus anything else you think is appropriate."

"No, that's not it." He was still looking at his phone, his expression slightly worried. "I'll happily pay for the work. I just didn't realize how late it was."

Rhea glanced at the tablet on its stand. She'd spent a little extra time setting up, but it wasn't even six o'clock yet.

"Sorry. I should have let you know what time it was when we got started. Did you have somewhere you needed to be?"

Leo slipped his phone into his pocket and gave her a slightly forced smile. "No, it's cool. I'm just not a night person. I like to be home before it gets dark."

"I suppose you turn into a pumpkin?"

Leo's laugh was nervous. "Something like that."

Rhea couldn't figure out what faux pas she'd made, but she'd definitely made one. "I shouldn't have assumed you'd want to jump right into it after your first day of work. We can schedule the rest of your touch-ups for whenever you want."

"Don't worry about it. It's not a big deal. And I love the tattoo, so it's all good."

She still felt she'd upset him somehow. Maybe a gesture of trust would smooth things over. Rhea twisted an extra door key off the shop ring.

"In case I need you to open or close sometime."

Leo stared as she placed the key in his palm. "You're giving me a key?"

"Is there any reason I shouldn't?" Damn, she really hoped there wasn't.

Leo's smile this time was genuine and a little heart-breakingly adorable. "Absolutely not. You've got my Social Security number, so you can track me down. Not that you'd ever have to track me down. Because you won't need to. You can count on me." Leo looked flustered at his own rambling. He held out the key. "Maybe you should keep this after all."

Rhea laughed. "No, take it. Just know that I *will* hunt you down if you ever screw me over." He looked a little worried. Which was perhaps a little worrying. Why hadn't she just taken the key back?

"Well, I thank you." Leo gave her a dramatic little bow and slipped a length of ball chain out of his shirt from around his neck. He unhooked the clasp to slide the key onto it to hang next to the pendant he wore, an image of a wide-branching tree with roots that mirrored them. "I shall keep it close to my heart." He patted his chest after he'd slipped the chain back into his shirt, emphasizing the firm definition of his pecs.

* * *

After Leo headed out, Rhea tidied up and checked to make sure all the valuable equipment was locked in a cabinet. She was almost home when she remembered she'd left the damn tablet.

A strong wind drove the light snow still falling across the highway, making Rhea more cautious than usual—while also keeping an eye out for wayward ghostly riders. Luckily, she saw none of those, but it was almost seven by the time she got back to the shop.

She'd left a light on in back. Had she let Leo Ström's soulful eyes and potent scent rattle her that much? She grabbed the tablet off the counter without bothering to turn on the light and headed into the back to switch off the lamp—and gave a little yip of surprise. Leo Ström, speak of the devil, was sitting in her chair.

Correction: he was *shackled* to her chair.

Chapter 4

Rhea dropped her bag in the doorway. "Leo? What the hell happened?"

Leo looked embarrassed as Rhea examined the restraints at his wrists. "I came back to get my hat and surprised these two guys. I guess they were looking to steal your equipment or something. One of them pulled a gun and ordered me into the chair and cuffed me."

The restraints were professional looking, heavy-duty leather cuffs secured with a pair of electronic padlocks. Rhea turned one of the locks in her hand. "These look serious. I'm going to have to cut the cuffs off." She probably had a pocketknife or a box cutter in the toolbox in the back of her car. Rhea pulled aside the curtain and headed back out. "I might have something I can use."

Leo called after her. "Maybe we should leave it. They said the locks were on a timer and they'd open automatically when the time was up. It can't be that long. They probably just needed enough time to get away, right? We should just wait."

"Wait?" Rhea glanced over her shoulder, incredulous. She shook her head and opened the door. "I'm not waiting around to see if they were telling the truth. Let me find something."

There was no pocketknife, but she found a fish-gutting

knife she'd forgotten about. It had belonged to her father, whose toolbox she'd been hauling around since leaving for college. Some girls kept letters and stuffed animals to remember the dead. Rhea had a toolbox.

A bell tolled distantly as she crawled out of the hatchback, some church clock chiming the hour. The mark of passing time brought her focus back to Leo's claim. Who would use a timer on a padlock? Why would a couple of crooks even have wrist restraints with padlocks? Something didn't add up.

When she returned, Leo had one leg crossed jauntily over the other as though he was just relaxing in the tattoo chair. He no longer looked embarrassed but completely at ease.

"Ah, you're an angel." He nodded at the knife in Rhea's hand. "I knew you'd come through." His eyes looked different somehow. Darker. Or bluer. Maybe it was just because he wasn't wearing his glasses.

"You're lucky I came back." She unsnapped the sheath and slipped the knife out.

"Guess it's a good thing I stopped in, though. Otherwise you'd have been robbed."

Rhea paused with the knife at the edge of the first cuff. "But you're tied up. How does that keep me from being robbed?"

"I guess finding someone here spooked them and they didn't want to hang around."

There hadn't been much to rob because she'd locked up her machines and needles, and even the ink. The only thing of value had been right on the front counter in plain view of the door. The tablet hadn't been touched. But they'd hung around long enough to threaten Leo with a gun and strap him to a chair with timed electronic locks?

Rhea regarded him. "So where's your hat?"

"My what?"

"Your hat. You said you came back for your hat."

"Oh." Leo shrugged. "Yeah, guess it wasn't even here. How dumb am I?"

Rhea straightened. "You don't even remember telling me about a hat, do you?"

"Of course I do. It just wasn't the most pressing thing on my mind." He wriggled his wrists in the restraints. "Come on, doll. These are starting to chafe."

Rhea slid the knife back into its sheath. "Don't call me doll."

Leo's smile was mischievous. "What would you like me to call you?"

"How about my name? Rhea will do fine."

"All right, then, Rhea, sweetheart, would you please get these off of me?"

Rhea folded her arms. "Is this some kind of joke?" She glanced around, half expecting to see a hidden camera. "Are you punking me?"

"I wouldn't even know how to 'punk' you—unless that's a euphemism for something. I wouldn't mind euphemizing you, now you mention it."

"Leo, this isn't funny. I thought you seemed like a nice, normal person, so I gave you a chance—"

Leo's laughter interrupted her. It infuriated her, and, at the same time, there was something deeply sensual about the way he laughed. It somehow managed not to be mocking. It was as though he genuinely found the idea amusing.

"*Nice* and *normal* aren't words I would use to describe myself."

"I'm beginning to sense that."

Leo laughed again, and the timbre of his laughter tickled along her skin. "Come on, Rhea. Just release me. I promise to make it worth your while."

"You're kind of creeping me out right now." Or maybe the fact that she was aroused by his laugh was creeping her out. She shivered as he chuckled softly. Nah, it was him.

"I'm sorry. I promise to be good." He straightened in the chair and blinked at her from behind a messy lock of hair. "I solemnly swear I am not a creep."

"You just said you weren't nice or normal, which kind of leaves creep."

"Oh, come now. There's plenty of room between nice and creep. There's interesting. Fun. Unusual. Exciting. You don't really like nice, normal people. Admit it." Rhea blinked back at him, matching fake innocence with fake innocence. "*You're* not nice or normal."

"What's that supposed to mean?"

Leo studied her, taking stock with a frank gaze that made her blush. "You don't dress like every woman your age."

"What do you mean, *my* age? You can't be much older."

He ignored the question as if he hadn't heard it. "So many tend to wear tight, revealing, bright colored clothing, as if they're afraid of not being seen. The plain white shirt with the sleeves rolled up, loose cotton pants in black, practical boots—they speak of comfort, both physical and with your own individuality. Your dress is confident and unconcerned with being 'right.'"

"I see." She shifted her weight, feeling downright *un*comfortable under his scrutiny, appreciative though it was.

"And your hair… I've never seen anything like it. How many colors have you got in there? I see dark roots beneath an almost platinum fair and little streaks of pale blue, pink, lavender—"

"Okay, so I like color." Rhea ran her fingers through her hair, trying to get the floppy point out of her eyes.

"And then you put something in it to make it do that, to separate it."

"Look, why are you going on about my hair?"

"It's not nice or normal. It's rather exceptional. I quite like it."

Rhea could feel the heat in her cheeks. "Well, goodie for you. I didn't ask for your approval—"

"I know. It's extraordinarily sexy, you not wanting anyone's approval."

"And you're trying to distract me from the real issue here, which is that you're up to something weird in my tattoo shop. I don't believe for a minute that you came back here for your hat, and a couple of random thieves happened by and locked you up at gunpoint with restraints and timed padlocks."

"Don't you?" Leo's eyes glinted with amusement.

"No, I don't. I think somebody else tied you up. And you let her. Or him. But I'm guessing her."

"Sex games, you mean." Well, there it was. Blunt and out in the open.

"Maybe you didn't play by the rules, so she left you to cool your heels. Or you were paying for it, which is more likely—paying for sex in *my* tattoo shop—and she robbed your ass and took off after she'd tied you up like a sucker."

Leo seemed pleased. "I like that story. That's really good. I should use that. But why would I do such a thing in your tattoo shop?"

"I don't know, because you're obviously a freak? I don't care why. Because I'm calling the cops."

Leo's plump lower lip protruded in a mock pout. "That's not very nice."

"Yeah, well, as you've pointed out, neither are you."

"Why don't you cut me loose and find out how not nice I can be?"

"Cute. Enjoy your jail cell." Rhea pocketed the knife and took out her phone.

"Well, it's not ideal. But so long as *somebody* cuts me loose, I'll have won the contest. I can work with that."

Rhea paused and sighed. "What contest?"

Leo looked surprised and chagrined. "Contest? Did I say contest? There's no contest."

"Uh-huh. Good luck with that, then."

"All right." Leo sighed audibly. "All right, you caught me. It's a little game I play with a friend. He bets me I can't escape before the time runs out on the clock. If I'm free before dawn, I win the whole pot. And the pot is substantial. We've been at this a long time. If you help me win, I'll split it with you, eighty-twenty."

"Eighty-twenty."

"Seventy-thirty, then."

"You're so completely full of shit. Tell you what. Let's pretend there really is a game, and I won't call the police. If you're gone when I come back tomorrow morning, good riddance. And if you're not? If your 'friend' doesn't return to let you loose because you've been such a very naughty, naughty boy, *then* I call the cops. And you can tell your bullshit stories to them. Have a super night." She switched off the light and left him sitting in the dark.

"Rhea." The way he growled her name sent a shiver up her spine. *"Rhe-a."* The musical lilt to his voice this time, deep and rich, made goose bumps skitter over her arms, the slight accent making her name into a promise of unspeakable pleasure.

She dug her nails into her palms, steeling herself to ignore him, and went out, locking the door behind her. There was nothing he could steal. She had the tablet. Let him get out of his own mess. And hopefully she'd never have to see him again. Which sucked, because she'd really wanted to like him.

It was a long, boring drive back to Cottonwood, and she couldn't stop rehashing the strange scene she'd walked in on. Leo had to be on drugs. It was the only explanation for his odd behavior and for the bizarre change in his demeanor. It would be just her luck to have hired a meth head. Though he didn't look like a meth head. He looked like Thor. The snug T-shirt fit him like one of Chris Hemsworth's costumes in the Marvel Avengers movies. Did he own anything that wasn't stretch cotton and snug? Who was he to talk about Rhea's clothing, anyway?

His amber-resin scent still lingered somehow, and Rhea let out a quiet, frustrated growl. It wasn't often a guy really got to her physically. She appreciated a hot body and a pretty face as much as the next person, but she was more likely to be affected by cerebral attraction. And there was nothing cerebral about Leo. At least, not the Leo she'd met yesterday, not the Leo she'd tattooed this evening. The Bizarro Leo currently shackled to her tattoo chair, however... Maybe not cerebral, exactly, but he certainly seemed to have a layer of depth the "other" Leo lacked.

A familiar thundering drew her out of her reverie, and Rhea gripped the wheel and slowed the car. The spectral hunting party galloped out of the darkness several yards ahead. Beside the leader, a woman in a long, flowing and utterly impractical gown rode a white horse that lacked the skeletal features of the others. *She* lacked them, in fact, green eyes bright in the headlights reflecting off the snow and healthy, rosy cheeks visible, as if an altogether different light shined on her. Or perhaps she refracted light differently. The gown was layers of brilliant cobalt blue fluttering in the wind, with a kind of leather breastplate covering the bodice, and flowing copper hair streamed out behind her.

Rhea slowed to a stop. The female rider did the same in the center of the highway, while the others thundered onward. She turned and smiled, and it was by no means a friendly smile. It sent a little chill up her spine. Or maybe that was the frigid air seeping through her windows. Rhea turned up the heat, her gaze drawn away for a second as she sought the knob. When she focused on the road once more, the huntress was gone.

Chapter 5

In the morning, Rhea took her time getting ready. She wasn't looking forward to getting the police involved if Leo was still there. By the time she finally made herself head into town, the midmorning sun was brilliant against a clear winter sky—crystalline blue, although the air was icy. The snow had stopped falling sometime in the night, leaving the red rocks of Sedona's dramatic landscape striped and dotted with white, like a spice cake dusted with powdered sugar.

She parked in back, making a mental note to take care of the spray paint on the wall of the building. She couldn't make out what it said. Probably just some stupid tags. So much for Leo being able to help her with the cleanup. To her relief, when she unlocked the door, the shop was empty.

There was no sign of any hanky-panky Leo might have gotten up to in the back room. No leather cuffs and no electronic locks. And speaking of locks, she was going to have to change hers. That was another hundred bucks she didn't have.

The little bell on the door jingled, and Rhea went through the curtain, hoping someone finally wanted to make an appointment. Her jaw dropped when Leo turned from closing the door behind him and smiled as if showing up this morning were the most ordinary thing in the world.

His smile faltered at her expression. "Is something wrong?"

"Seriously? That's how you're going to handle this? Just act like nothing happened?"

Leo frowned. "Like...what happened?"

"I'm not in the mood for this." Rhea held out her hand. "Just give me the key."

He stood blinking at her, baby blues wide with innocence behind his glasses, and she thought he was going to keep playing dumb, but he sighed and fished the chain out of his shirt inside his coat and slid the key off.

"You were here last night, weren't you?" Leo placed the key in her palm. "I had this vague idea I'd spoken to you. I was hoping it was a dream."

"Very funny."

"I'm not trying to be funny. I kind of...blacked out last night. I should have told you about my problem."

"What, that you're a meth head?"

"I'm not a meth head." Leo took off his hat and tousled his hair, which made him look even more like a meth head. "I...have a dissociative disorder. I usually lock myself in my room when I feel it coming on. It mostly happens around this time of year, after dark. That's why I try not to be out late. It only lasts a few hours, so I came up with the idea of using timed padlocks."

Rhea laughed sharply. "That's the lamest story yet. You've gone from 'a man came in the window' to 'I can't help myself, it's a mental disorder.'"

"It's not a story." Leo stuffed his hands into the pockets of his dopey plaid hunting jacket. "I said a man came in the window?"

"It's from an old comic routine. Except the guy's not funny anymore."

"I see. What *did* I say?"

"You're honestly going to stand there and tell me you don't remember."

"I *don't* remember. I hope I wasn't rude to you. But I can't apologize properly if you don't tell me what I said."

Rhea curled her fist around the key. "You said you came back to get your hat and surprised a couple of thieves who'd broken in, and they shackled you to the chair."

"That's it?"

"Pretty much." She wasn't sure why, but she didn't want to acknowledge the game he'd played with her.

"But I was still here this morning. You didn't try to cut me loose?" Leo blushed. "I mean, not that I'm blaming you."

"I didn't believe you last night—and I don't believe you now—so I left you to get out of your own mess. And it looks like you did, so I guess your dominatrix came back."

"Dominatrix?" The slight pink in his cheeks went crimson. "I swear to you, that is absolutely not what happened. When I'm dissociating, I do a lot of weird things, say a lot of weird things. It's like sleepwalking. That's why I use the restraints. But there was *no* dominatrix. I just stayed out too late and didn't think I'd make it back to the motel in time, so I slipped back in here after you left."

"And you just happened to have restraints on you. You carry them around."

"Yes, as a matter of fact. I can't always afford to rent a motel room around the clock, so I usually check out in the morning and take all my belongings with me." Leo sighed. "Look, I don't expect you to believe me, and I'm really sorry for anything weird I said or did last night. I'll have to find some other way to pay you back for the ink." He went to the door. "But I will. You have my word."

"Why don't you just pay for it now?"

Leo paused in the doorway, looking back. "I really only have enough cash to cover the motel."

"You can clean off the graffiti in the parking lot."

She wasn't sure why she wasn't just letting him go and being glad to be rid of him, but something about his little sob story of not being able to afford the motel room around the clock rang true. She wasn't buying the dissociative bit, but if he was essentially homeless, it didn't feel right to toss him out on his ass in the snow. What had he really done, anyway? Used the key she'd given him willingly to let himself into her shop after hours and maybe got kinky with some crack whore in her tattoo chair? Yeah, okay. That was pretty bad. But he hadn't done anything *to* her, and he hadn't robbed her. So that was something. Sort of.

Leo was still staring at her, uncertain.

"I mean, if you want to prove you're not some kind of creep, you can at least work off your debt."

He nodded emphatically. "Sure. Absolutely. Just point me in the right direction."

"There's a bucket of cleaning supplies in the bathroom. I've had to do this a few times already. These damn kids keep coming back and tagging things."

Leo nodded, looking like an eager pup, and fetched the supplies.

"The lot's down the back stairs. Paint's on the wall next to the red MINI. You'll see it."

"Got it. I'll take care of it." Leo paused once more in the doorway as he headed out. "Thanks."

"For what?"

Leo shrugged. "For not calling the cops on me, I guess. For giving me another chance."

Rhea raised an eyebrow. "It's early yet. Don't make me regret it. And no more weirdness."

Even though she was still glaring at him, his face broke

into an unexpected and disarming smile. "You won't regret it. No more weirdness. Cross my heart." He made the quaint gesture, finger making an X over his heart, before heading downstairs. If he was a meth head, he was a damn adorable one. Rhea sighed and set up her tablet and got to work.

Leo stopped at the bottom of the stairs and leaned against the wall, closing his eyes. How the hell had he been so stupid and careless? He should never have stayed for the tattoo touch-up that close to twilight. He was usually good for a stretch of time after the sun initially set—he had an app on his phone to determine when civil and nautical twilight began and ended so he wouldn't get caught out like he had. Because after full dark, all bets were off. Sometimes he recalled the transitional time—what he referred to as his own personal twilight—but more often than not, it was like drinking to excess, with only fuzzy memories of the time leading up to the episode. And the headache he had in the morning only emphasized the similarities. Christ. He might as *well* be a meth head.

He pushed away from the wall, rubbing at the serpent tattoo through his sleeve as he went down to the back of the touristy little shopping complex. Jörmungandr was the last of the marks, the one he knew a little something about, even if he still couldn't remember getting it. He couldn't even say how he knew, but something told him the symbolism of the Midgard Serpent contained the destructive energy of his illness. The part that would be unleashed if he wasn't careful, if he didn't follow the rules he'd set for himself. And last night he'd played fast and loose with the rules because of Rhea Carlisle's touch.

Something had happened when she touched his skin. Not just the little tingle of pleasure at the softness of it or the desire to be near her, but a connection that made him feel as if he could almost remember whatever it was he'd forgotten about the marks and his episodes and his entire life. Little silent movies had played for an instant in his head as she'd worked the ink. And he was certain Rhea had seen those featurettes, too. Her reaction, that little shock of stillness, echoed his own. *Snow kicked up by the hooves of horses—the sturdy, stocky horses of war. The smell and creak of leather and mail. The tang of blood and ice on his tongue.* But wars weren't fought on horseback in leather and chain mail. Not anymore.

Leo stopped in the parking lot to catch his breath, the familiar muscle spasm tugging at his ribs, as if someone had thrust a knife under them. Then it was gone and forgotten. There was Rhea's red MINI, and there was the graffiti. Leo's brows drew together as he contemplated the tags. This wasn't gang graffiti. These were runes.

He set down the bucket and got to work. A brush and some paint thinner took out some of the color, but the paint had set into the wood—probably done while Leo was still tied up upstairs raving like a lunatic. When he'd done all he could with the thinner, he started on the sandpaper-backed sponge. As he scrubbed the runes from the wall, the shapes gave up their meaning. *Soiled...impure. Throw*—no, *cast out. The impure shall be cast out.* He pieced the rest together. *And the pure shall inherit the land.*

Leo set down his sanding sponge and wiped his brow. Something about this made him really angry. Murderously angry. And, as with so many things that similarly affected him, he had no idea why. Or even why he could read the symbols in the first place. Odder still was why some shift-less punk would be spray-painting Norse runes on the walls of an outdoor shopping mall in the middle of Northern Arizona. Because these were definitely Norse.

Leo's spine twitched, as though someone had walked

on his grave, and he rolled his shoulders. Under his right sleeve, Jörmungandr was prickling against his skin. The ink irritated him more in winter. Probably from going from the cold and damp to the dry air of heated interiors. He could feel the outline of the tattoo through the sleeve as he rubbed at it, slightly raised, the skin inflamed.

But it wasn't dry skin. It was these runes. They were a message for him. Somehow, he was certain of that. And the mark was responding to the message as though to a threat. He pondered the faded symbols on the wall as he sanded out the last of them. Leo straightened and frowned. That little spidery shape at the end—that wasn't part of the runes. He'd thought it was messy punctuation or maybe a stray mark, but now... Another shudder traveled down his spine, this time one of revulsion. It was a crudely drawn swastika.

It brought new meaning to the words spelled out by the runes. It wasn't the first time some nasty little vermin had tried to drag him into their racist bullshit. And nothing made him angrier than being mistaken for one of them. They'd appropriated his heritage, sullied the beauty of his ancestors' mythology, twisting it to their own purposes. He wanted to find the little shits and crack their skulls.

He tossed the sanding sponge into the bucket and went around to the front stairs and checked to make sure his bag was still safe underneath them. Of course, the cat, so to speak, was *out* of the bag. He might as well take it upstairs. The army surplus duffel bag contained a change of clothing, the restraints and locks, and his beard trimmer. Everything he owned in the world. Leo slung the bag over his shoulder and mounted the stairs.

Rhea made a face at the spreadsheet on her tablet. Numbers were so not her thing, much less this annoying program. Theia was the one who had always been good with calculations. They'd talked about owning a shop together for years. Not a tattoo shop, of course. Coffee and books had ranked among the top five. They'd both liked the idea of a cat café. But in every iteration of that idle dream since high school, cats or no cats, Theia had been the one doing the books and the finances while Rhea was the artist and the public face of the business. Now she was stuck doing everything herself. Which wasn't exactly Theia's fault— she wouldn't have been interested in opening a tattoo shop, but it still rankled that Rhea couldn't even count on her for emotional support.

True to Theia's pattern, as soon as Rhea started stewing about her, a text notification chimed on her phone. In addition to having prophetic dreams, one of Theia's gifts was an uncanny—and annoying—sense of knowing when someone was thinking about her.

Thinking about you, Moonpie. Also an irritating gift for synchronicity. And for coming up with cutesy names.

Rhea switched the screen off and glanced up as Leo came in. "How'd it go?"

Leo rubbed absently at his right biceps. "I think I got most of it. Did you happen to see what it was?"

"It looked like scribbling to me. I thought maybe it was gang symbols. Why?"

"It was in the runic alphabet. Norse runes, specifically." His expression said this was significant.

Rhea set down the tablet. "Were you able to read it?"

"It was a message about racial purity. Have they done anything like this before?"

"No, just stupid gang tags. At least, I thought they were gang tags." Rhea tried to remember if she'd ever seen anything overtly racist. "You're sure the message was about racial purity?"

"There was also a swastika."

Rhea's stomach clenched. "Fuck. I guess that's pretty unambiguous."

Leo's eyes were hard. "The next time you catch them at it, you should call the cops."

"I'm not a big fan of calling the cops on kids, but I've never actually caught them." Rhea considered. "To be honest, I'm not even sure they're kids. I just assumed."

"Does anybody around here have a security camera pointed on the lot?"

"Not that I know of."

"You should get one. Or a security guard. These groups usually escalate."

"I can't even afford to pay someone to clean up graffiti. How would I pay for a security guard?" Rhea noticed the duffel bag slung over his shoulder. "What's in the bag?"

Leo glanced down as though he'd forgotten it. "My stuff. I was keeping it under the stairs so you wouldn't think I was squatting here. Which I guess I kind of was. Sorry. It wasn't my intention."

"So you really are homeless."

"I'm not an addict or anything. I just move around a lot during the winter. It's hard to hold down a job and an apartment when you have to spend dusk to dawn restrained. People kind of frown on it when they find out."

Rhea fiddled with the edge of the counter. Maybe she'd misjudged him. She liked to think she was open-minded about mental health issues. She wasn't exactly the poster girl for neurotypicality. She was probably going to regret this, but that had never stopped her before.

"Why don't you sleep here, then? You could keep an eye on the place."

Leo's eyes narrowed. "Are you messing with me?"

"I need a security guard, you don't have anywhere to stay… It seems like a natural solution."

Leo still looked skeptical. "You got the part where I'm not in my right mind and I have to be restrained until dawn, right?"

"But the vandals wouldn't know that. If they see a light on, they'll be less likely to try anything. And you can always call me—you have a cell phone?"

"Yeah, I've got a phone."

"So if you see something, you could give me a call to alert me, and I could come by and catch them in the act. Assuming they stuck around that long."

"You're also assuming I'd be levelheaded enough to remember to call you—or to care. I don't really know what goes on when I'm 'out.'"

"Well, I do. I was here talking to you. You seemed perfectly lucid, just—kind of an ass."

Leo laughed, that genuine laughter of surprise that made his whole face light up. "A lucid ass, huh? You know, I've never had anybody tell me what I'm like in that state. It might be useful to have an observer to document it. I mean—I'm sure you've got better things to do than babysit my lucid ass personality. But if you wanted to stick around to verify that I'm not doing drugs or calling pro-dommes to spank me in your back room, you'd be welcome to." He grinned, running his fingers through his hair in a gesture that belied the easy self-deprecation.

Rhea pondered the idea. She'd be a fool to completely take him at his word. It wouldn't hurt to keep an eye on him and see if he was putting her on.

"Why not?"

Leo cocked his head, studying her. "You're serious. You'd let me sleep here—or not sleep, as the case may be."

"Let's just try it out for one night." Rhea gave him her patented half smirk. "I'll let you know what I think in the morning."

Chapter 6

After locking up, Rhea finished off their Chinese takeout while Leo set up. It was like watching Houdini prepare for a straitjacket stunt. He was well practiced in setting up the restraints on each arm of the chair so that all he had to do was slip one arm in, tighten the strap and snap the lock into place, slip in the other arm, pull the strap with his teeth and wrap his fingers around the lock to close it. It was actually kind of hot. And now he was at her mercy, which she hadn't thought about. She wondered if he'd thought about it.

Leo leaned back against the headrest, the scholarly glasses set aside as if his other personality didn't need them. "I should warn you I'll probably say anything to try to get you to release me once I've slipped into 'lucid ass' mode."

"I'm aware." Rhea raised a suggestive eyebrow without elaborating on what he'd said the night before. "I think I can handle you. It."

It was Leo's turn to raise an eyebrow. "There's a reason I use the restraints. I might seem persuasive, even pleasant when I'm trying to manipulate you into releasing me, but I have it on good authority that I'm anything but when I've managed to wrangle my way out of them."

Rhea was skeptical of the need for all this drama. She

suspected his fear of being set free was all part of the illness. "You've wrangled your way out before?"

"I'm told I have, yes." Leo didn't elaborate, though he looked uncomfortable.

"Are you saying you become violent?"

"To my knowledge, I've never done anything totally random, like attack someone out of the blue. But it's kind of like a blackout drunk. I've been jailed on assault charges for fights I've apparently been goaded into." He colored slightly. "Or started."

She realized she hadn't even run a background check on him. She wasn't off to a very good start with this business stuff. "I'll keep that in mind."

"I just want you to understand the seriousness of the problem. I wouldn't go through this if I didn't think it was absolutely necessary. I haven't attacked anyone unprovoked, but I'd hate for there to be a first time. And I'd really hate for it to be with you. Promise you won't let him charm you."

"Duly noted." Odd that he'd referred to himself in the third person. "And I promise." She tried to keep her tone light, but she was starting to wish she'd let someone know where she was tonight. On the other hand, it was almost dark and nothing had happened to convince her he even had this dissociative disorder. "So what do you do all night while you're tied to a chair? It has to be pretty boring. Isn't there some medication you could take that would be easier than going through this?"

"If I could afford the medication, sure. But it also makes me kind of lethargic and dull. And it isn't foolproof. Since I only have these episodes for a few weeks out of the year, this works well enough."

"Why do you suppose that is? These few weeks, I mean. What's significant about them?"

Leo smiled. "Are you analyzing me?"

"I'm just curious. I've never heard of a dissociative disorder with a time element."

Leo lowered his eyes, like she'd caught him in a lie. "I have a confession to make."

Rhea swiveled the stool back and forth idly. "What's that?"

"I've been screwing with you." He looked up, blue eyes twinkling. "I don't have a dissociative disorder. When you caught me last night I was embarrassed to admit I was messing around in here with my toys and got myself stuck. So I made up the whole thing when you confronted me this morning."

A rush of anger propelled her off the stool. She'd always hated being the butt of a joke. And she'd always been too gullible, which people like Leo tended to pick up on. People who thought it was funny to see how far they could take something before she caught on. Rhea wanted to punch him.

"You're a goddamn jerk."

"I really am. I'm sorry." He seemed genuinely contrite, but she wasn't falling for that. "To tell you the truth, I never thought you'd believe me. But I couldn't help myself. The only disorder I have is that I'm a compulsive liar."

"You're a compulsive liar." Rhea folded her arms. His eyes had taken on the darker hue or deeper intensity she'd noticed the night before. Maybe it was just the light in here. Or maybe it wasn't. "If you're a compulsive liar, why would I believe anything you just said?"

"Ooh. You're good." Leo's expression changed from contrite and slightly chagrined to an almost sultry gaze of appreciation. "You're very good. I like playing with you."

"Playing with me."

"Isn't that what we're doing? I suppose dull-as-a-sackof-hammers Leo told you I was dangerous. Are you my babysitter?" He waggled his eyebrows. "Care to sit closer?" Rhea followed his gaze to his lap without thinking and quickly looked away from the prominent bulge in his pants. If this was all an act, he was one sick puppy. "Don't tell me you and he haven't been intimate."

Rhea met his eyes once more, glaring defiantly. "Me and who, exactly?"

"Candy-ass. Leo the Dull."

"So you're not Leo. Is that what I'm supposed to believe now?"

"Me?" Leo smiled, utterly charming. "I'm Leo's *munr*."

"Munr?"

"His subconscious. The distillation of his will and desire. His id, if you like. I occupy the skin and retain control over the vital processes, the *hamr* and *líkamr*. Leo the Dull is ruled by his *hugr*, the essence of his conscious thought. You might call it the soul. I call it fucking annoying. Happily, it's off doing some dull soul thing. But he doesn't trust me, so he locks me up. It's really unkind." He gave her an adorable pout.

"So this is real, then. This isn't just more compulsive lying?"

Leo—or Leo's id—gave her a dramatic sigh. "If I said I was lying about being a compulsive liar, would you believe me? So many layers of meta. And so boring. When we could be having fun." He gestured with his hips, and Rhea almost made the mistake of looking down again but caught herself. Leo laughed good-naturedly. "Come on. You don't really think I'm dangerous like he told you? He's a puritanical child. I'd never do anything Leo isn't capable of doing himself. He's repressed and he expects me to sit here all night, a slave to his tight little repressed ass, just because he's afraid to be his authentic self."

Rhea leaned back against the cabinet. If this was an act, it was Oscar worthy. It also didn't seem like a dissociative episode. Not that she was any judge. But she'd seen magic before, and this had the air of a magical transformation.

"Have you made up your mind about me?" Leo smiled up at her.

"If you mean have I made up my mind about whether you're telling me the truth—"

"No, I mean, have you made up your mind about whether you're going to satisfy your curiosity? He won't remember any of this tomorrow. You could have your way with me. But be gentle. Technically, I'm a virgin."

"You're unbelievable."

"You have no idea."

"And neither do you, according to you. If you're never allowed free rein when you're in control of the—what did you call it?"

"The *hamr* and *líkamr*. Appearance and form. The skin, if you like."

"So if you're never in control of the skin, how do you know you're any good?"

Leo laughed, the rich, deep laugh that made her loins tingle. "Because, darling, I'm the one with the hard-on. Trust me, I know how to use it." He gyrated his hips again, making Rhea suck in her breath involuntarily. "Ha, I knew it. You want me. Come on. You don't even have to let me go. Just come closer. Please," he added, and that one little word sounded sincere.

Rhea gritted her teeth. "I'm not coming over there, so you can forget it."

"Why?" He growled the word in frustration. "I'm not trying to trick you. I just want a little kiss. A taste of your lips. Just to satisfy what we're both feeling. What do I have to do to convince you I'm sincere?"

"You're *not* sincere. You think this is a game."

"Rhea. A hard-on is not a game." He sighed, head back against the headrest once more. "It's not as if I could pretend to have one." He had a point. One that didn't bear examining.

"I think my hanging out here while your soul is supposedly off skipping the light fandango was a bad idea. You're going to spend the entire time trying to manipulate me into letting you go, and I'm going to spend the entire time being super annoyed." Rhea took her coat from the rack. "I agreed to observe your transformation to validate your claim that you have a dissociative disorder, and I've done that." She pulled the coat on. "So good luck to you."

As she started through the curtain, Leo's voice stopped her. "Did you tattoo me?" He sounded surprised.

Rhea turned, adjusting her collar, to see him studying what he'd called the allrune on his right forearm. "You asked me to touch it up. You don't remember?"

"I tend to ignore Leo the Dull. He spends his time studying chemistry or something. It's a snooze fest."

"Molecular biology." Rhea shrugged when he looked up at her with a look of curiosity. "That's what you said. You dropped out of the molecular biology graduate program at NAU."

"NAU."

"Northern Arizona University. In Flagstaff. Where you met Theia."

"Theia." Leo's eyes registered sudden recognition. "That's why you look so familiar to me. You're Theia Dawn's sister."

The usual irritation at having someone make the connection prickled on her skin. "And that, I presume, is why you're sitting there sporting your misplaced 'admiration' for me."

His eyes seemed to go a shade darker, and he leaned forward sharply, jerking against the restraints with such ferocity that she jumped back even though she was several feet away. "Don't do that," he snapped. "Don't you dare stand there and try to tell me I don't know my own feelings."

"I wasn't exactly talking about your feelings."

"*Desire*. That's my purview. I know all about desire, and I'm not some stupid animal ruled by my prick who'll just wave it at anybody with tits."

Rhea's face went hot. "I didn't say you were an animal, and I don't appreciate the way you're talking to me. Being Leo's id—"

"*Munr.*"

"Whatever—doesn't give you a free pass to be an asshole."

Leo looked taken aback. "*I'm* an asshole?"

"Yeah, you are. Pretty much."

"You're the one who just accused me of being attracted to you because you look like your sister. I'd say you're the asshole."

Rhea flicked the hair out of her eyes in frustration. "How does that make me an asshole? You dated my sister! When you walked in here two days ago, it was because you thought I was Theia. It doesn't take a genius to conclude that your interest in me—your *desire*—is misplaced."

"I'd show you how misplaced it is if you weren't such a chicken."

As Rhea opened her mouth to tell him to go to hell, the realization struck her that she'd been drawn into an argument with a man's id, and she burst out laughing.

Leo glowered at her. "What's so damn funny?"

"This…" She lifted her arms, encompassing the room, the evening, the two of them. "I can't believe I'm arguing with you about the sincerity of your hard-on."

His glower wavered, curving upward into a slight smirk. "I'd have to concede that it's a first in my experience."

Rhea returned the smirk. "I thought you didn't have any experience. Except you obviously remember Theia."

"But I didn't sleep with Theia." That he had no memory of it now didn't necessarily mean he hadn't, but the admission was more satisfying than it ought to be. "At any rate, when Leo isn't boring me into a coma, I can retain some of his memories, but I can't recall ever having such an argument with anyone. You'd think I'd remember being tattooed, though." He glanced down, his gaze drawn to the other arm. "Are you going to do this one, too?"

"I was."

He looked up. "But you're not now?"

"No, I— He's working it off. I mean, *you're* working it off. So I may do the next one. If I let you stay."

"And you don't know if you're going to let me stay." Leo nodded thoughtfully. "That's fair. Just once, I'd like to remember getting tattooed, though."

"I'll talk to him about it. He said he might want another new one." She was starting to talk about Leo in the third person, but it seemed easier to treat them as two different people. "Might be a good way to pass the time while you're locked up."

"So you *are* letting me stay."

"I didn't say that."

"But you are." Leo looked smug. "And what about you? Are you sticking around? Going to keep that coat on?"

"Maybe. Going to keep that hard-on?"

Leo laughed in that incredibly sexy way Rhea was starting to want to keep being the cause of, the sort of laughter one would describe as being genuinely "tickled." Not to mention the throaty richness of the sound he made. He also closed his eyes when he did it. It was probably a good thing he was tied up. She wasn't sure what she'd do if he were able to reach out and touch her right now.

"So what is it with those tattoos, anyway?" She folded her arms, still wearing the coat, maybe subconsciously— or not so subconsciously—trying to keep herself closed to him. "They look older than you."

Leo opened his eyes, the smile slightly less joyful. "They've been there as long as I can remember."

"But you don't remember all that much from the times you're not in control of the skin."

"True. But I also don't remember a time when the marks weren't there."

"This soul-splitting-off thing with the other Leo—"

"Leo the Dull." His blue eyes twinkled.

"Okay, *Leo the Dull* going off to do whatever and leaving you here in restraints—how long has that been going on?"

The smile faded as he pondered the question. "I guess I don't remember a time before that either."

"Not even when you were a kid? This was going on back then?"

"I—don't remember being a child. I suppose that's a bit peculiar, isn't it?"

"Maybe not. Maybe it only happened after puberty. If it's a dissociative disorder, that might make sense. Maybe something traumatic happened to you around the time you got the tattoos."

"Except it's not a disorder. I told you that was bullshit Leo the Dull made up to explain me away. It's Leo's self-righteous *hugr* going off to be self-righteous without me."

"That's how you see it, anyway." She realized she was leaning toward the mental illness hypothesis after all.

"And you're back to analyzing me."

"Maybe I am. You're right, I am. Sorry."

"I'm not objecting. I just find it interesting. Because it means you find *me* interesting." He grinned broadly. "Which I can't imagine is something I share with Leo the Dull."

"Or maybe I find your tattoos interesting. It is kinda my thing after all." But she did find Leo interesting, with or without his *hugr*. "They've been there as long as you can remember, and they're home jobs with significant fading—at least the two on your forearms. The other one looks professional."

"The other one?"

"On your upper arm." He was staring at her blankly. "The Midgard Serpent." He'd worn the long-sleeved Henley today, with the sleeves pushed up to his elbows. What he couldn't see, apparently, he wasn't aware of.

Leo's face clouded. "He's marked me with the serpent? That son of a bitch."

"What's the significance of the serpent?" She'd noted it with some trepidation. Serpents seemed to be intimately bound up with the Carlisle sisters' lives. It all went back to the Lilith blood.

"The Midgard Serpent—Jörmungandr—it's supposed to bring about Ragnarök. The twilight of the gods. The end of the world. Jörmungandr rules the waters surrounding the visible world. It's a sea serpent. A dragon."

Of course it was a dragon. It was *always* dragons.

Rhea sat on the stool once more, rolling it closer to the chair. "So why is it significant that he marked you with it?" It was no use trying not to differentiate between the two of them. "Is he trying to end *you*?"

"Oh, I'm sure he'd love to. But that's not it. It's a way of containing my energy just as Jörmungandr contains the world. I assume it encircles my arm and swallows its tail?"

"I only glanced at it, but, yeah, I think so." She pondered for a moment. "Do you want to see it?"

Leo's eyes danced with amusement. "I don't see how you're going to be able to get my shirt off without undoing the restraints. Or are you planning to cut the shirt off me?" He looked hopeful.

"Yeah, nice try." Rhea wheeled the stool up next to him and pulled down the right shoulder of the stretchy fabric, baring his upper arm. "Take a look."

Leo's breath was warm against her hand as he stretched his neck to see the tattoo. "Can you pull it down a little more?"

As she did, her hand brushed the ink, and the vision from the allrune came back to her, only far more forcefully and in vivid detail. Where her earliest visions had encompassed a series of images answering a question in the client's mind, the ones she'd had without the client's awareness were more like impressions, a peak into memories or desires swirling about inside the person's head. But this…this was like actually being there.

Ice-cold air rushed up at her as she plunged toward the frozen ground, and the force of the impact knocked the air from her lungs. Blood made a spattered trail in the snow ahead of her—her blood. She struggled to stand, fumbling headlong toward the frozen thicket while the groans of the dying and the clash and thud of conflict sounded on the hill behind her.

Her feet were becoming numb as her boots sank into the snow, the creak and crunch of her weight compressing it the only evidence she was still touching it and not floating above the ground. Her chest ached, her lungs having trouble taking in air, and blood was flowing from a hole between her ribs. Blood and sweat ran into her eyes, and she collapsed into the snow and muck and mud, a yard from the covering trees. And from within them came the howling and snarling of wolves.

"What the hell was that?" Leo's growl penetrated the vision, tearing her out of the icy snowbank and grim daylight into the warmth of the heated shop and artificial light.

Rhea broke her grip on Leo's arm and staggered backward off the stool. "What was what?"

"Don't give me that. What just happened? Are you going to pretend you didn't see any of that?"

Rhea was still trying to catch her breath without showing she was doing it. "Why, what did you see?"

"Snow and blood and a pack of wolves."

"Have you ever seen this before? Do you…remember any of it?"

"Why would I have seen it?"

"Because it's your memory. Your reading." Rhea sighed. "I wasn't trying to get a reading. It's an ability I have—I read tattoos. I've been trying to avoid doing it lately, especially when the person hasn't asked for a reading. But when I get anywhere near your tattoos…it just sort of happens."

He scrutinized her face, maybe trying for a reading himself. "It happened with Leo? I mean, when he was occupying the skin?"

"A little bit, yeah."

"And what did he say about it? Is it something that happened to us?"

"He didn't say anything. *I* didn't say anything. I don't know if he saw it. Sometimes it's like that, especially if the person hasn't asked for a reading." Rhea paused. "It's not always a memory. It could be a premonition."

"So I may be stabbed and eaten by wolves in my future?" Leo scowled. "Do it again. I want to see more."

Rhea kept her distance. "I don't think that's such a great idea."

"Why? It's not as though seeing something is going to make it happen. I want to know what's going on, where the wolves are, who stabbed me." He gestured with his head. "Come over here and do it again." He seemed to realize his tone wasn't being appreciated. "Please."

Rhea sighed. "I can't guarantee it will be the same vision. I don't even know if it *is* a premonition. I'm still trying to get a handle on this ability, which is why I haven't been doing it lately." His sleeve had slipped back up over his shoulder, and Rhea pulled it down again. The amber-resin-and-spice scent he'd exuded before rolled off him in waves, a personal pheromone designed just for her. Rhea bit her lip and let her hand move down the firm musculature toward the knotted pattern of the snake.

This time, there was no snow, no blood, no fighting. Only Leo's body under hers, hard and hot…and naked. They were both naked, in this very chair, and Leo was bound to it while Rhea straddled his lap, full of him, riding him, moaning as he pumped his hips into her, grasping for his mouth with hers as the beating of their hearts and their rapid breathing rose toward a crescendo. She arched her back and tilted her hips deeper into his lap, feet off the ground and hands gripping the chair behind her as Leo dipped his head and closed the heat of his mouth over her breast, sucking the nipple in roughly against his teeth. And with a melodic shout, she—

"Holy fuck." Rhea sprang back so forcefully she slammed into the cabinet behind her and hit her head on the corner of the shelf above it.

Leo's eyes were on her, warm with amusement and desire. And his erection, she couldn't help noticing, was back with a vengeance. "Well, that was different. Was that your future or mine?"

"I…" Rhea shook her head, trying to form words, her

face giving off heat like a radiant coil. She managed, finally, four small words in a breathless rush—"I have to go"—and darted past him through the curtain.

Chapter 7

A clock tower in the distance struck seven as predawn light reached the back of the shop, and the locks, right on schedule, clicked open. Leo yawned and rubbed his wrists after working the buckles out of the restraints, disappointed that Rhea had left sometime during the night. He wondered idly if his presence in the building would actually be a deterrent to vandals. He'd kept his cell phone within reach, but would his alter ego bother to call Rhea if he heard someone outside? For all Leo knew, he was the sort of person who would cheer them on.

Leo frowned. God, he hoped his alter ego wasn't a neo-Nazi. Could that be the source of the tattoos? *No.* He refused to accept the idea that he could harbor something so antithetical to his own morality. Rhea had said he was an ass, but she hadn't said anything about him being a neo-Nazi ass.

As long as he was sleeping here—assuming he hadn't done something reprehensible last night and Rhea was still letting him stay—he might as well make himself useful. After checking downstairs to make sure there was no new graffiti, he found more cleaning supplies in the bathroom and gave all the counters a good scrubbing, along with the bathroom tile and the wood floors in the rest of the shop. There was no shower, but he managed to give himself a decent sponge bath before changing into his other clothes. He wrinkled his nose as he sniff-checked the T-shirt. He was going to have to find a laundromat soon.

The door opened as he was pulling the shirt over his head, and Rhea made a sharp little noise like she'd caught him naked.

He tugged the fabric down, head emerging through the collar, and grinned sheepishly as he put his glasses back on. "Sorry. Guess I could have changed in the bathroom."

Her eyes were even wider than usual and her cheeks were flushed. Maybe it was from being out in the cold. It wasn't as if he hadn't been wearing any pants.

"Must have been boring sitting around with Lucid Ass Leo last night, huh?"

Rhea peeled off her gloves and unwound her scarf as she headed into the back. "I wouldn't say boring, no." She returned, sans hat and coat, with that little spike of silvery-lavender hair hanging in her eyes.

Goddamn, she was cute. The word wouldn't have done her justice if he'd used it to describe her to someone else, but it was the best word to capture the sum total of her mannerisms and quirks—the wide, dark-rimmed eyes that crinkled with easy amusement and sarcasm, the combination of almost haphazard yet defiant dress that at the same time managed to seem completely unselfconscious and totally endearing, the no-nonsense way she spoke as if she didn't give a damn if she impressed anyone; they could take her as she was or get bent. But the wild, punky hair had its own separate personality, rebelling from and complementing her at the same time.

She was staring at him like he'd forgotten to zip his fly. He checked to be sure.

"So…was I rude to you again? I hope I didn't do anything out of line."

Rhea studied him. "You absolutely don't remember anything that happens when you're in that state?"

"No. Shit, I did something, didn't I? That's why you left. I'm sorry, I wish I could—"

"You didn't do anything. I mean, you tried to get me to sit on your—"

"No."

"Yeah. But it was nothing I couldn't handle. I mean the come-ons," she added hastily. "But he—*you*—said some curious things about your tattoos."

"Did I?" Leo leaned back against the front counter, palms braced against the edge. Was he finally going to get some answers his conscious mind didn't have access to? Having Rhea talk to his alter ego might turn out to be useful. Unless she found out something he didn't want her to know. He only wished he knew what there was to find out. "Like what?"

"He didn't remember getting them. And he didn't even know about the Midgard Serpent. He thinks you got it to punish him in some way. To control him."

So the other him didn't have a clue about the marks either.

Leo tried not to let the disappointment show on his face. "You realize you keep talking about me in the third person."

Rhea shrugged in acknowledgment. "It's a little weird trying to have a conversation with someone about their other self. He kept using the third person when he talked about you. He calls you…"

Leo waited, but she didn't finish the sentence. "He calls me what?"

Her cheeks reddened slightly. "Leo the Dull."

"Really." He wasn't sure why that annoyed him so much. "Did you tell him we call him the Lucid Ass?"

"It didn't come up."

"Well, maybe next time you can let him know." The rush of air filling his chest and the tightness in his jaw were confusing until it dawned on him that he was jealous of his own alter ego. The idea of him spending time with Rhea—*propositioning* Rhea—made him want to call the asshole out and challenge him. But the "asshole" was himself. It occurred to him that perhaps this response wasn't entirely healthy.

Rhea's expression was guarded. "So, did you? Get the tattoo to punish him, I mean."

Why did he get the feeling she was mad at him about it? "Maybe. I don't know."

She laughed, obviously disbelieving. "How can you not know?"

This was starting to go places he really didn't want it to go. On the other hand, she already knew more about him than he knew about himself. What was the point in keeping what he did know a secret?

"Because…I don't actually remember getting it." There. It was out. She was looking at him the way he'd expected her to. Not only did he have an alternate personality he had to tie up at night, he had blackouts and giant gaps in his history no sane person would have.

"Neither of you remember getting the tattoo?" She glanced at his wrists. The way he was gripping the counter made the allrune and Mjölnir prominently visible. "Do you remember getting those?"

He didn't want to answer. But she already knew.

"I only know they weren't always there and they weren't by choice. But *when* they were put there and by whom…?" He shrugged. "I couldn't tell you. Jörmungandr…" He paused, the memory of buzzing tattoo needles tugging faintly at him. He remembered the aftercare, peeling back the gauze bandage and seeing the intricate black designs, holding his arm before the mirror and turning until he could see the shape of the coiling snake. "Jörmungandr, I think I had done myself. But that's all I know."

Rhea studied him, trying to determine, no doubt, whether he was full of shit. "Do you have any long-term memory?"

Leo gave her a half smile. "Are you analyzing me?"

Her eyes narrowed. "That's what he said."

"Well." Leo shrugged and pushed away from the counter. "We both share the same skin." He put his hands in his pockets, uncomfortable with her scrutiny. "So I promised to work off my debt. What else do you need done? I checked downstairs earlier and didn't find any new graffiti, and I cleaned up a bit in here."

Rhea glanced around, her eyes taking in the gleaming hardwood. "Did you scrub the floor?"

"Yeah."

She looked at him curiously. "I don't have a mop."

"I just used a sponge and some warm soapy water. I followed up with a towel to make sure the water didn't soak in."

She was still looking at him funny.

"What?"

"Nothing, I just— Well, I didn't expect you to be crawling around on my floor on your hands and knees." That little flush was back in her cheeks. "But thank you. It looks great." She glanced around once more, avoiding his eyes. "I did want to go over the inventory. It's not much yet, a dozen bottles of ink, a small supply of needles and accessories, and the disinfecting supplies. I started a spreadsheet to estimate how much I'll need and how much this is going to set me back before I start to turn a profit, but I couldn't get all the columns to add up."

"I can take a look at it for you."

"Could you? That would be great. Even if you could just finish entering the physical inventory and tallying it, that would really help. The more complex stuff can wait."

Leo smiled as Rhea fished the tablet out of her bag. "I'm pretty good with data. I'm used to working in a lab."

While Rhea pulled up the spreadsheet to show him how far she'd gotten, the bell on the door jingled. A woman who looked as much like Rhea as she could without being her twin—except for the long, dark chestnut hair in a high ponytail and bangs—stepped inside, blowing on her bare fingers and stamping her feet.

"Goddamn. It's colder than a witch's tit." She grinned as Rhea turned in surprise. "Hi, brat! I figured I'd come by and see your new digs while Rafe is busy dealing with the frozen pipes at one of his worksites."

"Phoebe." Rhea's expression was a mixture of pleased and annoyed as she went to greet her. "It's not ready yet. I told you I'd have everyone in for the grand opening. How did you even know where it was? I didn't tell anyone I'd signed a lease."

"Seriously, Rhe. A new tattoo shop opens up in Uptown Sedona with the name Demoness Ink? Give me some credit."

Leo studied the spreadsheet as if greatly interested in it. If Rhea didn't want to introduce him, that was her business.

But he hadn't escaped her sister's notice. "You already have a client?"

Rhea cleared her throat. "This is Leo. He's my employee."

"Employee, huh? Well, aren't we fancy. Hi, Leo. I'm Phoebe, the sister that doesn't look just like her."

Leo stepped forward to shake her hand. "I wouldn't say

that. There's actually a striking resemblance. If I hadn't already met Theia, I might have guessed you were the twin."

"You've met Theia?"

Rhea's posture had gone stiff. He realized he'd stepped in it.

"We were in the same program at NAU." He figured mentioning they'd dated would compound the mistake. "Well, I'd better get started on that inventory. Nice to meet you, Phoebe." He slunk away into the back room before Rhea murdered him with her eyes.

Rhea switched on the electric kettle on the little table in the waiting area after Leo tactfully pulled the curtain closed behind him. "Do you want some tea? I've also got cocoa."

Phoebe was giving her the eye as she took off her coat. That I-know-what-you're-up-to eye that had often led to bargaining and blackmail when they were younger and Phoebe had caught one of the twins trying to keep something from Ione.

"Stop looking at me like that."

"You *like* him." Phoebe's voice was low but not low enough.

"Shut up. What are we, twelve?"

"You're blushing." Phoebe pinched her cheek, and Rhea smacked her hand away. "And that was your work on his arm. So I know you've read him. Spill. I want details."

Rhea lowered her voice, hoping Phoebe would take the hint. "There are no details. You're out of your mind. He's just my employee." She got some mugs and spoons from the shelf and brought the bin of assorted tea and cocoa packets, choosing a jasmine green for herself as she sat on the funky red leather couch she'd found at a flea market.

Phoebe grabbed a cocoa packet and plopped down beside her. "This is me you're talking to." She ripped open the packet and dumped the powder into one of the mugs. "I know that look." She glanced at the curtain. "And *damn*. Is it hot in here or is it just him?"

"Jesus, Phoebes. Would you please keep your voice down?"

Phoebe grinned. "Not so funny when the shoe's on the other foot, eh? You and Theia were merciless when I met Rafe. I think turnabout's fair play."

"Yeah, well, your *sex tape* was all over the internet. I think you had a little ribbing coming."

Phoebe grimaced. "You are forbidden from mentioning the sex tape. We all agreed never to speak of it again. How was I supposed to know there was a reporter hiding in the bushes outside his house?"

The kettle beeped, and Rhea poured water into Phoebe's cup. "You might have thought about closing the curtains, Slutina."

"Ouch. The claws are coming out." Phoebe stirred her cocoa. "You don't usually get this defensive unless there's something to defend. Does this have anything to do with Theia?"

Rhea kept her expression neutral as she poured the water over her tea bag. "No, it has nothing to do with Theia."

"She says she doesn't know why you're mad at her."

"Phoebe." Rhea closed her fist around the hot mug. "I told you not to talk to her about it."

"I didn't. She called me to see if I knew what was going on with you. She's worried about you."

"So you told her."

"I *didn't*. I said she'd have to talk to you because it wasn't my business. But we all think it's a little weird."

"Phoebe!" The heat of the mug was becoming intense, and Rhea uncurled her fingers before it burned her palm.

"I can't believe you. I tell you something about Theia in confidence and you not only discuss it with her but you decide to bring Di into it?" It was the nickname the three of them used for Ione. Her given name was actually Dione, but she hated it.

Phoebe blew on her cocoa before taking a careful sip. "There was no 'bringing.' You know I don't volunteer information to Ione. But apparently Rafe and Dev got together—Dev's looking for work now that he's no longer employed by the Covent, and Rafe might be able to use him in operations for the construction business—and I guess Rafe might have mentioned something about you two not talking."

Rhea growled as she wrapped the string of her tea bag around her spoon. "Which he knew because you told him."

Phoebe had the grace to look chagrined. "I talk about things I care about with Rafe. And I care about you. So, yeah, I told him. Which was kind of your fault, if you think about it. Because you told me to ask him about the ghost riders and I had to provide context."

"Which included, 'Oh, by the way, Rhea's being a bitch and not talking to Theia.'"

"Nobody thinks you're being a bitch. And yes, of course it did. I'm thorough." Phoebe tried to hide her smile. "Anyway, don't think I haven't noticed that you've steered me away from the subject of hot Thor in there."

Rhea slapped Phoebe's arm with the spoon, which turned out to be still hot from the tea bag, and Phoebe made a little squeal of protest.

"So what's the story?" Phoebe rubbed at the spot. "You didn't just happen to hire somebody who was in Theia's grad program. What's his deal?"

"There's no deal. He saw my Help-Wanted sign and came in, thinking I was Theia. After a little awkwardness around the confusion, I hired him."

"Why is a molecular biology student looking for work in a tattoo shop?"

"Ex-molecular biology student, and how do I know?"

"How well did he know Theia?"

Rhea sighed and drank her tea. "They dated, apparently."

"Oh, honey." Phoebe was giving her another one of her looks, only this one was akin to pity. "You're doing that thing again."

"What thing?" Rhea looked over her shoulder to make sure the curtain was still closed. "There's no 'thing.'"

"That thing where you try to compete with Theia when she's not even competing with you. You know you're your own person, unique and interesting and sexy."

"Jesus, Phoebes."

"You don't need validation from someone who was into Theia to prove you're valuable."

"That is not what I'm doing, and shut up, I don't do that." Rhea set her mug down forcefully. "Sometimes you're worse than Ione."

Phoebe set down her own mug with a glare. "Okay, *that* was mean."

"Then stop being bossy and judgmental."

"Rhea."

Rhea leaned close to her, keeping her voice to a low murmur. "If you must know, I did read him. And the vision I got was of me riding him like a Brahma bull on Rodeo Day. So don't tell me I'm looking for validation, because I got it without even asking for it, and I've never even had sex that good in my actual life."

"Wow." Phoebe raised her eyebrows and looked pointedly in the direction of the curtained back room. "That wouldn't have anything to do with that snake tattoo peeking out of his sleeve, would it?"

Rhea scrubbed her hands over her face and smoothed her hair back, palms pressed to her crown. "I am so screwed." She and Phoebe locked eyes at the inadvertent pun and burst out laughing.

When the laughter subsided, Rhea sighed. "There's a lot more I can't get into right now, but the tattoo is apparently meant to contain the destructive energy of the Midgard Serpent."

"The way Dev's tattoo keeps Kur caged inside him?"

"Not exactly." Rhea glanced nervously over her shoulder again. "It's more like his own negative potential."

"So you don't think he's like Rafe and Dev."

Rhea stared into her empty cup. How was this happening? Was she really "destined" somehow to be with Leo because of serpent energy and Lilith blood? Were all the Carlisle sisters cursed because of crazy Madeleine Marchant being burned at the stake in 1462?

"Rhea?"

"Hmm? Sorry. No, I don't think he's a shifter." What she thought seemed even more improbable. That he was something more than just a mortal man with a mystical propensity to transform into something serpentine, like Rafe Diamante or Dev Gideon did, at the touch of the Carlisle sisters' demon blood. She had also seen the visions of the Wild Hunt, and a battle in a field of snow, and talking foxes.

She was about to say more when the curtain opened with a loud scrape of the wooden rings on the rod. Unusually loud, like he'd been waiting for his moment to emerge and wanted to make sure they noticed. Crap. How much had he heard? She thought back frantically over the last several seconds.

"I think I've got your spreadsheet sorted." He held up the tablet.

Rhea couldn't tell from the look on his face whether

he'd heard anything embarrassing. "That was quick. I was tearing my hair out over that thing."

"You just had a couple of little errors in your formula."

Rhea laughed. "Very diplomatic." She rose and went to the shelf to get him a cup, trying to keep from being awkward. "Do you want some tea or cocoa?"

"Actually, I realized I hadn't eaten, so I thought I'd go out and get a sandwich or something if you can spare me?"

"Of course."

Leo grabbed his coat and hat from the back room and set the tablet on the counter. "Would either of you like anything?" If he'd heard anything mortifying, he wasn't letting on.

Rhea picked up the tablet and pretended to look over the spreadsheet. "No, I'm good."

"I'm good, too." Phoebe paused a little too long; Rhea should have seen it coming. "But Rhe's *very* good. Or so I've heard." She was too far away for Rhea to kick her.

Leo laughed awkwardly, pulling on his hat, and let himself out. A blast of cold air was sucked in before he shut the door behind him.

Phoebe was smiling smugly.

"You suck, Phoebe."

"You and Theia always take such pleasure in tormenting me about my sex life, and I never could figure out what was so damn appealing. But, you know, this is actually pretty fun. I get it now." She beamed. "I like it."

Rhea gave her a murderous glare. For once, she was completely without a comeback. She'd created a monster. At least Leo hadn't overheard anything crucial.

Phoebe took a sip of her cocoa. "So have you seen any more ghost riders?"

"They're not ghost riders. They're riders and they happen

to look like ghosts. And I refuse to answer that question on the grounds that it may incriminate me."

Phoebe grinned. "I've taught you well. Guess all that law school I wasted money on paid off. Anyway, Rafe agrees."

"With what?"

"They're shades, in a manner of speaking, but not ghosts. Not the spirits of the dead. More like wraiths. Especially given the presence of that fox you mentioned. He says it sounds like you encountered a *fylgja*. It's an aspect of the Norse concept of the self. Apparently, there are several aspects that can act independently of one another, projecting outside the physical body. The *fylgja* is a sort of familiar spirit projection. It can also appear as a warning."

It fit with Leo's talk last night about the *munr* and *hugr* being separate parts of himself. But if Vixen's appearance had been a warning...what was it a warning of?

Chapter 8

Leo had heard every word of Rhea's conversation with her sister. He'd tried not to, but the sound in the little shop carried extremely well and they were unbelievably terrible at keeping their voices down.

At least he knew now why Rhea had left last night. He'd never heard it put quite so colorfully before, but "riding him like a Brahma bull" painted a vivid picture. He was going to have to find out more about this "reading" skill of hers. It explained the images he'd seen while she was working on his tattoo. And if he was going to have her do more work, he'd have to find some way to shield himself from being read—or straight-up admit he knew about her ability.

As he walked in the brisk air, he tried not to dwell on the image she'd conjured and instead pondered her talk of "shifters." It had followed the discussion of the Midgard Serpent. Rhea apparently knew more about that than she'd let on. Could she have lied about what his alter ego knew? It was frustrating having only part of the story of his own life, and knowing the other Leo might have information he didn't was infuriating. As if they were two separate people competing with each other. And now they were competing for a woman's attention.

Not that Leo was pursuing Rhea, or that he could even afford to pursue anyone, but she'd had the vision while reading the other him, not Leo himself. Which, coupled with the propositioning he'd reportedly done, meant the other him already had detailed images of being with Rhea in his mind. Or were her readings premonitions? Heat rushed to his face with a surge of anger at the thought of the other Leo occupying his skin while being intimate with Rhea—without him.

Gods, he was losing his mind. And he was *not* going to think about Rhea in that fashion. It was getting him nowhere. He concentrated once more on the idea of shape-shifting. Did Rhea actually know shape-shifters—this Rafe and Dev her sister had mentioned? And if she did, what would his tattoo have to do with it? Rhea didn't seem to think Leo was a shifter. But the fact that her sister had even asked was just weird. Like it was common enough that she'd expect it. Could that be why he'd always been so determined not to let his alter ego get free? Would Leo *shift*?

Deep in thought about the terrifying prospect of actually becoming Jörmungandr, he wasn't paying attention to his surroundings, and he nearly ran smack into someone coming from the opposite direction.

Slipping precariously on the icy sidewalk, he grabbed for the other man's arm to steady them both. "I am *so* sorry." Leo let go and took a step back. "I wasn't paying attention to where I was going."

"I can see that. You really ought to… Leo? Leo Ström, right?"

Leo pushed up his glasses, trying to place the face. Early thirties, fairly nondescript brown hair and eyes—he looked vaguely familiar, but—shit, what if this was someone he should know but had forgotten along with so much else?

"Brock Dressler." Dressler held out his hand. "We met at a conference at NAU a few months ago. *Genetic Imper-*

atives in Biotechnology. We talked briefly about eugenics while we were waiting for the elevator."

Leo shook his hand and nodded. Maybe he'd forgotten him because he hadn't made much of an impression. "Right, right. Of course. Brock. How have you been?"

"Can't complain." Dressler turned up his collar against the wind. "What brings you to Sedona?"

"Oh, just the scenery. I hadn't been down here before. I'm taking a break from my studies."

"You picked a great time. Sedona's beautiful any time of year, but there's something special about snow in the desert. We don't usually get it this early. Looks like we're going to have a white Christmas." He winked conspiratorially. "I'm allowed to say that now, right?" Dressler laughed like he'd said something clever.

Leo thought about ignoring it, but he was feeling contrary, still riled up by the thought of the other Leo being with Rhea. "Why wouldn't you be allowed to say that?"

"White and Christmas." Dressler grinned. "Thank God we don't have to tiptoe around trying not to offend the elites pushing their agenda anymore."

Leo folded his arms, perhaps subconsciously aware of their intentions. "What 'elites' would those be?"

"You know, the liberal Zionist media."

He took a deep breath, trying to be the better man, trying to think of what the better man would say to such an appalling expression of idiocy.

Dressler's smile faltered. "Don't tell me you're one of them? Not with those tattoos."

Leo glanced down. The sleeves of his coat had ridden up when he'd crossed his arms, revealing the gauntlets.

"Why else would you have the allrune and Thor's hammer tattooed on your arms? I know a brother when I see one."

In retrospect, coldcocking a virtual stranger on the street

probably wasn't his finest hour. But it felt like it was as his fist impacted with Dressler's jaw.

Dressler's head snapped back, his eyes wide with surprise, and he stumbled backward, ducking belatedly. "What the *hell*, Leo?"

Leo stepped in close before Dressler could back away farther. "I'm not your goddamn brother. Don't you ever mistake me for one of yours. And if you want my advice, I wouldn't throw away your toe shoes just yet either, because you're going to need to go back to tiptoeing. There are still plenty of people who find your kind of talk disgusting. Thank the gods." He turned on his heel, grateful he didn't slip on the ice again and make a fool of himself after his outburst.

"I ought to press charges, you maniac!" Dressler called after him. "That was assault!"

Your face *is an assault.* He choked back laughter at the childishness of the thought and waited until he'd rounded the corner before shaking out his hand and flexing his bloodied knuckles. He wasn't sure if it was Dressler's blood or his own. He'd hit the guy pretty good. At least he'd made his position clear. And maybe the little worm would think twice about assuming his bigotry was somehow acceptable now. Leo would be just fine with his kind going back into the closet for fear of public ridicule. Or face punching.

He remembered the conversation at the conference now. The panel they'd come out of was on balancing the strengths and weaknesses of inherited traits, and Dressler had spouted some drivel about the ethics of breeding out inferior genes. Leo hadn't taken his words as hinting at racial purity at the time, but in retrospect, Dressler's agenda seemed fairly transparent. He remembered hoping the elevator would hurry up and come. He'd been about to meet Theia for drinks—they'd gone out only once before—and he'd brushed off Dressler without paying him much mind. Combined with the graffiti at Rhea's place, what Leo had dismissed as xenophobic wing nut babble took on greater significance. Maybe there was something bigger going on here.

By the time he got back to the shop, Rhea's sister was gone. He'd forgotten to get his sandwich, but then that hadn't really been the purpose of his walk. Rhea stood behind the counter, absently twisting a pastel multicolored spike of hair, the tablet's screen asleep in front of her.

He smiled and tried for nonchalance as he closed the door against the cold air. "So how many of you are there?"

Rhea paused with the strand around her index finger. "*Me?* I'm not the one with a split personality."

"No, I meant sisters." He grinned. "I want to be on the lookout in case I stumble across another one."

Rhea pushed the hair back from her forehead with a look of annoyance. She'd probably heard that one more than once. "There are four." She scrunched up her nose. "Or seven, depending on whom you ask."

Leo dropped onto the leather couch, realizing it wasn't quite made for his weight as it creaked beneath him. "Sounds intriguing."

"It's not."

"Sorry. I didn't mean to pry."

"No, that's okay." Rhea folded her arms and leaned against the counter. "It's just kind of a sore spot with me right now. It's not a secret or anything. Or maybe it is. I don't know. But it might be nice to talk to someone other than my sisters about it."

Leo leaned back, stretching his arms across the couch back. "I'm all ears."

"Theia was doing this genealogy thing a while back.

Genetic research is kind of her hobby. She was interested in plotting various traits throughout our lineage, and with our parents dead and no living grandparents, there was no one to ask." Rhea looked up at the ceiling as if carefully choosing her words. "And she stumbled upon this other Carlisle family. It turns out our father was a secret biga- mist, and there are three half sisters out there we've never met. Well, except one, who's a nutjob and left roadkill on our doorsteps after she found out about us."

Leo's hat was slipping into his eyes and he pushed it back on his head, as if he needed to see better to process the story. "Damn."

"Yeah. Damn."

For once, he didn't have that nagging desire to know where he'd come from. There were certain benefits to not having a family. No one to totally betray you and leave you feeling stabbed in the gut.

"But you and your sisters are pretty close, I take it? The ones you grew up with. It must be cool to have a twin."

"Usually." The dark rings around the gray of Rhea's eyes seemed especially vivid. He decided not to pry further, but apparently Rhea didn't need any more encouragement now that she'd gotten started. "I thought I could trust Theia, but she never told me about any of this. I had to find out when the nutjob was trying to kill Phoebe."

He wasn't quite sure what to say to that. "She literally tried to kill her?"

"She got taken in by this asshole my older sister Ione used to date, and he kind of…recruited her to do his dirty work while he's in prison."

Leo shifted on the couch. He'd had to ask.

"Too much information, right?" Rhea laughed and picked up the tablet, studying the spreadsheet. "Anyway, that's why Theia's not exactly my favorite person right now."

A funny little pang of disappointment accompanied the realization that jealousy over his involvement with Theia had nothing to do with it, and he spoke, as usual, before he thought. "That's why?"

Rhea eyed him over the top of the tablet. "Why else?"

"I don't know." *Think fast, Ström.* "I guess if I had a twin, I wouldn't let that come between us."

Rhea looked at him pointedly. "You can't even get along with your own id."

He couldn't help but laugh. "You've got me there." He scratched at his knit cap. "Id. That's an interesting way of looking at it."

"Well, he said the term was *munr*. I mean, *you* said." The word had a sharp zing of familiarity, but he couldn't place it. It was like trying to read something in a dream.

"Munr?"

"I think it's Old Norse. He said it was the self of will and desire."

"The self." He scratched at the hat again.

"He claims your soul goes off on some business of its own, which is why he's in charge of the skin."

"My *soul*?"

"He called it the *hugr*. The self of conscious thought. You really didn't know any of this?"

The hat was bugging him, and he pulled it off his head. "I...did not." Leo combed his fingers through his hair. The idea that parts of him were engaged in activities and conversations he knew nothing about was unnerving. "You said he—my *munr*—thinks I got the Midgard Serpent tattoo to keep him in line. I think that's true. I've had the idea since I got the tattoo that the serpent is a symbol for his destructive energy, and, that if he were to escape, he could use that energy to cause a great deal of harm."

He'd been pondering how to broach the subject of shifters without letting on that he'd heard her entire conversation with Phoebe, but he lucked out, and she did it for him.

"Do you think that energy could be literal?"

"Literal?"

Rhea's unruly strand of hair slid back into her face as she looked down at the counter, pondering the answer. "Like... do you think he has any unusual abilities? Maybe the ability to actually...change the form he's in? I mean, he talks about being in control of the 'skin,' which I think he sees as another aspect of self. What if he could manipulate it?"

"You think my *munr* could turn into a snake."

"Well, maybe not a snake exactly, but...something physically different from the form you're in now." She was dancing around it. Maybe he was going to have to say it after all. But Rhea straightened and put her hands in her pockets. "Do you believe in magic?"

He took his time answering. "Well, since so much of what I know about my life is somewhat murky, I can't say that I definitely *don't* believe in magic."

That crooked half smile, half smirk that drew undue attention to her lips slid into place. "So you're not *not* licking toads."

Leo pulled his gaze away from her mouth. "I... What?"

"It's from an episode of *The Simpsons*. Bart asks Homer if he's licking toads and he says he's not *not* licking toads."

"What's *The Simpsons*?"

Rhea's mouth dropped open in exaggerated horror. "Don't tell me you've never seen *The Simpsons*. It's only been on television for nearly thirty years. They must have had it in Sweden."

Leo lifted his shoulders, giving her a helpless smile.

"I don't really watch television." The truth was, he might have watched hundreds of television shows, but that sort of thing didn't seem to stick.

Rhea shook her head. "I'm starting to worry about you, Leo. I may have to do an intervention. Lock you up at my place instead of here some night and force you to watch *The Simpsons* best-of. Maybe some 'Treehouse of Horror' episodes—the Halloween specials."

Something inside him did a little flip-flop at the idea of Rhea locking him up. He moved his hat into his lap. "You realize you'd be showing the Lucid Ass your House of Horrors and I still wouldn't have seen it. In fact, why don't you ask him? He's probably already seen some. I often leave the television on in the motel to give him something to do at night."

"It's Treehouse of Horror, and I suppose you're probably right." She shrugged. "Maybe I will ask him."

"So you plan to stay again this evening? That is, if you're going to allow *me* to stay again this evening?"

Rhea studied him, her expression giving away nothing. "Yes, I'm going to let you stay. I don't know if I will. We'll see." She drummed her fingers against the counter. "In the meantime, you're here to work, remember?"

"Right." Leo jumped up, making a strategic wardrobe adjustment. "Sorry. I got a little too cozy, huh? So what's next?"

Rhea took a stack of flyers from behind the counter and set them on it with a heavy plop. "I've been setting up digital ads and working on the website, but I figured some old-school advertising couldn't hurt. I need these posted around the Uptown area." She brought out a staple gun along with a heavy-duty roll of cellophane tape and set them next to the stack. "Use whatever method works. Staples for telephone poles, tape for the sides of newsstands. Whatever. Just don't get arrested."

Leo smiled, putting his coat back on. "I think I can handle it." As he put on his hat, Rhea came out from around the counter and surprised him by grabbing his hand.

"What the heck is this?" She held up his bloodied knuckles. He'd forgotten all about Dressler and the ill-conceived but immensely satisfying action he'd taken in response to the man's bigotry.

"I, uh…" *Oh, hell, just say it.* "I punched a Nazi."

"You *what*?"

"This asshole I ran into while I was out. I'd met him at a genetics in biotech conference a few weeks ago, and he assumed my attendance at a panel on selecting for beneficial genetic mutations meant I was sympathetic to his cause. Well, that, and my tattoos."

Rhea studied him, clearly trying to decide if he was putting her on or just insane. She was still holding his hand. She noticed at the same moment he did, and she let it drop. He'd kind of been enjoying it. More than "kind of."

"Should I be checking to see if you have a prison record?"

She didn't seem too serious, so Leo laughed. "Maybe you should be. For all I know, I could be a felon."

She frowned. "That's not encouraging. But I don't necessarily disapprove of punching Nazis."

"So…" He smiled. "You're not *not* licking toads."

The grin he got in return was totally worth the bruised knuckles.

He had to get creative with posting the flyers. There weren't many accessible utility poles or newsstands. A few crystal shops and bookstores had boards where postings were encouraged, so he hit up as many of those as he could, pinning the flyers among advertisements for Reiki and yoga and cupping. He couldn't help a little juvenile smile at that last term.

But the smile faded as he stopped to put up a few flyers on the planks lining a temporary covered walkway. Right in the middle of the advertisements for indie bands and metaphysical retreats, a bold poster, larger than the others, had been tacked up. Red-and-black print repeated the phrase from the graffiti he'd cleaned up, this time in English, complete with swastikas.

Intending to tear it down and rip it to shreds to deposit it in the nearest recycling bin, he met with an unpleasant surprise. Something sharp lined the back of the poster, slicing his fingers open as he yanked on the poster board. Leo swore and pulled his hand away to find his fingers dripping with blood.

Chapter 9

Rhea looked up when the bell on the door announced Leo's entrance, the smile on her face quickly turning to open-mouthed shock as she saw his bloody fingers.

She hurried out from behind the counter. "*Now* what happened?"

"This time it wasn't me. But it *was* Nazis." He held up the bloodied strips of poster board, showing her the razor blades he'd found glued to the back along the edges.

"Are you kidding me? Who would do that?" Rhea took the strips from him and set them on the counter. "Come on. We'd better clean you up. You don't want to get sepsis."

A flash of something went through his mind, not quite a memory, but an image of a fallen comrade dying of a festering wound. *Comrade in what?*

"No," he agreed and let Rhea lead him to the bathroom.

Having Rhea fussing over him was almost worth the sting of the soap and alcohol as she cleaned him up and bandaged his fingers.

"I don't think I really need bandages," he protested, but Rhea was insistent.

"For all we know, you need a tetanus shot." Rhea glanced up from taping the last of the adhesive bandages over his right pinkie. "Have you ever had a booster?" When he opened his mouth to say he wasn't sure, Rhea held up her hand and shook her head. "Never mind, don't tell me— you have no idea. Jesus, Leo. How do you even know what your name is?"

Leo shrugged and smiled. "It's on my passport." He was only half kidding. Rhea rolled her eyes as they headed back into the reception area.

She carefully picked up one of the bloodied poster strips from the counter. "Why did you bring these back?"

"I thought we might need the evidence. I don't know. I suppose the police can't do anything."

"The police might be complicit." That wasn't encouraging. Rhea laid out the strips on the counter, piecing it together, and frowned. "'The impure shall be cast out.'"

"That was the same thing that was written on the wall downstairs."

Rhea's expression hardened. "That's not good."

"Does it have some special meaning?"

"My half sister Laurel—she kept using that phrase when she was delivering threatening notes from the necro—from Ione's ex."

Leo looked bemused. "You think her ex is involved in this?"

"I wouldn't put it past him. He's the reason the police are a no-go. They were in on some ugly shit with him when he was a high-powered attorney." Little frown lines formed between Rhea's eyes. "Damn. I'm going to have to let Ione know about this. She'll totally freak. She's kind of controlling when it comes to the three of us—she raised us, basically, after our parents died." Rhea leaned back against the counter. "But if this has something to do with Carter, I have to let her know. And Phoebe. And Theia. Dammit."

Leo started to brush his fingers through his hair but paused as he remembered the bandages. "Maybe it's a coincidence."

"Nothing is ever a coincidence around this guy. He's powerful and spiteful. We took his little apprentice away from him, which has to have pissed him off. Maybe he's found another way to get to us."

Leo studied her. She was seriously rattled. "What you started to say a minute ago... This guy, your sister's ex—is he actually a necrophiliac?"

Rhea laughed, and then shuddered. "He's certainly twisted enough to do it. But that wasn't what I was about to say." She put her hands in her pockets and studied the floor. "I suppose I might as well tell you. Carter Hamilton and my sister Ione both belonged to the same coven. Until Carter decided regular witchcraft wasn't enough for him and he started using magic intended to give him power over the dead." She glanced up, a combination of defiance and determination in her eyes, as if daring him not to believe her. "He's a necromancer."

It was one of those words he knew he'd heard before in another context, in another time, but the significance eluded him.

"Or he was. We stripped him of his power." She was watching him, waiting for his reaction.

"Who's 'we'?"

"My sisters and I. And Rafe, Phoebe's boyfriend."

"And your sister Ione is...?"

"A witch. Yes. So is Rafe."

A lot of people called themselves witches these days. It wasn't that unusual. Necromancy, on the other hand... But he wanted to know more about these "shifter" abilities.

"You said Rafe is able to shift into another form. Is that because of this 'necromancer'?"

"You don't have to say 'necromancer' like I'm talking about my imaginary friend. It's fine if you don't believe me, but don't condescend to me." Rhea went to the electric kettle and switched it on. "You should get something hot into you. You're freezing and your fingers are bleeding through those..." She'd turned away to get him a mug from the shelf, but she paused with the mug in her hand and turned slowly back to face him.

"What's wrong?"

"When did I say Rafe could shift into another form?"

"When you were suggesting the Ass might have the ability to transform into something serpentine."

Rhea shook her head slowly. "No. No, I'm pretty sure I didn't." Her cheeks went slightly pink. "I mentioned it to Phoebe. We were talking about your tattoo and about Phoebe's and Ione's boyfriends. And you...heard the entire conversation." The pink was now a delightful fuchsia.

Leo tried to find something to do with his hands. He ended up crossing his arms awkwardly, his fingers splayed. "I caught a few things here and there."

"You didn't hear me talking about reading you."

"Reading me?"

"Stop it, Leo." Her eyes narrowed with irritation, the dark brows contrasting with the glowing cheeks. "Just stop. You heard me tell Phoebe that I..." She obviously couldn't bring herself to say it to his face.

Leo looked down at his boots. "That you had a vision where you rode me like a Brahma bull, I believe it was." He couldn't help smiling, and he snuck a glance up at her from under his lashes.

Rhea groaned, forehead in her hand. "Is the ground opening up? My eyes are closed. I can't tell. Please tell me the ground is opening up to swallow me whole."

Leo laughed. "Nope. Sorry. The ground appears to be pretty stable."

"I've sexually harassed my own employee." Rhea sighed, still not looking up. "Let me get you the complaint form to fill out. I think I should warn you in advance that I don't have much for you to sue me for. Just my shop. And my entire life savings that I've sunk into it."

"I think you're making too big of a deal about this."

Rhea peered up at him through her fingers. "Isn't that my line? Is this where I get dismissive and make an accusatory comment about what you were wearing? I'm new at being a lecherous douchebag."

"Rhea." He couldn't help laughing at her miserable expression. "I'm not going to sue you. I was a little surprised. More about the reading part than the...riding." That, of course, wasn't true, but he *was* curious. He realized he needed to phrase this just right. "Can you tell a person's fortune by reading their tattoos?"

She was still looking through her fingers. "I've been known to...read certain information about a person's life from their tattoos, yes." The kettle beeped and Rhea heaved an audible sigh of relief. "Tea or cocoa?"

"Cocoa." He watched as Rhea busied herself with the little packets. "So, is it like a tarot reading or a palm reading?"

"It's like I *am* the tarot." Rhea poured the hot water into the cups. "I pick up images. It used to be only when the subject wanted to know something. It was a shared vision, but lately...I don't know, it's kind of gotten out of control. I've been trying to quit."

"But you read me yesterday when you were working on the touch-up." Leo came to the table and took the cocoa from her. "I felt something. Saw...some kind of..." He sat on the couch, blowing on the hot beverage. "I don't know. It felt like a memory."

Rhea sat beside him at a deliberate, respectable distance. "Why didn't you say anything?"

"Why didn't *you*?"

"The visions I've been having recently have been one-sided. I didn't want to call attention to it." She took a sip of her cocoa while it was still too hot and winced. "I'm not even sure we saw the same thing."

Leo smirked into his cup. "There wasn't any bull riding on my end."

Rhea sighed and set her cup down, pressing her lips together against the cocoa burn, prompting a sudden urge within him to kiss them and make it better. "There wasn't any on my end either. Just a bunch of snow. Full-on subarctic winter. And you were running—or I was running. It got a little blurry identity wise. Like in a dream. I've never had a vision that dragged me into it that way before. But there was blood spattered on the snow. And I think someone stabbed me." They both shuddered at the same moment, and Rhea glanced at him. "Is that what you saw?"

"Pretty much. The blood and the snow. And there were wolves. But not the stabbing. Except, when you said that, it felt…true, I guess is the only word. I could almost feel it happening."

Rhea studied him. "There weren't any wolves in my vision. At least, not that one. I did hear wolves in the vision I had with *him*." Her cheeks went pink again. "The first vision. Before the…"

"The Brahma bull?" he offered helpfully.

Rhea glared. "You're just going to keep saying it, aren't you?"

"Sorry. It's just such a colorful description."

She made that soft little groan again that didn't help matters. "Anyway, there were hunting dogs in one of my visions, too." She was pointedly trying to get him off the subject of Brahma bulls. "Though they did look a bit wolfish. Except they had curly tails."

"Jämthunds."

"Sorry?"

"Sounds like they were *jämthunds*. A kind of Swedish elkhound. They have sort of wolfish faces. Probably descended from them." Leo sipped his cocoa. "I wonder what the hunting imagery means."

Rhea looked like she was about to say something but sipped her cocoa instead.

"So about your fortune-telling ability—"

"I call it pictomancy."

"You said you'd done readings for people based on their queries. I wonder if you could use it to find out about someone's past."

"You mean your missing past."

"Yeah, I…" He hadn't thought this through. He didn't know what Rhea might find. That was the problem with not knowing. "Never mind. Bad idea."

"Not necessarily." Rhea's look was guarded; maybe she was calculating the possibility of another intimate vision. "If you concentrate on a specific question, the reading should give us the answer to only that question. That's the way it's always worked before."

Was there a specific question he could ask that wouldn't be potentially disastrous? He vaguely recalled getting the Jörmungandr tattoo. That ought to be safe enough, to get clarity on where and when he'd gotten it done. Just *some* damned detail from his past, no matter how mundane, would be nice.

Rhea sipped her cocoa again. "Do you want me to do a reading?"

"How much do you charge?"

Her gray eyes flashed with apparent insult. "I don't *charge*. That would be unethical."

"Why would it be unethical? People charge for reading fortunes all the time."

"Well, I'm not 'people.' I only do readings for friends and family."

Leo smiled, cocking his head. "So I'm a friend?"

The smile she gave him in return seemed a little surprised. And pleased. "Yeah, I guess you are."

He was surprised by how this affected him. He couldn't remember ever having a friend. Which was sad and pathetic. Then again, he couldn't remember if he'd ever watched television. Maybe he'd had lots of friends. And maybe his alter ego had escaped and turned into a giant snake and killed them. *Sure, just go there immediately. That'll help with the whole "carefully selected past" concept.*

Rhea set down her mug. "So roll up your sleeve."

"Actually, I was thinking of the Midgard Serpent."

Rhea laughed nervously. "Right. Because that wasn't at all awkward the last time."

"I wasn't present the last time," he reminded her. "At least not mentally. And you said you could focus on an event from the past."

She looked suspicious. "Why does it have to be the serpent?"

"Because the question I want answered— Do I tell you beforehand?"

"It's not a parlor trick, so, yeah, that information would be useful."

"Right. Sorry. I want to find out exactly when and where I got the tattoo."

"And you don't want to know where you got the others?"

Leo gave her an apologetic smile. "Not from you."

"Ah. Got it. Okay, take off your shirt." Her face went red again as soon as she'd said it. "I wasn't speaking as your employer."

Leo laughed. "It's okay. The lines here are sort of blurry, anyway." He stripped off the shirt before she could object.

Rhea pointedly avoided looking at his bare chest, turning her body on an angle to face his shoulder. Mindful of the cold, she rubbed her palms together briskly before placing her right hand over the tattoo. There was no immediate flash of imagery. He wasn't sure if that was good or bad.

"Now think about your question. Hold it in your mind. Make it as specific as you can."

Leo concentrated on what he remembered about the time around the tattooing. He'd been in Sweden, he thought. Working on his undergraduate degree. He was dating someone… "Oh." As he spoke the word aloud, the vision came, and he could see Rhea was sharing it. *Faye.*

Somehow, he'd forgotten Faye. *She was with him in the tattoo shop, bundled in a fur coat like the place was cold. Fire-red hair flowed down her back, blending with the russet hues of the fur. She was laughing at something the tattoo artist said, flirting with him, green eyes alight with pleasure. Faye flirted with everyone. "He can take it," she was saying. "I've seen him take much worse." She winked before turning her attention on Leo. "Can't you, beautiful one?" Leo could feel the endorphin high from the tattoo blending with the helpless state of desire Faye could reduce him to with a word. The scene changed swiftly to a bedroom, Faye displayed in all her glory against the deep blue sheets, a poppy floating in the ocean. "What would you do for me, pretty Leo? Will you do anything for me?" He leaped onto the bed on all fours like a wild dog. "Gods, yes!"*

"That's about enough of that."

The vision ended abruptly, and Leo suffered an instant of disorientation, trying to remember where he was. The moment had seemed utterly real. Mortified, he realized where he was when Rhea, scowling beside him, withdrew her hand.

He grabbed his shirt and pulled it on. "Sorry. I didn't mean for that— I had no idea—"

"Of course you had no idea. That was the point of the reading, wasn't it?" Rhea rose and busied herself tidying the cocoa things. "It's not like you conjured the vision deliberately. The pictomancy took you there. That was the moment. That's when you agreed to get the tattoo."

"What do you mean, that was the moment? How do you know?"

Rhea turned back to him, her expression annoyed. "'Will you do *anything* for me?'" She copied Faye's sexy, purring inflection rather well. "She was asking if you'd get tattooed for her. That was the answer to your question. And I'm guessing you had the kind of relationship where she tested your loyalty to her in a number of…interesting ways. If you catch my drift."

Leo crossed his arms over his chest, bandaged fingers still making it awkward. "No, I don't catch your drift. What are you talking about?"

Rhea looked at the ceiling and made an exasperated growling noise. "She was topping you. Idiot."

"Topping…"

"Oh my *God*. BDSM! Bondage. Discipline. Dominance and submission. Ringing a bell yet?" She made a little motion with one of the empty cups like she was ringing a servant's bell.

Heat rushed up his neck to the tips of his ears. And there was nothing he could say in his defense, because he remembered Faye now. Faye had treated him like a plaything—and he hadn't objected. He remembered crawling on all fours for her, sitting up and begging like a dog while his cock raged, her angry, willing standard raised between his legs. He'd licked his own cum off her boots.

Rhea went back to putting things away. "I'm beginning to see why it didn't work out between you and Theia. If you even suggested anything kinky, she'd throw you out of a moving car on the highway without looking back to see if you'd gotten road rash. She can be surprisingly prudish about sex."

"Which you're not, I take it."

"Me?" Rhea turned away from the shelves, glaring fire. "Who the hell said anything about me?"

"I— Nobody. I just meant— You sounded dismissive. I wasn't trying to— This isn't about you and me."

"Oh, heaven forfend!"

"Heaven...what?"

"Fuck off, Leo." She grabbed the tablet from its stand and dropped it into the bag she kept behind the counter. "You can close up tonight." She turned back at the door. "I mean *lock* up. By yourself. Since that's your thing."

Chapter 10

Rhea sat in her car and screamed for five minutes before starting the engine. She didn't even have a real reason for being mad at Leo. It wasn't like he'd chosen the memory deliberately. She couldn't say why his habitual cluelessness had pushed her over the edge, but if she'd heard one more of her own words repeated back at her as if it were in a foreign language, she'd have lost it. Like she was losing it now.

As she started the car, she remembered she'd meant to call Ione about Leo's Nazis. Christ. Not *his* Nazis. The Nazis who'd shown up…around the same time he had.

Rhea frowned, warming her fingers while she waited for the window to defog. Was there some connection? Leo's reaction to the incidents seemed genuine. She didn't harbor any suspicion that he was part of it. Not directly. But it did seem to be centered on him. The graffiti, the poster, the random white supremacist he'd run into on the street who'd provoked Leo into punching him in the face. What were the odds some guy Leo had met at a conference in Flagstaff would run into him on the street in Sedona a few weeks later? Not astronomical, she supposed, but still.

She took out her phone, thumb poised over Ione's number. Maybe she should call Phoebe and let the Carlisle grapevine do her dirty work for her. Not for the first time, she wished she could call Theia and tell her about all this weirdness. Ask her what *she'd* do. WWTD: What Would Theia Do? It was a mantra she'd fallen back on many times. Instead of going off half-cocked as she was prone to, she'd pause to think for a minute how Theia would respond to a situation. Theia was the thinking one, the one who looked at something from all angles before making up her mind about it and the one who gave everyone the benefit of the doubt.

Rhea was the one who said the first thing that came into her head, no matter how inappropriate. It sucked not having Theia on her side. She felt like she was missing a limb. Or like she was no longer grounded, and she might float up into the air and dissipate in the atmosphere if she didn't maintain constant vigilance.

She had to suck it up and call Ione. But maybe it could wait until morning.

The setting sun was throwing purple shadows over Snoopy Rock. Leo's "episode" would be starting soon. And the other Leo wouldn't remember anything that happened between her and daytime Leo. Probably. As she contemplated going back upstairs, movement in the shadows caught her eye. A dog sat on its haunches, staring. A wolfy-looking dog with pale blue eyes. She'd seen this hound before—the vision of the Hunt that had overtaken her on the highway. Which begged the question: Was she having a vision now?

There were no other indications of magic in the twilight. Snow had begun to fall. The wolf-dog stared at her. Her windshield wipers thumped quietly as she put them on intermittent. No trumpeting horns sounded. No great white birds flew at her. No thundering hooves.

"Shoo." Her window was rolled up. It wasn't as if the dog could hear her. "Go away. Go home."

It gave her one more look before standing and trotting

off, swallowed up into the darkness. Its tail curled over its rump. Maybe it was part basenji. Because sure.

Christmas lights were sparkling to life around the shopping center as she backed out of the parking space. She loved this time of year. It wasn't religious for her anymore. That ship had sailed a long time ago for everyone in the family except Ione. The pagan high priestess. Not that Ione let that keep her from going to church. But the lights and pageantry, even the stupid holiday music, both secular and religious, made Rhea happy. She hadn't bothered putting up a tree at her new place, but now she was regretting it.

Before she pulled out of the lot, her phone buzzed. Rhea glanced at the message on the screen. Theia.

Just wondering about your holiday plans. Phoebe says you're really busy with your new business (congrats!) and might not make it for Christmas Eve dinner.

The screen went black.

Rhea reached for the phone, her thumb reactivating the screen. Maybe she was being stupid about Theia's secrecy. Maybe it was time to let it go. Another text balloon appeared.

I heard from Laurel. She's not ready to do a big family holiday or anything, but she says she'll meet me for coffee the day after Christmas.

Rhea jammed her thumb against the button and tossed the phone facedown on the seat beside her. Unbelievable. She felt like screaming again. How could Theia even consider that woman family? Had she actually *invited* her? Dinner was going to be at Phoebe's—because there was no way Ione would have people eating food in her cream-colored fortress of solitude. *Phoebe*, whom Laurel had tried to freaking murder.

It didn't matter to Rhea that Laurel had been under Carter's influence, poisoned by Carter's lies. And it didn't matter that she'd thought she was only consigning Phoebe's soul to the underworld to give Carter control over her. "Soul death," Rafe called it. Murder was murder. And you didn't invite your sister's would-be murderer to Christmas dinner, for God's sake, or have fucking coffee with her. She didn't even know Theia anymore.

The last of the sunlight had faded by the time Rhea hit the road, and the glow of the luminarias at Tlaquepaque as she drove by to take a peek had the look of a sacred ceremony under the deep cobalt sky. As the blue turned to black outside the city limits, the little pockets of cheery holiday lights along the highway seemed all the cheerier, and yet somehow lonelier at the same time.

Thunder rumbled in the distance despite the falling snow. But of course it wasn't thunder. Rhea pulled over to the side of the road preemptively. Sure enough, the rumbling grew louder, the ground shaking with the impact of hooves. This time, a rider on horseback, who looked wholly human, barreled out of the brush from a trail up ahead and began galloping down the highway, throwing panicked looks over his shoulder as the first of the Hunt emerged from the trail moments later to the sound of horns—car horns, this time, because the rider they pursued was going the wrong way in the opposite lane of traffic.

Presumably, the drivers who honked and swerved around the startled man and his equally startled horse saw only the one being pursued and not the terrifying assembly swiftly gaining on him. From Rhea's vantage point, she saw the leader of the Hunt charge forward, ignoring the oncoming traffic, and beside him, the woman Rhea had seen with the Hunt before, hair covered this time with an impressive horned helmet, her gown pieced together with some kind of flowing metal armor. She pulled ahead of the leader and came alongside the terrified rider, mere feet away from Rhea's car, and with a sweep of her deceptively graceful arm, she dragged him from his horse and onto the back of her own.

The leader of the Hunt raised his sword in the air with a wild shout, and Rhea stared openmouthed as the female warrior's horse galloped past her MINI into the air. Wings stretched out behind the warrior, not from the horse rising into the air but from the back of the woman herself, the wingspan broad—and bright white.

The riderless horse panicked, ears thrown back and eyes wild as it galloped toward the swerving traffic. Someone was going to get killed here. And if Rhea wasn't careful, that might include her. After the next car passed, she pulled out onto the highway and tried to overtake the horse, with no idea what she was going to do about it if she did. But before she had to confront the stupidity of her lack of a plan, the leader of the Hunt drew up beside the horse on the other side and leaped from his spectral mount onto the living one. The horse immediately calmed as the hunter took the reins, while the rest of the Hunt, including the hounds and the leader's own mount, rose into the sky and thundered away after the female warrior and her prize.

Only the corporeal horse and the leader of the Hunt remained on the highway, while Rhea's car kept pace with it. As distant headlights grew larger, she realized she was going to end up getting the poor horse killed—and who knew about the hunter?—if she didn't get out of the way. She picked up speed. In her rearview mirror, she saw the horse pulling behind her into what was at least the right directional lane. And following it loped a smaller, dark shape: the black wolflike hunting dog.

The hunter turned his mount onto a trail and disappeared into the darkness, but the dog somehow kept up with Rhea's car. She was driving cautiously, but she couldn't imagine how it was trotting steadily behind her at forty miles an hour. She started to feel guilty, even though she hadn't encouraged the dog to follow her. How did she even know it was part of the Hunt? It didn't look spectral. Maybe someone's dog just—happened to be running with a ghostly hunting party. Because sure. She couldn't shake the feeling, though. And she couldn't shake the dog.

Rhea slowed as she turned into her neighborhood, and when the dog continued to follow, she pulled into a convenience store parking lot. If it was rabid or something, or some crazy shape-shifting necromancer, at least there were bright lights and people around. The dog simply sat on the pavement watching her, its tongue out, panting, while her engine idled. She supposed she'd be panting, too, if she'd been running behind a car for twenty minutes at forty miles an hour.

After a moment, she opened the car door, carefully watching the animal as it watched her. It didn't look rabid. Then again, she wasn't sure she knew what rabid looked like. Didn't they say rabid animals showed no fear? This wolf-dog—*jämthund*, maybe—certainly wasn't showing any. She put one foot outside the car, the toe of her boot on the pavement, and the dog stood. Rhea yanked her foot back inside and slammed the door. Its blue eyes blinked deliberately before the dog nonchalantly trotted around the side of the building. Rhea took a deep breath and backed out of her parking space, slowly cruising around to where the dog had disappeared. There was no sign of it.

It occurred to her as she drove home that the dog was

perhaps the least weird thing in this whole bizarre scenario. A winged woman warrior had just swept some dude off his horse and flown away with him, accompanied by spectral hunters, and the leader of the Hunt had ridden off on the dude's horse.

She unlocked her door to find the weirdest part of it, in fact, sitting in her living room.

Rhea jumped when she switched on the light. "Vixen." She'd almost managed to convince herself the fox had been a hallucination.

The Guardian of the Hunt sighed with annoyance. "You're distracting him."

Rhea dropped her bag onto the chair by the door and folded her arms. "Distracting whom?"

"The Chieftain. You have him worrying about stray horses. He ought to have dealt with the prey himself. He is the leader of the Hunt."

"Dealt with how? And what does it have to do with me?"

"He should have taken the head as a trophy for the pleasure of the gods. As for you…" Vixen studied her and shook her head, clearly finding Rhea lacking. "You don't believe in the gods. You are not a huntress or a warrior. And yet you are in the middle of this hunt, and so you are a part of it, worthy or not."

"So why doesn't anyone else see this stupid hunt? If you don't think I'm 'worthy,' why can't someone else who's more suited to it have the Hunt revealed to them and deal with it themselves?"

"You see because you have the gift of second sight."

Rhea laughed. "I hate to be the one to break it to you, but a lot of people in Sedona have the gift of second sight."

"None like you."

"Well, that's flattering. I guess."

"It wasn't meant to be flattering. There is some aspect

of your gift the Chieftain has clearly responded to. Something he needs."

Rhea's stomach growled. She hadn't eaten all day and she was tired of talking to this stupid fox. "Maybe he needs someone who'll distract him from taking people's heads as trophies," she offered as she headed to the kitchen to get a frozen dinner. "That was a human being, you know." She spoke into the freezer as she worked a box out of the ice. "So what did he even do? Why was he being hunted?"

"Perhaps you should ask the Chieftain."

"And how am I supposed to do that, exactly?" Rhea popped her dinner into the microwave and set the timer.

Vixen pursed her downy muzzle. "It seems the Chieftain has chosen you as his earthly protector. When he travels by night, he is vulnerable. You have the power to protect him or destroy him."

Rhea's hand dropped to her side. "Wait...you don't mean Leo Ström is the Chieftain?"

Vixen ignored the question. "Because of your disruption, Kára was forced to take the lead."

"Kára?"

"The warrior who took the prey as her prize."

The microwave timer dinged and Rhea opened the door to take out the steaming little tray and stir the half-frozen noodles in the center. "So what's she going to do with him now that she has him? Is she planning on taking his head for her own trophy?" Rhea popped the tray back in and punched in another minute. "Or is she taking him to Valhalla?"

"His kind does *not* belong in Valhalla." Vixen's voice was tight with disdain and anger. "Valhalla is for heroes, for those slain in battle, not for cowards."

When she looked up from pressing the start button, Vixen was gone.

"She's a Valkyrie, though, right?" Rhea said to the empty room. "I totally nailed it, didn't I? That was a Valkyrie I just saw." She shook her head with a sigh. "And now, not only do I have conversations with talking foxes, I'm talking to myself *as if* I were having a conversation with a talking fox. Because that's totally not weird."

It was clearly time for alcohol.

Chapter 11

Rhea woke in the morning with a throbbing headache and an upset stomach. Microwaved macaroni and cheese and Guinness in a can apparently didn't mix.

She was late getting into the shop but found the door locked and the lights out. Leo wasn't there. Rhea realized she didn't even have his cell phone number. She looked up his application on her tablet. He hadn't provided it. Maybe he'd decided to bail after she'd ribbed him for being Faye's boy toy. Maybe she'd done a little more than rib him. Maybe she was a bit of a jerk, and now she was out a perfectly good employee. And a hot, mysterious nutjob her subconscious clearly wanted to ride like she was a rodeo queen.

He'd helped her out a lot already, though. The place was even cleaner than when she'd come in yesterday, inventory was officially counted, and the accounting system was all set up and ready to go. She might actually be able to get this business off the ground. All she needed now were some clients.

As if she'd conjured one, the door jingled open and someone walked in. Someone who was not Leo. This guy was a much better dresser—if not quite as sexy in his natty suit—and his hair lacked the undisciplined chaos of Leo's.

She gave him her best professional smile. "Looking for a tattoo?"

The natty dresser smiled back. "I saw one of your flyers and thought I'd come check it out." He glanced around at the flash Leo had helped hang on the walls. "Is this all your work?"

"None of it is, actually." Rhea came out from behind the counter and picked up the leather-bound book on the coffee table. "This is my portfolio, if you'd like to take a look. We're not officially open yet, but I'm taking appointments beginning the first of the year and I'd be happy to do a consultation if you see something you like." She handed him the book. "I'm Rhea."

"Brock." He held out his hand, his face lighting up with a genuine smile of interest. The handshake was firm and brief. No nonsense. The day was looking up. "Are you the only tattooist?"

Rhea's smile faltered. "I'm hoping to bring in some other artists once I've opened, but for now it's just me. Is that a problem?"

"No! Sorry, no. I was just curious." He opened the book, looking embarrassed.

"Why don't you have a seat? I've got tea and cocoa if you want to take your time looking it over."

"Cocoa sounds great, thanks." Brock sat and flipped through the book while Rhea took the kettle into the back to fill it. He raised his voice to carry to where she was. "This one's interesting."

Rhea came back out to set the kettle on the heating plate and leaned across the table to see what he was looking at. It turned out to be Theia's sacrum tattoo: a multicolored sunrise with dark curls of filigree in front of it.

"That one uses a sort of combination watercolor/airbrush technique I've been experimenting with."

"It's really stunning. Not exactly the kind of thing I'd get, but I love the effect." He glanced up. "How long have you been tattooing?" It was the question she'd been dreading. But it was only fair.

"Honestly, only about six months professionally. I practiced on friends for about a year first. And on myself."

"On yourself? Any you can show me?" Brock brushed the carefully styled hair across his forehead. "I mean… that's not a rude question, is it? I didn't mean to get personal."

Rhea laughed. "Well, I did volunteer the information that I've tattooed myself, so I kind of stepped right into that, didn't I? I don't really have any I can show you without a wardrobe malfunction—oh. Wait, I do have one." She put her foot up on the edge of the couch and rolled up the left leg of her pants before pushing the thick woolen sock out of the way. "I did this a few days ago. I have some more fine detail work to do on it, but it's mostly done."

"Wow." Brock leaned in to get a better look at the Black Moon Lilith. "That's an amazing color."

"I know. I just love it. I found it at a convention recently. A custom blend. Hopefully, it stays true when it's done healing." She rolled down her pant leg and took her foot off the couch, feeling self-conscious. She didn't usually show off her own ink to strangers.

"I've never seen that symbol before. Does it have any special meaning?"

Rhea hesitated. She hadn't even shown her sisters this tattoo yet. She certainly wasn't going to tell some guy who'd walked in off the street about the Lilith connection. She hadn't even told Leo about *that.* Not that it was any of Leo's business. But she knew more about his business than—

Rhea realized Brock was staring at her curiously while she waged her internal debate. "It has some personal meaning."

Brock smiled. "Those are the best, huh? I've been thinking about getting a quote from one of my favorite books. I should probably think it through carefully, though, if it's going to be words. That's what everyone tells me."

"Good advice. Never tattoo someone else's name on your skin is better advice." Rhea grinned. "So this will be your first tattoo?"

Brock nodded, thumbing through the book. "I've been thinking about getting one for years but never had the guts to go through with it. But when I saw your flyer, it seemed like the time was right."

"While you're thinking it over, I can put you down for an appointment for when the shop opens after the first. You can always cancel—with twenty-four-hours' notice, of course—if you change your mind or haven't decided on the right tattoo by then."

Brock smiled, but the smile drooped as he considered. "After the first. I'm going to be traveling for a while on business. There's no way you could do it before? I promise not to tell anyone I got it early."

There wasn't much else she needed to do before opening, and turning down her first client didn't seem like a good start. "Well…I guess I could. If I have the color you want in stock."

"Oh, it's going to be all black, whatever I decide on."

"Then I've got your color." Rhea smiled. "Okay, let's put you on the calendar." She grabbed the tablet from the counter and pulled up the booking app. "Just so you know, I charge one fifty an hour with a one-hour minimum." He nodded when she looked up. "How's next Friday at one o'clock?"

"Perfect."

"I can call or send you a reminder the day before if you want to enter your name and contact information in the app."

Brock typed in the information and handed the tablet back.

Her new client glanced at his watch and rose as the kettle beeped. "Guess I'm going to miss out on that cocoa. I need to get going. But it was great meeting you, Rhea, and I'm really looking forward to next Friday."

After he'd left, Rhea turned on some music and indulged in a little victory dance. She paused to text Phoebe—after shaking off the millisecond's impulse to hit Theia's number first—to tell her she'd bagged her first client, leading to a *squee* of congratulations and a follow-up phone call moments later.

"That's awesome, sweetie!" Phoebe was always Rhea's biggest cheerleader, but something in her voice said this wasn't the reason for her call.

Rhea sighed. "Okay, what is it?"

"What's what?"

"What is it you're waiting a polite three minutes into this congratulatory call to tell me that has nothing to do with my first official client?"

"I keep forgetting you're psychic."

"Ha. And yet you haven't let me tattoo you or let me anywhere near your existing tattoos since the one I gave you to help find Rafe when Carter was trying to drain him of his blood."

"Yeah, thanks for the reminder, Theia. I'd almost stopped having nightmares about it."

Rhea felt her teeth grinding together. "You just called me Theia."

"Oh, shitballs. I'm sorry. It's just—Theia says you've blocked her number, and she called to tell me she had a dream about you and asked me to pass it on."

"Oh, for God's sake."

"She's worried about you, Rhe. And you know her dreams are always significant."

"And always vague enough to read like a horoscope everyone thinks makes perfect sense after the fact."

"Why are you so pissed at Theia?"

"Just tell me the dream."

"She said someone came to your door to take something from you, and you let them in. She says to tell you to be careful reading the ink of a stranger because you may read what you want to and miss the—" Phoebe paused as if reading from something herself. "And miss the meaning of the words beneath the skin. And she dreamed about a black wolf. She couldn't figure out if it meant you harm."

Goddammit. It figured Theia's dreams about her would be right on the nose.

"Rhe? You still there?"

"Yeah, I'm here. Thanks for the message."

"Is that a thanks for Theia or for me?"

Rhea made an exasperated noise. "Whomever you want it to be for."

"So other than your awesome news, how are you doing? Any more visits from the ghost riders?"

"Nope. Not a one." She didn't feel like telling Phoebe she'd had another conversation with a talking fox. Or about being stalked by a wolf. Elkhound. Whatever. It would only wind up getting back to Theia.

"Huh." Phoebe didn't sound convinced. "Why would they show themselves to you for no reason and then stop?"

"How would I know?"

"Do you think it has something to do with snake boy?"

Rhea growled. "He's not a snake boy, and, again, how would I know?"

"Uh-oh. Trouble in paradise?"

"Phoebe—"

"I'm just saying, you had this hot vision, and your visions are never wrong, so—"

"I've also had visions from creepers fantasizing about me. Those didn't come true. They were just nasty little 'wishes' I made damn sure weren't going to be fulfilled."

"But you were in control in the vision with Leo. You experienced it physically."

"Maybe it was *my* wishful thinking. Anyway, I need to get going."

"You still haven't RSVP'd for Christmas Eve. You're coming, aren't you?" Phoebe tried to sound stern.

"I'll think about it."

Rhea turned the volume back up on the music after the call and broke into dance once more, rocking out to Lady Gaga and Beyoncé. As she spun about with a particularly vigorous hair whip, she careened unexpectedly into Leo's arms. He looked as surprised as she felt.

"Holy shit, Leo." Rhea steadied herself and backed out of his grip, trying not to blush. "You nearly gave me a heart attack. How long have you been standing there?"

"I just walked in. I said hello, but I guess you couldn't hear me over the music." He was kind of shouting over it even now.

Rhea hurried to turn it down. "Sorry, I was celebrating. I booked my first client."

Leo smiled. "That's terrific. Sorry I wasn't here."

"Where were you, anyway? When I found the place empty, I thought maybe you'd quit."

He glanced down at his boots, rocking back on them slightly, with his hands in his pockets. "I kind of did. Or I was going to." He looked up and met Rhea's eyes. "And then I realized I hadn't worked off my tattoo yet."

"I see." Rhea leaned back against the counter. "Well, if you're uncomfortable here, I don't want you to feel obligated to stay. You can pay me back when you have the money."

Leo blinked at her, the same blue eyes as that damn dog's. "Are...are you firing me?"

Rhea's temper flared—the way it did when she realized she was the one being an asshole. "I'm confused. Do you want to work here or do you not want to work here?"

"Okay, I guess I should go." Leo drew his hands out of his pockets—gloveless and pink from the cold—and turned to leave.

Rhea glared at the ground for a second, like the ground was the one being the asshole, before reaching out and grabbing for his hand. "Leo, wait. I'm sorry. I'm being a jerk."

Her fingers brushed the Thor's Hammer tattoo at his wrist as he turned back toward her, and the vision hit her before she could pull away. *The thundering hoofbeats of the Hunt, the Viking she'd seen in her first vision in her living room leading the charge, blue eyes bright with excitement. The hair was longer and wilder and the beard fuller, and the thick fur garments and leather armor made him seem bulkier, but it was unmistakably Leo. He raised his sword and gave a hair-raising cry.*

Leo was the one to break the connection, pulling Rhea's hand from his wrist and grabbing her arms to give her a sharp shake. "All right, what the hell was that?"

Rhea stared up at him. "That was you, Leo. I don't know how, but it seems you're the Chieftain of the Hunt."

He dropped her arms and took a step back. "Sorry, *what* am I?"

"You lead the Wild Hunt. Or your *hugr* does. I think."

"My conscious thought-self."

"The other Leo said it was comparable to your soul."

Leo pulled off his hat and messed up his hair. "My *soul* is riding around in the middle of the night...leading Odin's Hunt."

"So you know about the Hunt."

"Of course I know about it. I minored in Norse mythology."

"You never mentioned that before."

"No, because I—just remembered it." Leo shook his head. "This is too much. Why would I be leading Odin's Hunt? I'm starting to think you're feeding me these visions."

A prickle of outrage rippled through her skin. "You think I'm making this up?"

"No. No, I—" He sank onto the couch. "I am *really* confused." Leo glanced up at her, suspicion still lingering in his gaze. "So how do *you* know about the Hunt?"

"I've been seeing it for a few nights now. Ever since you arrived in town. It doesn't look quite like the vision. The horses and riders are more spectral, more contemporarily dressed. It only happens when you're here, locked up."

"And when were you going to tell me about this?"

"I wasn't sure it had anything to do with you. I see weird things sometimes. I mean, never this weird, but it started with my own tattoo before I'd even met you."

"What tattoo?"

She'd shown it to a stranger. She might as well show it to Leo.

Rhea rolled up her pant leg once more and propped her boot on the edge of the coffee table. "I did it the night before you came into the shop, and while I was finishing up, I had the first vision of the Hunt."

Leo studied it. "Oh, the Black Moon Lilith."

Rhea let the fabric of her pants drop back over it, removing her boot from the table. "You know the symbol?"

"Of course. From Theia."

That familiar surge of anger was back. "Theia talked to you about Lilith?"

Leo gave her a peculiar look. "She has the same tattoo."

It was all Rhea could do not to kick the table across the room. "Theia has a tattoo I don't know about? A tattoo I didn't *do*?"

Leo blanched. "I just assumed you *had* done it. It's exactly the same except for the color. She just has the black outline inside her left forearm. I asked her what it was and she called it the Black Moon Lilith symbol."

Visions having nothing to do with pictomancy or Wild Hunts were going through Rhea's mind—visions of putting a pillow over Theia's face and holding it down. "But she didn't tell you anything else about Lilith?"

"Like what?"

"You didn't ask her what the significance was?"

"No. It didn't seem like any of my business, and she didn't offer."

Rhea walked back to the counter and fiddled with the tablet. "And did she offer any information about the tattoo I *did* do?"

"I didn't see any other tattoos."

Rhea laughed. "Come on. You didn't notice the giant sunrise above her ass cheeks?"

Leo looked annoyed. "I never saw her ass cheeks."

"I suppose she's missionary only."

He straightened his glasses. "If you must know, I didn't see *any* parts of her that weren't clothed."

"Um, how did you have sex if you never saw her naked?"

"I never said I had sex with Theia. You just assumed."

Rhea looked back down at the tablet to hide her surprise. Nighttime Leo had been telling the truth. "Well, that's a first." She glanced up and met his eyes. "You know, because she's a super slut." She grinned and fiddled with the accounting program for a minute before giving up with a sigh. Rhea took the tablet off the stand and came around the counter to bring it over to him. "I added a column and I think I broke the spreadsheet again. Would you mind fixing it? If you're here to work, that is."

"Absolutely. If you're not firing me, I'm not quitting." His thumb hit the home button as he took the tablet, and he ended up in the booking app. Leo paused, reading the entry, and his eyes darted up to meet Rhea's. "What is Brock Dressler's name doing in here?"

"That's my new client."

Leo stared at her. "That's the Nazi I punched."

Chapter 12

There was no way to be sure Brock Dressler hadn't come to the shop by coincidence. But Leo wasn't buying it.

"He must have followed me back. Or he saw me later putting up the flyers."

Rhea had the urge to rub her arms, like bugs were crawling on them. "He seemed so normal."

"They always seem normal. Because they believe they are. It's everyone else who's brainwashed. Everyone else who's attacking them for their beliefs. They're the most persecuted sons of bitches in the world." Leo looked down at the scabs on his knuckles. He should have gone in for a second punch.

"It sounds like you have a lot of experience with them."

Leo's head shot up. He searched Rhea's face, trying to determine if there was more behind the statement than the words on the surface. "Maybe I do. I don't remember."

Rhea sat on the arm of the couch. "It seems like all this Nazi stuff must have something to do with you." She held up her hand as he opened his mouth to protest. "I'm not saying you're part of it. But that it's, I don't know, following you."

Leo slumped forward with his head in his hands. It did seem to follow him, and he didn't know why. Dressler had made a beeline for him at the conference, and then there he'd been on the street while Leo was going for lunch. Not to mention the graffiti and the posters. And now Dressler showing up wanting a tattoo? What the hell was the connection? He wanted to grab hold of his brain and shake it until he remembered. And the horrible fear was that he'd find he somehow *did* have something to do with these bastards. That he wasn't who he thought he was. That maybe he wasn't a good person at all.

Rhea's hand settled gently on his shoulder. "We could do another reading. Maybe read one of the earlier tattoos. Go further back and find out how you got it."

Leo lifted his head.

"Unless there's a reason you don't want me seeing that, which is totally your call."

"What reason would I have for not wanting you to see how I got the earlier tattoos?" Even as he said it, he realized he'd told her yesterday he didn't.

"I don't know, Leo. You tell me."

The fear of being exposed gripped him again. And he didn't even know what he was afraid of having exposed. That he was crazy, maybe, and this would give her the proof. Or that he really was associated with scum like Dressler.

"What I'd like to know more about is this Hunt thing," he said finally. "If my soul is actually leaving my body to *hunt* something—"

"Somebody."

"What?"

"Hunt some*body*. Last night, I watched them chase down some guy and snatch him off his horse and take him…"

"Take him where?"

"They rode off into the sky."

Leo laughed, but she was serious. He was starting to

wonder which one of them was the crazy one. "Okay. Well, then, I'd like to know who I'm hunting and why."

"You want the reading, then."

He nodded. "Yeah. I want the reading." He pushed up his sleeve and held out his arm, hand in a tight fist. "Let's do Mjölnir."

He screwed his eyes shut and held his breath as Rhea placed her hand on the tattoo, repeating "not a Nazi" in his head like Harry Potter begging the Sorting Hat not to put him in Slytherin. So he'd seen *Harry Potter*, he realized. Or maybe read it. That was something.

And then he had one boot in a stirrup and he was swinging himself onto the back of a sturdy horse. *He didn't feel like himself. He felt stronger. More in control. And incredibly angry. "No mercy!" he bellowed. A woman beside him answered, "For Odin and Freyja!"*

The horse thundered forward at his command, but before he could catch his breath, the scene changed. Searing pain seized his arm. Leo looked down to find his hand had been severed. Someone grabbed his bleeding stump as he drifted toward unconsciousness.

"We had a bargain, damn you!" It was the woman's voice, the one from the Hunt.

"You said nothing of limbs," said another woman, her voice toneless, beyond cold. "Only head and heart."

"He will have no heart if the blood drains from it!"

"Will you give us his mind?"

"His mind? I have given you his will!"

Leo was shivering and everything was going dark.

"Think quickly, Kára. The skein unravels as the heart winds down. He is nothing but clockwork. A mind for a body. We think it a fair exchange."

"Leo." Someone was shaking him. Or he was shaking.

Shaking apart. Something crinkly draped his shoulders. "Leo, snap out of it. You're scaring me."

He realized his eyes were still screwed shut, and he opened them to find Rhea hovering over him with concern. She'd wrapped him in some kind of space-age silver blanket.

"Are you with me?"

"Rhea?"

"Thank God. You scared the crap out of me. I think you were going into shock. I grabbed the Mylar blanket from the first aid kit. You should lie down and elevate your feet. Get the blood pumping back to your heart."

Leo let her ease him back onto the couch and lift his feet to slide a pillow under them. Blood to his heart. What the hell had he just seen? He pulled his right arm from the blanket to make sure his hand was still attached.

"It felt so real," he murmured.

"I think it was real." Rhea put his arm back inside the blanket.

"How could it be real? I lost my hand."

"I don't understand exactly how, but you asked why you were hunting—"

"I also asked who."

"True, and we didn't really get a who, but I might have an idea about that. My point is, you seem to have been part of a bargain. Kára said she'd given them your will, and then she apparently bargained your mind to keep you from bleeding to death."

"Who the hell is Kára?"

"That's what the voice in the vision called her. I think it's the woman I saw hunting with you—or with the Chieftain, anyway—last night. I think she's a Valkyrie."

Leo sat up, no longer shivering so hard he thought he might come apart. "A Valkyrie? That's ridiculous."

"About as ridiculous as a flying hunting party, yeah."

Nervous energy propelled him to his feet as he pulled off the Mylar blanket. "I don't know what to think about any of this." He held out his right hand, alternating between making a fist and flexing his fingers. "But I think I'm good on the whole reading thing for now. Until I can get a better idea of what's real and what's my mind supplying images in some semi-dream state."

Rhea picked up the blanket, folding it into smaller and smaller squares. "But the reading last night—that seemed to ring true."

Heat rushed to Leo's face as he remembered the vivid images conjured by the reading and the even more vivid memories that followed when the reading ended. "Yes. Faye is someone I actually knew. I don't remember when I stopped seeing her or even how long ago, but the vision…yeah, it definitely happened." He tucked his hands into his back pockets. They felt like extra appendages he didn't know what to do with. "Sorry. I know it made you uncomfortable."

Rhea gave him an odd little smile he couldn't interpret. "I wouldn't say it made me uncomfortable, exactly."

Unconsciously, he'd stepped closer to her. Close enough to see the faint glow of heat in her cheeks. Why would she be blushing if she wasn't uncomfortable? Unless… *Please. Dude. She is* not *into you. She's into* him.

The rings around Rhea's irises seemed extra dark. "I guess I was a little jealous, if you want to know the truth. Not that I have any right to be. It's not like we—" She paused, biting her lip. "I mean, I'm your boss."

He couldn't seem to stop staring at her mouth. With another step, Leo had breached the distance between them. The folded Mylar slipped from Rhea's fingers, exploding back into a full-sized blanket at their feet in slow motion as she stared up at him.

Before he could second-guess himself, he took her hand, his fingers weaving between hers. "I could quit again," he said. "If you think that would help."

The corners of her eyes crinkled, her smile slight and secretive like the Mona Lisa. It was as good a sign as any.

Her eyes went wide when he cupped the back of her neck and lowered his head, but she melted against him as he drew her close and kissed her. She was surprisingly slight and soft in his arms, her lips slick and sweet. She gave off such a prickly, self-reliant vibe, he'd half expected her to be built like a wiry, hard-muscled boy. But there was nothing boyish about the way her petite curves pressed into him.

After a moment, self-consciousness kicked in, and Leo stepped back, letting their fingers separate, uncertain now whether he'd been projecting. "Sorry. I hope I didn't misread…?"

Rhea's tentative smile faded. He'd blown it.

She snatched up the Mylar, cramming it back into little folded squares. "For future reference, Leo, 'sorry' is not what a girl wants to hear after intimate contact."

Rhea kept things light for the rest of the afternoon, trying not to let on how conflicted she was about the kiss. He'd taken her by surprise, sending the blood rushing to her extremities in the best way possible, and her lips still tingled—she had to keep stopping herself from touching her fingertips to them to be sure his mouth wasn't somehow still pressed against them—but his tentativeness afterward was weird and disappointing. She couldn't get the memory of the vision she'd shared with the other Leo out of her head. There had been nothing tentative or uncertain about what they'd been doing.

Leo was gamely trying to pretend the kiss hadn't happened, which made the disappointment worse. She couldn't help thinking about the passion he'd shown for Faye. Maybe he only responded that way to dominant women. Rhea certainly wasn't submissive, but actively dominating someone wasn't really her thing either.

By late afternoon, she figured making a lighthearted exit before dusk was the best course of action, but after they shared some Indian takeout, Leo posed the question she'd been hoping to avoid.

"Are you going to stick around tonight?"

Rhea didn't raise her head as she boxed up what they hadn't finished. "Do you think it matters?"

"Matters?" Leo's expression was wounded when Rhea looked up.

"I mean, you won't remember whether I was here, anyway."

"True. But it's nice to know someone's here before it happens." Leo took the dishes to the sink. "You're probably right, though. I don't blame you for not wanting to deal with my out of control id."

"He's not *that* out of control." Rhea bagged up the garbage and set it by the door. She turned to find Leo watching her with a thoughtful expression. "Do you like board games?"

The expression went from thoughtful to confused. "Board games?"

"I've got Scrabble and some other games on my tablet. Maybe the Lucid Ass could use something to occupy the time."

Leo laughed. "I suppose he could. I can't speak for him, of course, but presuming we share the same interests, sure. Sounds fun to me."

They started playing Scrabble while Leo was still himself, strapped in and waiting for the light to fade. But there was a definite moment when Rhea could almost see the change come over him: Lucid Ass Leo's Mr. Hyde eclipsing Leo the Dull's Dr. Jekyll.

He paused with his finger poised above the tile he'd been about to move while Rhea held the tablet for him, and Leo's habitual hesitant tension relaxed into an easy self-confidence.

Crisp blue eyes rose to meet hers with amusement beneath the pale lashes. "Well, now. What fresh hell can this be?"

"Feeling all right, Leo?"

"Marvelous. I missed you last night."

"Did you, now?"

"You doubt my sincerity. Do you doubt my tumescence?"

Rhea forced herself not to follow the downward flick of his gaze. "Unless you were about to put that word on the board, that's a losing move, mister."

"The board?"

"The game board. We're playing Scrabble. I have to warn you, I come from a Scrabble family, and I'm very competitive."

"What's the purpose of it?"

"We build words onto existing words on the board by placing our letter tiles on the squares, and each tile has a specific value—there, above the letter—while certain squares multiply the points of a letter or a word."

"But what's the *purpose* of it?"

Rhea sighed. "I thought you could use something to pass the time. It's a game. Entertainment."

"Is it? I can think of much more exciting entertainment."

"I'm sure you can." She tapped the board. "It's your move."

Leo perused the board while Rhea averted her eyes to

avoid seeing his tiles, which he'd failed to hide at the bottom of the screen. "What was *his* last word?"

"Tinsel. He added the *S-E-L* to my *tin* for six points."

"Tinsel?" Leo laughed with that deep, warm vibration his laughter had when the *munr* had the skin. "He could have made it *tins* and spelled *sensual*. Or *sexual*. He's an idiot."

"I don't disagree."

Leo uncrossed his ankles to poke his stockinged foot against her shin. "Oh, dear. What did the fool do?"

"Nothing."

"That's what I was afraid of. You have to see what an idiot he is." The foot remained where it was, his big toe slowly stroking her through the fabric. "We share the same skin. He shares my desires. I *am* his desires. Only I'm honest about it. I'm direct and forthright. What you see is what you get."

She forgot not to look where his gaze was trying to draw hers. *Jesus.*

His grin reminded her of the Cheshire cat. "And you obviously like what you see."

Rhea folded the tablet into her crossed arms. "That's your opinion."

"I swear, if I had him in front of me, I'd beat the snot out of him for being too stupid to see how much you desire him in return. The flush in your cheeks, the sparkle in your eyes, the way your breath is rising and falling in your chest."

"Stop looking at my chest."

"Honestly, I can't imagine what you see in him—other than the obvious fact of our rather impressive skin. If he can't act like a man and respond to those signals, if his all-important dull little soul can't recognize what he has right in front of him, he doesn't deserve you."

Was he trying to make her feel better? Giving her a pep talk about the guy—who was *himself*, no less—who'd failed to make a move?

"You sound like one of my sisters." She jumped as the stockinged toe slipped beneath her pant leg and stroked her skin.

"I assure you, I am nothing like one of your sisters." He was goddamned adept with that one toe—through a *sock*. It made her wonder what he could do with the rest of his body. "Why don't you put that fancy game board down and let me show you just how unlike them I am?"

"It's not just a fancy game board, it's a computer. Honestly, Leo, how do you not know anything?"

"Is that a reason to keep hugging it?" His foot slipped from her pant leg and hooked beneath one of the wheeled legs of the stool, and with a sharp tug, he managed to drag her close to him, making her lose her grip on the tablet as she threw her arms out to catch herself against the armrests. Which meant grasping his forearms. The tablet tumbled into his lap.

Leo shifted his weight and the tablet slipped between his legs—where it remained propped at a forty-five degree angle.

Leo's smile was amused at her hesitation. "Are you planning to cede that to me for the rest of the night?"

The tablet gave a little jump as she moved one hand from his arm.

"You seem happy to have it."

"I'd be much happier with something else there."

"I'm sure you would."

"Don't be silly. Just pick it up. It's not as if I can do anything." He jerked lightly on his wrist restraints. "I'm completely at your mercy."

The image of Leo on his hands and knees at Faye's bidding sprang to her mind. "Right. I forgot that was your thing."

"Sorry?"

Rhea snatched the tablet from his lap and pushed off with her feet against the base of the chair, sending the stool rolling backward. "That's what *he* said."

"I'm not following you."

"You seem to enjoy being at a woman's mercy."

Leo's red-gold brows drew together. "What woman's mercy? Yours? I don't exactly have a choice in the matter."

"Faye's, for instance."

"And who is Faye?"

Rhea laughed. "Surely you remember the woman you swore you'd do anything for. The one who marked you as her own."

"Marked…?"

Leo turned his head toward the Midgard Serpent tattoo, though it was hidden beneath his shirt. He'd worn the long-sleeved one again today. Rhea really needed to give him an allowance to buy some new things. She could write it off as a business expense.

"She gave me the tattoo?" His vision turned inward. "*She* gave me the tattoo. She marked me so I couldn't escape the skin."

"You wanted to escape the skin?"

"She'd already bound me." He turned his wrists in the restraints. "As you can see. Bound Leo's will so that he had to obey her. Convinced him to engage in this stupid ritual. But if the *hugr* can leave temporarily, so can the *munr*. Except not now. As Jörmungandr constrains the waters of the sea, the mark constrains the will."

She'd bound his will. "Kára." They'd said the name together.

Leo's eyes fixed on hers, narrowed with suspicion. "How do you know that name?"

"I shared a vision with Leo. Two visions, actually. One of Faye having him marked and one of Kára...bargaining his mind for his life. They're the same woman, aren't they? The Valkyrie."

"The Valkyrie." Leo's fists curled tightly against the armrests. "The accursed Valkyrie."

Chapter 13

Leo leaned back against the headrest. Rhea couldn't help but notice the enthusiasm of his erection had faded. "I can't say whether it was willing submission on Leo's part—without will, how is anything willing? But you're correct that the Valkyrie owns me. She has enslaved me."

He'd been pretty damned willing in her vision, but Rhea decided not to go there. "How much do you remember?"

"You said she bargained Leo's mind."

"He was bleeding to death and going into shock. He'd lost his hand."

Leo's eyes flicked toward his presently whole limbs with little interest, perhaps checking to see if they were there. "And that's why both he and I are absolute shit at remembering things. A pretty stupid bargain, if you ask me. Plenty of people have survived the loss of a hand. But I suppose no one did ask me." He sighed, staring at the ceiling. "I remember... I don't know. Chronologically, very little. But Kára, I cannot forget. She's like staring at the sun—intensely and damagingly beautiful."

Rhea must have reacted in some way she wasn't aware of—a breath of disappointment or a slight movement that gave her discomfort away—as Leo turned his gaze on her.

"Such beauty is hardly a personal merit. It's something cold, like a diamond, to be admired and coveted, perhaps, but not truly desired." He gave her an ironic half smile. "I should know."

"A lot of people covet you, do they?"

He laughed, a little sound of delight. "I didn't mean myself. I meant that I know what it is to desire something truly. You dismiss my desire as soulless gluttony, when it is the purest thing I can offer you. Far purer than anything *he* will ever express. He's a coward."

Okay, *now* she was uncomfortable. It was one thing to think he was toying with her, trying to get into her pants because she happened to be there—and maybe as a ploy to get her to set him free—but the way his eyes looked into hers as he spoke made her feel naked. He wasn't goddamn kidding. He *wanted* her. And he'd obviously gotten over whatever had momentarily...deflated him.

Leo tilted his head. "You want me, but my wanting you seems to distress you."

Rhea cleared her throat awkwardly. Which she was sure was totally hot. "It's a little weird. You're..." She gestured at him helplessly.

"Tied up and kept here against my will? A mindless, soulless animal?"

"In my employee's body, for God's sake."

He was still studying her with curiosity. "So it's because you've entered into a financial relationship with him? Would it be like paying me for sex?"

"Jesus, Leo. *No.*" Rhea flipped the irritating spike of hair out of her face. She had to get him talking about something else. "What do you know about the Wild Hunt?"

His face clouded, but he shook his head. "What is that?"

"A spectral hunting party that roams the night in the weeks between All Souls and Yule. It's mainly found in Norse and Germanic folklore. At least, I thought it was just folklore. Until I saw it."

Leo shrugged. "What has that to do with me?"

"I think that's where your *hugr* goes at night."

His quizzical look turned into a scowl. "It's not *my hugr*. It's his."

"Right. Well, that's what he's doing when he leaves the 'skin' to you. He's out riding, hunting people—murderers and oath-breakers, I guess."

"Bully for him. Sounds right up his self-righteous alley."

"I believe he rides with Kára. I saw her last night, flying off with someone she'd hunted down."

Leo shifted restlessly, wrists chafing against the bonds. "I don't want to hear any more about Kára."

"But if she's a Valkyrie and she controls him, I'm just trying to work out why—"

"Enough!" Leo punctuated the shout with a swing of his foot, sending the rolling worktable beside them spinning across the room and onto its side with a bang that made her flinch. "I said I didn't want to hear any more about her." He seemed slightly subdued by Rhea's reaction, but his eyes were flashing a warning.

"All right. Sorry." Rhea picked up the table and the scattered supplies from the shelf it had collided with and closed the cover on the tablet. "Maybe I should go."

"Please don't." Was it her imagination or had his voice shaken a bit? "You have no idea what it's like sitting here for hours waiting to die."

"You don't actually die, Leo."

"It feels like dying. He has the days, and his miserable soul has the freedom to fly where it will at night, hunting the profane, while I sit imprisoned. This is my entire life, dusk to dawn. And then I'm gone, snuffed out. Reborn again the next night but knowing each night that I have one less before I die again for an entire year."

She was tempted to tease him for being melodramatic.

It wasn't as if he was *actually* gone when the other Leo was awake. Like a split personality, he was integrated once more with the whole. At least, that's what she assumed. But it had to suck sitting here by himself. If she were tied to a chair even for a single night, she'd probably go a little bit bonkers.

"All right." Rhea pulled up the wheeled stool once more and sat beside him. "I'll stay for a bit."

The sudden urgency in his eyes was intense. "Stay the night."

Rhea laughed, trying to lighten the mood. "And we're back to that."

"That wasn't a proposition. Although I'm up for it, of course. Always." The smirk was back. "Just stay. Keep me company."

"I have to sleep sometime, you know. *I* don't disappear with the sun."

"Oh." He closed his eyes and turned his head to the side dramatically, as if she'd struck him a sudden blow. "She has a heart of stone." Leo peeked at her out of one eye and laughed at her dry expression. "If you get tired, you can share the chair with me. It's quite comfortable."

She shook her head at him despairingly. "So you don't sleep at all?"

Leo shrugged. "It seems wasteful when I have so little time. But I confess to having fallen asleep out of sheer boredom on occasion."

"Then I'll do my best to keep you entertained."

"I can think of a few ways."

Rhea groaned. "You never stop."

Leo winked. "You don't want me to. But let's set that aside for the moment. Tell me about this gift of yours. This reading tattoos."

"I'm not reading you again."

"Too much for you last time, was I?"

Rhea looked away, trying not to think about the truth of that statement.

"No worries. I'm not asking for a reading. Even if you do hand them out to *him* like candy."

"You do realize you're the same person, right?"

His eyebrow lifted. "Are we? At any rate, I'm curious about how it works. Have you always had the ability?"

"Why are you so interested all of a sudden?"

"Must everything have an ulterior motive? I'm simply trying to pass the time. You said you would entertain me."

"God, I did, didn't I?" Rhea leaned back on the stool with her arms folded, debating how much she ought to tell him. It wasn't as if he'd remember any of this once he'd gone dormant or whatever it was he did. The idea that, in a few days, this Leo would be gone gave her more than a twinge of regret. "All right. Why not? All of my sisters have gifts—"

"How many do you have, anyway?"

"Gifts?"

"Sisters."

"Oh." Rhea swallowed the familiar irritation. "Well, that depends."

Leo looked amused. "It doesn't usually."

"There's nothing usual about us. There were four of us. But, recently, Theia discovered we have three half sisters."

"Seven sisters. Like the Pleiades."

"In this case, the Titanides. Each of us is named after one of the original female Titans." It was sufficient for the story. "And each of us has a gift corresponding with our namesake. Although mine's a bit off. Rhea is associated with wild music and ecstatic rites, and a chariot pulled by a pair of lionesses—"

"Is she really? You know, the goddess Freyja rides in a

chariot pulled by two cats. She's the Norse goddess of love and war. Sex and death, intimately intertwined."

"*Okay.* Charming and weird."

"You don't think sex and death are intertwined?"

"Well...I didn't until just now."

Leo laughed, his eyes crinkling with pleasure. "Sex is generative power. Death is a kind of birth, a passage from one life to the next. And of course there is the *little* death."

Rhea cleared her throat. "Moving right along. For years, I tried to figure out what my 'power' was. Ione is a powerful witch. Phoebe can talk to dead people. And Theia—" Her chest tightened at the thought of Theia. "She's always had visions and prophetic dreams. But I never had anything. Until I started doing tattoos. Then the visions just came to me."

Leo studied her with a secretive smile. "And do they always come true, your visions?"

"Ah-ha-ha." She waggled her finger at him. "There you go again."

His eyes twinkled. "I have so little to occupy my thoughts. What with not having a mind. I'm nothing but will."

"You seem to have more of a mind than Leo the—" Rhea stopped before she finished the epithet. She hadn't meant to call him that.

"You see? He *is* dull, isn't he? A complete bore." He made a little motion that encompassed his shoulders and hips, almost a shimmy. "I can't help that I have all the best attributes." The shimmy set off that tingling in her extremities again.

"Except modesty."

"If I had any, it would be false modesty." He winked one sparkling blue eye. "So where do these gifts of yours come from? Did your parents have them?"

Rhea chewed her lip. "I haven't told Leo this. The other Leo."

He leaned forward in the chair. "Ooh, a secret. Just between you and me."

"Supposedly, we have demon blood. From the first demoness, Lilith."

"That, my dearest dove, is…" He shook his head slowly, letting his gaze roam over her. "Fucking hot."

She wasn't sure whether it was the endearment or the hungry, appreciative gaze or the unexpected "fucking hot" that was melting her pussy like the well of wax around a candle's flame. Probably all three. His biceps were flexed, hard and well defined beneath his sleeves as his fists clenched and unclenched in unconscious chafing against his bonds. He was at her mercy, as he'd said. She was sitting here with one of the hottest guys she'd ever seen—who wanted her with a refreshingly naked lust— resisting his tacky, relentless come-ons. And suddenly, it seemed absurd that she was sitting a foot away from him.

Leo's eyes widened as she pushed herself off the stool and swung her leg over the chair to straddle his hips. The seat was too wide to straddle comfortably, so she balanced her knees on the vinyl cushion on either side of him.

"If I'd known vulgarity was all it took—"

"Shut up, Leo." Rhea gripped his shoulders—*good lord, the muscles*—and silenced him. He tasted of cardamom and caraway and a bit of mint from the Indian food they'd eaten earlier. She supposed she tasted the same. His tongue teased as he alternately nipped and licked at her lips, humming softly into her mouth when she grew impatient with his teasing and pressed in closer. The vibration of sound made her damp between her thighs. Relaxing her hips against his, she felt his answering appreciation pressed firmly against her.

It wasn't quite her vision—they weren't naked, for one—but there was definitely something to be said for having a man at her mercy. In past experiences—admittedly not many and pretty much exclusively with horny undergrad dudes with one single-minded collegiate goal—this part, the kissing and sensuous grinding, was usually swiftly eclipsed by artless groping and undressing. The simple art of "making out" had been sorely lacking in those past experiences. She lost track of time, just kissing and moving with Leo in his lap in a gently rolling and perfectly synchronous wave, enveloped in his captivating scent.

Leo groaned when she pulled away at last, his hands grasping uselessly at the air. "Don't go."

"I'm not going anywhere." She took off his glasses—daytime Leo had kept them on to play Scrabble—and set them aside, settling back in his lap to look at him. His lips had reddened like cherries, wet and swollen. She could relate.

His tongue slid languidly across his bottom lip, making it slicker. "That was unexpected. And quite pleasurable. I wish I had my hands free." He stretched his pinky out to stroke one of her thighs, barely reaching. "Just one, perhaps?"

Rhea let go of his shoulders finally, letting her hands glide down his chest, feeling the hardness of his pecs, the sharp little peaks of his nipples beneath the fabric, his heartbeat.

She traced the outline of his pendant through the fabric. "You could at least pretend not to be using me just to get free."

The vibration of his laughter rumbled beneath her hands. "I've not pretended to be a saint. But I do have to object to the use of the word *just*. There is no *just* about you. You're very complex. As is my desire for you. Do I want to be free

Jane Kindred   147

of these damn shackles? Of course. But if I had to choose between freedom and having you in my lap, it would be a very difficult decision."

Rhea withdrew her hands and folded her arms. "And what would you choose?"

Leo leaned back, observing her, deciding, no doubt, whether she was worth his freedom. "How much freedom would I be bargaining? All of it? Or a single night?"

"Would your answer be different?"

"Of course. It would be no hardship at all to remain bound for another night if it meant spending that night with you."

"Now you're just trying to flatter me." Rhea grinned. "But I'll take it."

"No flattery at all. You make me forget I'm here against my will—in the most literal sense of the term."

Rhea uncrossed her arms and rested a hand on one of his. Leo threaded their fingers together. They sat that way, oddly comfortable in each other's silence and company, until the text notification on her phone broke the spell. He tightened his grip on her hand to keep her from letting go as she slid off his lap and dropped her feet to the floor.

She tugged against him. "I need to grab my phone."

"Do you? I'm not sure you're well enough acquainted with need to make such an assertion."

"Leo." She pried at his fingers with her other hand, and he released her reluctantly, his mouth drooping into a pout. "I'm only going two feet across the room."

She snagged the phone from the counter and opened the message. Phoebe had sent a picture of Puddleglum, her fat Siamese tabby, wearing a tiny sombrero, with the caption "We're going to party, karamu, fiesta...all night long." Rhea stifled a snort-laugh and switched off the screen.

When she looked up, Leo's expression resembled Puddleglum's resigned glower. "Are you leaving?"

Rhea tucked the phone into her back pocket and slid onto his lap once more. "I said I'd stay, didn't I?" She found the pedal beneath the chair and lowered the seat back, to Leo's pleased smirk.

"You might have let me know the chair reclined."

"Sorry, I hadn't even thought of it." Rhea rested her crossed arms on his chest.

"So this demon blood of yours—that's what gives you the power of…?"

"Pictomancy. But we're done talking about me."

"Are we?"

Rhea silenced him once more. While they kissed, her hands roamed over his obliques, stroking the taut muscles. With a shiver and a sudden jerk, Leo began to laugh. His skin twitched beneath her touch.

"You're ticklish." Rhea grinned. That was unexpected. And adorable. "You really are at my mercy, then."

"Cruel mistress. You wouldn't dare."

She tugged his shirt from his pants and moved her hands over the hardness of his abs, flirting with the edges of his waist to see where he'd twitch. *Goddamn.* It wasn't as if he'd been hiding much beneath the tight shirt, but he was even more ripped than she'd imagined. His abs formed a sharp V dipping down into the waistline of his pants. He wasn't ticklish there.

"Careful." The tone of his voice made her look up from unbuckling his belt. His eyes were intense. "There's only so much teasing I can take."

"Am I teasing you?"

"Aren't you?"

Was she? Rhea paused to consider. Was she really prepared to have sex with Leo right now? A man who was tied up and not in his right mind? The sincerity of his obvious desire notwithstanding, there was something more than a little unsavory about the circumstances. If the situation were reversed...

Rhea let go of the belt buckle and lowered his shirt.

Leo sighed. "Not quite the response I was hoping for."

"It wouldn't be right."

Leo dropped his head back against the headrest and rolled his eyes. "This is what it comes to. The absolute petty pointlessness of having a soul." He fixed his gaze on her. "Every part of your body and your mind desires me, wants to ride me with abandon and give yourself over to passion and lust as you did in our vision. But your silly little soul insists 'it wouldn't be right,' and so you deny yourself. You don't think *he*'s going to give you the opportunity, do you? He'd just as soon wear a hair shirt and castigate himself for his impure thoughts."

Rhea sat up, glaring at him through the errant lock of hair. "You don't have to be a dick about it." She regretted her choice of words immediately, given where she was sitting.

But Leo ignored the double entendre. "I'm not saying he doesn't want you, just that he's too pathetic to act on that desire. *Me.* I'm that desire. Right here in front of you, telling you to take what you want." Maybe he'd only been waiting to act on the wordplay. He punctuated the phrase with a movement beneath her that made her breath catch.

She managed not to show it. "People who take what they want regardless of anyone else's feelings are the reason the world is so messed up. I happen to care about Leo's feelings. *Your* feelings, as much as you like to think you're not him. And I wouldn't be able to look him in the eyes tomorrow morning if I acted on pure desire for my own selfish reasons without any thought for how he's going to feel about it when he's back in his own skin."

He studied her, his chest heaving with anger or passion— or both—and looking so hot she wanted to cry. And kick herself for not just saying "screw it" and going for it.

"He doesn't have to find out." The soft, hopeful tone in which he'd said it was so absurd she had to laugh. Leo gave her a reluctant smile and shrugged. "You can't fault a *munr* for trying."

It only made her laugh harder, tears springing to the corners of her eyes from the release of tension. She wiped them away, shaking her head, and let herself melt against him—moving subtly aside to avoid the frustration of continued friction. She'd almost gotten herself under control when Leo spoke again.

"Well, that was fun." The resignation in his voice rumbled through his chest beneath her ear where she'd rested her head. "What do you want to do now?"

Rhea buried her face in his shirt and laughed until the tears were flowing down her cheeks.

Chapter 14

The click of the locks woke him with a jolt. Something was different. Leo opened his eyes to find Rhea snoring softly on his shoulder. She'd lowered the seat back and curled up next to him on the chair. Or on him, mostly—one leg draped over his lap. Leo narrowed his eyes. His shirt was untucked and his belt buckle was open. What in the name of the gods had his alter ego done?

He was afraid to wake her, afraid to find out, but his bladder had no intention of being so accommodating. Leo turned his right wrist under the leather and worked the strap out of the buckle. Reaching over Rhea to unstrap the other woke her.

She glanced up with a quizzical look, stretching sleepily as if not quite aware of where she'd awoken, and he watched the realization dawn on her face.

Rhea scrambled up, wiping a bit of spittle from the corner of her mouth. "Leo, I..." She looked around helplessly, as if an explanation might show up somewhere in the room. "You wanted me to stay, so I—"

"Would you mind holding that thought?" Leo swung his legs over the other side of the chair, avoiding her eyes as he tugged his shirt down over the open belt buckle, trying to act like he didn't notice. "I really need to use the bathroom."

After he'd relieved himself and put his clothes back together, he stared into the mirror over the sink. "What the hell did you do?" His reflection blinked back at him without answering.

"Leo?" Rhea tapped on the door. "You okay in there?"

He must have been staring at himself, resisting the urge to put a fist through the mirror to get to his alter ego, for some time. "Yeah, I'm good." He washed his hands and face and his pits and came out to find Rhea pacing in front of the counter, hands in her back pockets accentuating the curve of her ass.

She turned at the sound of the closing door. "I can explain. Nothing happened. Mostly." Her face was flushed.

"We don't have to talk about it." The last thing he wanted to hear was what "mostly" meant.

"Of course we do. I violated your trust."

"*You* did?"

"I kissed him. And then I almost let things get out of control, but I realized it wouldn't be fair to you to take it any further because you wouldn't remember, so you couldn't exactly consent. So I stopped." Rhea took her hands from her pockets and scrubbed them over her face. "This sounds so awful. I'm sorry. I shouldn't have started anything."

"And he was completely innocent in the matter, was he?"

"Well, I—"

"Let's just forget about it. I don't want to know what he does with you."

"He's *you*, Leo. And we didn't do anything, I told you. Just kissed."

Just kissed with his pants undone.

"Would you have told me if I hadn't noticed anything?"

"I…am so sorry, Leo. It won't happen again."

"That was a nonanswer."

Rhea looked down at her feet. "I don't know. I doubt it." She glanced up again. "Because this is *so* awkward.

Which is precisely why I stopped. I realized how awkward it would be if we…" She didn't need to finish the sentence. The idea of her being with the other Leo—it didn't matter that it was his body—or maybe it mattered more—caused him actual physical pain.

Leo looked around and found his glasses, pulling them on and adjusting them to buy time. "I think maybe I should get a room tonight. I don't think this was such a good idea."

Rhea's face fell. "You're quitting? Again?"

He smiled despite himself at the added word. "Just finding someplace else to sleep. But to be honest…" He glanced around at the empty shop. "It doesn't look like you need me for much of anything else. I mean, the place looks ready. Have you considered opening the shop early? Why wait until the New Year?"

"You may have noticed the clients aren't exactly flocking in."

"What about the one you just booked?"

Rhea gaped at him. "Brock Dressler? Are you suggesting I actually tattoo that creep?"

"You could use your pictomancy to find out what he's up to. You said you could read people without them knowing. I could be here to make sure nothing happens, stay out of sight."

"What are you going to do, hide in the bathroom?"

"Why not? You could call him and tell him you have an earlier opening available. He doesn't know I'm aware of the appointment."

Rhea considered. "I suppose I could. But I'd have to get him in here tomorrow. Monday's Christmas, so I wasn't planning on being open this weekend."

Which meant tomorrow was the solstice. He'd been so wrapped up in his angst over Rhea's intimacy with his alter ego he'd almost forgotten. He just had to get through two more nights.

"In the meantime, I think I'm going to need a little time to myself, so unless you need me to do anything to set up for the appointment—?"

"No, it's fine. You go ahead." Rhea looked slightly wounded. Well, too bad. She'd wounded him first. "But you'll be back tomorrow?"

Leo managed a reassuring smile. "Definitely."

He eventually found a room for the night, though it cost him more than he'd planned. He hadn't figured in the effects of the holiday season tourism on the prices of even the most modest accommodations.

As dusk approached, he considered the usual setup for the restraints—the headboard of the bed in his room was essentially a piece of stuffed vinyl with nothing to secure them to, and the frame sat flush with the floor, so nothing usable there. There was a chair at the writing desk, but it was flimsy. He could see ramming the chair against the wall to break the supports and easily getting free. The only other options were the plumbing behind the toilet or the surprisingly sturdy metal shower rod permanently fixed to the wall instead of sitting in a bracket. Neither seemed a comfortable option for spending more than fourteen hours. Then again, why did the bastard deserve comfort?

He took perverse pleasure in pulling the restraints tight as he locked the two together over the shower curtain rod. It was oddly positioned, high enough that his arms were raised above his head—not painfully high, but high. It was probably part of the infrastructure, a piece of steel piping conveniently placed to double as a curtain rod. He supposed he'd regret it in the morning when the consequences became his, but the potential discomfort was worth knowing the other Leo would be miserable for a night.

The bastard had left him in the dark. Leo took a deep breath. The first in the absence of the miserable little *hugr* was always the sweetest.

What the hell? His arms were stretched above his head. Not the first time Leo had left him this way, but usually he'd been left with some kind of comforts. His eyes adjusted to the darkness. *A goddamn bathtub.* The son of a bitch had shackled him over a curtain rod in the bathroom like some damn hand-washed socks left to drip dry.

Despite the indignity, it brought a dark smile to his face. Leo had obviously leaped to conclusions after finding Rhea passed out in his lap with his pants undone. He supposed he could have nudged Rhea after she'd nodded off and asked her to put his clothes back together. But it was more fun knowing Leo would wake to the apparent evidence of how they'd passed the time.

The consequences of getting under Leo's skin were bittersweet, though. He had only a single night left after this one to see her—if Leo allowed it. Who knew where he'd wake up in a year? He was heartily sick of being Leo's bitch to be chained and imprisoned. And it made him more determined than ever to find a way to get loose before dawn came on the twenty-third and put an end to this game.

With Rhea's evocation of the word *Valkyrie* having jogged his memory, he now had an inkling of how long the game had been going on. It was difficult to piece together an accurate picture of the time after he'd lost his hand—and evidently had it restored by the Fates—since, with it, had come the fracturing of his mind. But before that, when he and Leo's other selves had been fully cognizant of the curse, he had been with Kára for more than three centuries. His death, which she had bargained with the Norns to forestall, had occurred in the year nine hundred and sixty-eight. He'd retained enough bits and pieces of memory over recent years to know it had been more than a thousand since.

He couldn't remember when Kára had marked him with the bond of Jörmungandr, but Leo was obviously stupid enough to have done it at her bidding without question. Judging from Rhea's comments about him being at a woman's mercy, he could just imagine the circumstances under which it had been done.

It meant that when he did escape, he would be confined to Leo's skin. Not a terrible hardship—especially knowing the *hugr* would be doomed to wander the Night Realm forever. Without the skin, the *hugr* would never know what it was like to be with Rhea. And that was an experience *this* Leo had no intention of letting pass him by.

As the evening wore on, Leo tried to find a more comfortable position, but there was no give in the link between the restraints. His arms ached and his fingers had gone numb. And he needed to take a goddamn piss. Not for the first time, he wished he could step outside the skin—not only now, to escape, but in general, so he could strangle the miserable little shit for stringing him up like a lutefisk.

The allrune tattoo itched something fierce beneath the suede backing of the cuff. Having the restraints rubbing against the healing tattoo couldn't be doing it any favors. The itching became intolerable, and Leo twisted in the shackles, cursing Leo the Dull. He let out a bellow of rage, not caring if the manager came and had him arrested for being a pervert. It would serve Leo right to lose the game that way.

The discomfort lessened with the expulsion of sound, but a tickling sensation remained. In the mirror across from him, barely visible in the black-and-white hues of night, a thin shadow, like a darkening vein, crawled down his arm.

Leo glanced up. The tattoo was bleeding from one corner. Rhea would probably have to repair it once it healed. And he might not even be aware the touch-up had happened for another year. They would be far away from Rhea by then. He cursed and kicked the back wall of the shower stall, and the heel of his boot stuck in it, cheap plaster crumbling into the stall as he wiggled it out. He laughed out loud, angry and yet feeling a strange sense of release. Fuck Leo.

The blocky shapes and angles of the bathroom had become a shade grayer. Dawn was coming. One more night left. One more chance to act on desire. One more chance to break loose once and for all and be free of Leo the Dull forever.

His arms felt like they'd been pulled from their sockets, and it took forever to work the link loose from the D rings on the restraints. Leo dropped to his knees in the shower stall and lowered his head to his knees.

"Son of a *bitch*." His alter ego had taken revenge on him by pissing his pants.

Chapter 15

She'd tattooed at least a dozen people, a few of them more than once, and never had a complaint. But her first official client had her feeling like an imposter—and not just because she was planning to spy on his nefarious plans through pictomancy.

Rhea glanced at the clock on her phone. Leo hadn't arrived yet and it was almost noon. She was beginning to think he wasn't coming back, that last night had been an excuse to split once and for all. If she was going to have to be alone with this creep, maybe she should rethink the whole thing and cancel. And maybe she should just give up this stupid idea of having her own tattoo shop since no one but some alt-right jackhole had expressed the slightest bit of interest, and she was going to die homeless and penniless and twenty pounds overweight.

The door jingled as Leo finally made an appearance. "Hey. Sorry I'm late. I had to do laundry."

"He's going to be here in half an hour. You decided to stop and do laundry first?"

"I had kind of a bad night."

She wasn't sure what constituted a bad night when one wasn't conscious of how one spent it, but she hadn't slept well herself. After heading home, she'd been restless and jittery. She hadn't seen any sign of the Hunt or Vixen and not even a glimpse of the black wolf-dog. How weird was her life that she'd been disappointed by that? She'd ended up elaborating on her tattoo design, adding some delicate filigree around the Black Moon Lilith symbol. It hadn't prompted any visions, but her dreams had been odd and dark—literal darkness, where she couldn't find anything or anyone and kept going in circles—and she'd woken up feeling more tired than when she'd gone to sleep.

"I thought maybe you'd decided not to come back."

"I considered it." Leo peeled out of his coat, revealing that the black long-sleeved shirt had been his choice today, but he left his knit hat on as though he'd forgotten it was there. "But then I realized I was making a big deal out of nothing. He's going to be gone after tonight, anyway. Then we can get to know each other without him in the way. Maybe even go out on an actual date or something." Leo gave her a tentative lopsided grin. "If you still want to, that is."

"Of course I want to." The other Leo was going to be gone after tonight? Somehow, she'd thought he had a few more days, despite knowing the time frame of the Hunt.

Leo glanced around awkwardly. "Anyway, I should probably make myself scarce." He disappeared into the bathroom not a moment too soon. Brock was early.

As the door opened, Rhea noticed Leo's plaid hunting jacket lying on the couch. There was no time to stash it, so she put it on. It was hip length on Leo but the hem hit Rhea mid-thigh.

Brock gave her a big smile. "So glad you were able to fit me in earlier. I really appreciate this." She hadn't noticed before, but his hair was cropped close on the sides, with a sort of pompadour-esque floop of longer hair hanging over it, oiled and slicked. God, how had she not pegged him for a Nazi?

Rhea resisted an automatic gag reflex as she shook his hand. "No problem. I realized I was going to be away for the holidays and I might not get back in time, so this works perfectly for me. Come on back." She led him through the curtain, casting an eye at the bathroom door to make sure it was shut. "You can hang up your coat on the rack."

"Looks like you have two," he observed as he removed his to hang it up.

"Oh, this?" Rhea lifted her arms at her sides, the sleeves hanging under her arms like flannel wings. "It's kind of my lucky work smock. It belonged to my dad. It gets pretty drafty in here. I wasn't expecting such cold weather this early."

"Yeah, this snow has been something, hasn't it? So much for those global warming gloom-and-doomers."

Rhea resisted the urge to tell him he was confusing climate with weather. "So, you said you have a mock-up of what you want?"

Brock handed her a piece of paper with the words *I am. I think. I will.* in a sort of retro serif typeface with fuzzy edges and missing spots, like it had been typed on an old typewriter. "Ayn Rand," he said. Rhea repressed the urge to roll her eyes. At least it wasn't Hitler.

"Is this the size you want it?"

"A little smaller." He took off his suit jacket and rolled up the sleeve of his pin-striped shirt. A little overdressed for getting a tattoo. "I want it right here, on the inside of my arm, starting below my elbow and heading toward my wrist."

Rhea reduced the image on her photocopier and copied it onto the transfer sheet once Brock approved it. "All right. I think we're ready to go."

She shoved Leo's jacket sleeves up to her elbows and had to roll the cuffs several times to keep them there, but she managed to act like it was part of her artistic ritual. Brock's skin was unusually taut, with an almost leathery quality to it, requiring a lot of pressure to pierce. She supposed he must get a lot of sun.

As Rhea worked through the outline, she let her arm above the glove rest lightly on the upper part of the tattoo, skin to skin, and concentrated on reading without "broadcasting" the reading to him. She'd done it deliberately once or twice, and the key was focusing on images close enough to the client's surface thoughts that they didn't intrude.

Rhea put out a little "feeler" question as though it were his own thought: *Did I eat enough before I came?* A clear image came to her of a bowl of muesli. How exciting.

She glanced up to see if the image had intruded on his thoughts. "How are you doing so far? Okay?"

Brock smiled a little nervously. "So far so good. It's both not as bad as I expected and a great deal worse."

Rhea laughed. "Sounds about right. Some areas are more sensitive than others, too, so it might feel like it's no big deal then suddenly become a big deal. Let me know if you need me to take a break. The endorphins should kick in pretty soon, though."

Time to try a little more specific test. She kept her thoughts focused on *how do I feel about this?* and then led him toward a loaded topic to see if she could pick up on what he really felt regardless of what he said.

"It's great to have someone breaking in the chair. I can't wait for the official opening, but getting this place ready has been a challenge. Some kids keep spray-painting graffiti on the walls. I swear, I've cleaned it off half a dozen times in the past two weeks."

"That's a shame. Have the police had any luck catching them?"

"I haven't called the cops. Hopefully, I won't have to. It

seems pretty harmless. They're obviously doing it for kicks. Trying to impress their friends and act like badasses. Although, the other day, they added a swastika to a tag. Who knows what motivated that? Actual hate? Or just, 'Ooh, look how edgy I am'?"

"Really? I wonder if they belong to a gang. Have you seen any of them?"

So far, his mental imagery was surprisingly blank. At least, she wasn't getting much of anything equating to *how do I feel about this?* Maybe she should try a different tactic.

"No, just the graffiti. I doubt they belong to any organized group, though." *Like the Nazi Party*, she thought deliberately and pictured a goose-stepping SS squad.

Brock flinched, and she took her foot off the pedal.

"Did I hit a nerve?" She was taking a chance with the double entendre, but what the hell.

"Yeah, it kind of took me by surprise when you got between the bones."

"Sometimes it's the spots you least expect to be sensitive. Tattooing over bone can be extra painful, but you never know what's going to be a trigger." She blotted the blood on the fresh part of the tattoo, letting their arms touch again, and projected the question with specificity: *How do I feel about Nazis?* This time, she picked up his own image of shouting skinheads and a white supremacist rally. It was pretty stereotypical stuff, and the feeling that accompanied it was a definitive wave of disgust.

She was starting to think Leo was wrong about him. If he was a Nazi, he certainly didn't think of himself as one. She wasn't picking up any images indicating he was at all sympathetic to such a cause.

Rhea tried a few more times but got nothing more definitive. She even tried more generally to see if she could pick up on an impression of why he'd come into her tattoo shop, but all she got was a flash of memory of him seeing one of her flyers.

He tipped her well and thanked her profusely. "This is really great. Absolutely fantastic. I'll be sure to spread the word."

Rhea beamed. "So glad you like it." She took a picture for her online gallery and wished him Happy Holidays as he left——her first client and a satisfied one.

Leo came out when he'd gone. "Doesn't sound like you tipped him off. Great job steering him. Did you get anything?"

Rhea uploaded the photo. "Not really. Are you sure about what he said to you? Maybe you misunderstood him."

Leo's eyes narrowed. "Are you kidding me?"

"He didn't react like he was on board with any of that—the swastika, the Nazis. I even tried picturing stuff myself, as a sort of subliminal suggestion, and the worst I got was a shudder."

Leo scratched his head through the cap. "I don't get it. He was very specific to me about the purity of the races and some pro-eugenics crap."

Rhea shrugged. "Maybe he's a racist asshole who thinks he's better than those other racist assholes."

"And you didn't get anything from him about why he showed up here after running into me?"

"Honestly, I think it must have been a coincidence. I floated the question and got an image of one of my flyers. Nothing about you. I doubt he's even aware you work here."

Leo sank onto the couch, shaking his head. "I don't get it. What are the odds? But maybe you're right."

"On the plus side..." Rhea held up the fifty he'd given her for a tip and grinned. "Demoness Ink is officially legit." She snapped the bill in both hands. "And now I've got Christmas spending money." She paused and grimaced.

"And the gas and electric bill on this place for the first month is probably going to be three times this."

Leo leaned forward, arms resting on his knees, looking rueful. "I feel bad being one more expense."

"Are you kidding? I've conned you into accepting ink for payment. You're the best thing I've got going here."

Leo grinned. "In that case, maybe you could pay me a little early? I've been thinking it would be fun to have both wrists itching at the same time."

"What the hell." Rhea popped the fifty into her cash box. "I'm in a generous mood, and I'm on a roll. After we close today, we'll get you set up."

Mjölnir was more complex than the allrune, a knotted pattern weaving throughout it. It was nice work but impossibly faded, as though the ink had blurred and run together over time. Time Leo couldn't possibly have had the tattoo.

"I may need to add some color to give it definition," she said as she looked it over. "Would you be okay with that? Or do you want to stick with black?"

"Actually, I really like the scarlet color you have in the tattoo you showed me. I was thinking that might look nice as a contrast inside the white space."

Rhea smiled. "I was just thinking that color would be awesome there." She took the bottle of ink out of her kit. "It's called Bloodbath."

Leo laughed. "Let's hope that's not prophetic."

Rhea pondered the job as she set up the supplies. "This one's probably going to take a bit more time than the other one did. Maybe two hours. Is that going to work for you?" She hesitated. "I mean...are you staying here tonight or do you need to get back to the motel?"

Leo considered. "I wasn't going to stay, but sometimes I have major memory problems after the final night. That's why I move around a lot. It's uncomfortable to wake up somewhere and have pieces missing that other people are expecting you to have. Maybe it would help to have a familiar face there when I wake up—if you're going to stay, that is."

"I thought I would." Rhea tried to play it casual. She didn't dare let him see how relieved she was at the prospect or how much she'd missed seeing his other self the night before. "And you have my word nothing untoward will happen." She crossed her heart, as he'd done the other day, with a lighthearted smile.

Leo's expression said he wasn't sure he could trust her, but he smiled, anyway. "Now if we could only get *his* word."

"Well, that's what the restraints are for, right? I'll keep my distance, and he can do his worst. As long as you trust me."

"I do trust you." This time the smile was genuine. "Him, not so much. But you, absolutely." His stomach growled, and Rhea paused in prepping his arm.

"When did you eat last?"

"I had an egg sandwich this morning."

"Leo. You know you can't get a tattoo without any food in your system. That's the first rule on the wall." She pointed to the plaque. "Let's get dinner first. If we run out of time, I can always do the rest while you're restrained."

"That's not exactly keeping your distance." The smile this time was more genuine. "But I trust you. So, yeah. Shouldn't be a problem."

They went for pizza, going out to pick it up down the block. The place was busy, and the light was already getting low by the time they walked back up the hill with their pie. Rhea had forgotten this was the longest night of the year.

Leo hurried inside and grabbed his bag to get the restraints in place before dusk fell.

Rhea helped secure them. "Sorry, Leo. I didn't think it would take that long. We should have gotten fast food. How are you going to eat like this?"

"I suppose," he said as the locks clicked into place, "you'll have to feed me, my little dove."

Rhea looked up into the *munr*'s amused eyes. "Wow. Just in the nick of time, it would seem."

"To you, maybe. I would have much preferred to skip this foolish ritual altogether." He glanced from Rhea to the pizza box to the little tray at the side of the chair all set up with the tattooing supplies. "I rather doubt those have anything to do with dinner."

"Leo asked me to touch up the other gauntlet."

"Of course he did. You realize what these marks are, don't you?"

Rhea shrugged. "Protective symbols from Norse mythology."

"Shackles. Stitched into the skin so that they become part of us. Far more effective than any cheap bondage gear."

"If you're trying to convince me you don't need the restraints, you can forget it."

"I wouldn't dream of it." His stomach growled loudly. "But you could give me something to eat."

Rhea opened the pizza box on the counter and took out a slice. "This is a little kinky for my taste, but I don't want you to pass out, so…" She shrugged and took a bite, to Leo's irritation, his brows drawing together and his sky blues clouding. Rhea laughed. "Don't freak out. I'm going to share." She held the slice in front of his mouth.

With a lifted brow, he leaned forward and took a bite. It was unexpectedly intimate to be feeding a man who was tied to a chair.

"I take it Leo didn't appreciate waking up with his pants undone, knowing he didn't get to participate in the fun."

"And letting me fall asleep without remedying the situation had nothing at all to do with trying to goad your own soul."

"Oh, it had everything to do with it." Leo grinned and took the next bite she fed him. "Do you know he strung me up from a curtain rod in the bathroom last night?" He rolled his shoulders. "My trapezius muscles are still killing me. Which means they've been killing *him* all day and damn well serves the miserable bastard right."

Rhea hadn't expected that. Leo was fighting over her… with Leo. "You know, each of you thinks the other is the miserable bastard."

"Well, he's wrong, because *he* is." Leo accepted another bite of the slice she held out for him, and Rhea finished off the crust. "He's the one who locks me up for fifty nights a year because he's afraid of his own free will. And you're just going to let him finish me off. Do his dirty work for him and watch me die at dawn. I hope it haunts you."

"Leo—"

"No, I don't want to argue. Sorry." He licked at a crumb on his upper lip but couldn't quite get it. "I want to enjoy this last night together."

Rhea wiped the crumb off with her thumb. "Do you enjoy it?"

"What, bondage? I think that's more Leo's thing, from what you've told me."

"Spending this time together." Rhea smirked. "I mean, aside from the other night, which it was quite clear you were enjoying."

Leo studied her, his expression serious. "I can't remember ever enjoying any moment more in my entire life than those I've spent with you these past few nights."

Rhea blushed and took another slice of pizza. "By your

own admission, what you remember isn't much." She took a bite and offered one to him.

Leo ignored it. "The more cumulative hours of consciousness I have, the more I retain. And the more I recall from past years. But from before my mind was bound by the Norns, I've begun to recall a great deal."

"How much, exactly, are we talking here? I mean, when did Kára…?"

"When was I spared on the battlefield from the death that ought to have been mine?" Leo tilted his head toward the slice she was still holding, and Rhea held it out for him to take another bite. He took his time chewing and swallowing, while Rhea nibbled on the pizza. "What do you know of Viking history?"

Rhea swallowed her mouthful. "Um…yeah…nothing, actually. Wasn't my area of focus at the university."

"The raid on which I received my mortal wound was in the last millennium."

She couldn't help the surprised little laugh.

"What's so funny?"

"The last millennium was seventeen years ago."

"Ah. Leo doesn't make much of an effort to keep me apprised of current events." Leo pondered a moment. "Then it was one thousand and…forty-nine years past."

Rhea nearly choked on her pizza. Not that it should have been a surprise. As soon as she'd made the Valkyrie connection, she'd suspected he wasn't exactly from the modern era. But more than a thousand years old?

"So you're, what…one thousand and…?"

"Seventy-four. I admit the age difference is a bit of a barrier, but I'm a young one thousand and seventy-four." His eyes twinkled, and all Rhea could do was wonder how he didn't have any crow's-feet. No wonder his tattoos looked faded.

"So the marks, as you call them, they're that old, too?"

"The originals, yes. Evidently, Leo has them refreshed every so often, because he's a complete twat."

Rhea glanced at the prepped table. "So I guess I shouldn't…"

"Of course you should. Why not? It's not as if he won't do it tomorrow anyway after I'm gone."

"But I'd have to remove the restraint."

"How could I possibly get away with my other arm still locked down?"

Rhea shook her head. "No can do."

Leo sighed. "You're a cruel mistress, Rhea Carlisle."

"I'm not your mistress." She tried not to think about the implications of the word. "I can do the handle portion, though." Only the top of the hammer was fully covered by the restraint. "I mean, what else are we going to do all night?" Rhea laughed as Leo waggled his eyebrows. "I promised him I wouldn't."

"Gods, that soul of yours. Almost as irritating as his." Leo pouted. "My last night, and I don't even get a kiss goodbye?"

"Well, maybe one. But only if you behave and let me work without being difficult."

"That promise, my dove, will keep me going for hours."

She put the pizza away and held a water bottle for him to wash it down before settling beside him and pulling up the tray. She'd already shaved his arm, so after a quick swab, she started on the black.

As unproductive as her attempts to read Dressler had been, Rhea hadn't even considered the potential for another inadvertent reading from Leo, but given her previous experiences with him, she should have seen it coming. The moment she made even proximal skin contact, it was like the tattoo was buzzing with anticipation, waiting to tell her stories.

Focusing on reinforcing the black lines of the design, she managed to shut out the images threatening to overwhelm her, but they were vibrating in the air, wanting to be read.

Leo watched her biting her lip in concentration. "Why not take a peek?"

Rhea kept her head down over the machine. "I don't think I want to see what you're thinking right at the moment."

"The vision you had before didn't reflect what I was thinking. Why do you assume it would work that way now?"

Rhea laughed. "It might not have been your uppermost conscious thought, but you were definitely thinking it." And judging by the visible bulge in his jeans she was trying to ignore, his current train of thought was similar.

"And what are *you* thinking?"

"I'm thinking this is going to be a long night."

"The longest," Leo agreed.

Rhea paused to switch out the needles and ink. "You know, I usually spend this night with my sisters."

"Sorry. Didn't mean to keep you from them."

"You're not. We didn't have anything planned this year. Theia's still up north—not that I'm talking to her, anyway—and Phoebe and Ione have other things on their minds."

"What sorts of things?"

"They're both in new relationships."

"Ah, so they're busy fornicating."

Rhea laughed. "Sometimes you have quite a way with words, Leo. But yes. They are, I'm quite sure, busy fornicating."

Leo watched as she readied the red ink cap. "He's adding color?"

"It was my idea. The old lines have lost a lot of definition around the edges, so I thought we could fill in some of the spaces between with color to delineate them better. He said to go for it."

"I doubt the Norns would be pleased." The last word was cut off on a sound of surprise in his throat as she put the needles to his flesh. The first stroke of the red ink seemed to have an instantaneous physical effect on him. And Rhea was feeling it, too. It was beyond arousal, beyond desire. It was a sense of *rightness*, as though they were kin. And not in a creepy incestuous way, just an overwhelming sense of belonging together.

"What is that?" Leo stared at his arm where she'd continued tattooing in a kind of trancelike state. "What did you do?"

"I don't know. Do you want me to stop?"

"No. It's...*nice* isn't quite the word. It feels a little like ants crawling through my veins, but I have to admit, it's strangely pleasant. Satisfying."

"Yeah." That was the word that had been eluding her. "I mean, I don't feel the ant-crawling thing, but this feels very satisfying. I don't want to stop."

"Weird," said Leo, but he didn't seem too disturbed by the odd sentiment. "It's like...an itch being scratched."

Rhea nodded, head bent over her work. "It's funny. My tattoo has been itching like crazy lately, but it stopped as soon as I started on yours."

In less than half an hour, she'd finished the knot work on the handle, which was super fast for her. Of course, the rest of the tattoo was still covered by the restraint. Rhea took her foot off the pedal. Leaving the tattoo incomplete was maddening. *That* was an itch that needed scratching.

Rhea pondered the fishing knife she'd tossed into a drawer that first night. He wouldn't be able to escape with one arm still shackled. Not unless he somehow managed to grab the knife from her and stab her so he could do it himself. She didn't think he was capable of that, soul or no soul, but she'd be on her guard.

She set down the machine and got up to get the knife.

Leo's eyebrow ticked upward. "And what are you planning to do with that? Is this some pagan ritual you've been leading up to culminating in a blood sacrifice on the eve of the solstice?"

"Just getting this out of the way." She slid the blade beneath the outside edge of the cuff pointing away from his skin and slashed downward and out. It barely made a dent in the leather. But it did make a dent.

"Careful," said Leo as she started sawing at it. "You don't want to slip with that thing. I've already lost this hand once. If the Norns wanted my mind in exchange for restoring it, I don't even want to think about what they'd want this time."

"Relax. I'm not going to cut your hand off." It took some doing, but at last the far edge of the leather came away, leaving him free to wriggle out.

Leo ran his fingers up her arm and drew her close. Rhea had enough presence of mind to toss the knife onto the counter out of reach before she gave herself over to the pleasure of his mouth. God, this man could kiss. This was master class–level kissing. She wrapped her arms around his neck and hooked her fingers in the hair at his nape, twisting it mindlessly until he made a slight noise of discomfort against her mouth.

Rhea drew back, releasing his hair. "Sorry. I got caught up in the moment. Forgot the hair was attached to anybody." She earned one of those surprised, delighted, deep-throated laughs from him. He was still wearing that damn knit cap.

Rhea took it off and tried to smooth the flyaway hair into a tidier semblance, but it was a losing battle.

Leo studied her as she played with it. "That was unexpected. What did I do to earn my partial freedom?"

"It's not freedom. I'm not going to cut the other one. I just wanted to finish this damned tattoo."

"Fair enough." He laid his arm across the armrest, and Rhea sat once more and went to work on the sections she hadn't been able to get to, switching out to do the rest of the black lines first so she'd have more control to fill in the red. Images tugged at her once more, but Rhea tuned them out.

He watched her quietly until she'd finished the rest of the black and started to switch out the ink for the final time. "I suppose Leo has filled your head with cautionary tales of horror about me turning into a giant snake or something if you were ever to set me free." His eyes were teasing, but the question seemed genuine enough.

"Actually, he said he thought it would unleash the destructive energy of Jörmungandr. It hadn't occurred to him that you might change form and make that energy literal until I suggested it."

Leo laughed. "But it's absurd. No one can change form. The physical selves, the *líkamr* and *hamr*, are just as distinct as the formless selves. They're governed by the laws of physics."

"What would you say if I told you I'd seen more than one person transform into something similar?"

"I'd say you'd been smoking too much cannabis."

She was sworn to secrecy about Rafe and Dev, but he would remember none of this tomorrow. Which was depressing. She tried not to think about that and started working on the red fill. Both of them relaxed into the peculiar "rightness" from before.

"No weed necessary. I know a man who regularly

sprouts wings and can take various animal forms temporarily."

"Do you, now? Who's this magical fellow?"

"He's called a quetzal. He's the human embodiment of the Aztec god Quetzalcoatl. He also happens to be my sister Phoebe's boyfriend."

Leo leaned back against the headrest. "You're serious."

"As a heart attack."

"So this is the new relationship she's in, the one you mentioned before."

"The very same."

"You said there was more than one person you'd seen transform."

"Ione's boyfriend. He shares physical form with a dragon demon. Not simultaneously. Only one of them occupies the skin at the same time. Kind of like you and Leo. I mean you and your *hugr*."

He was regarding her dubiously. "How is it that two of your sisters happen to be involved with these shapeshifters?"

She wasn't sure she wanted to get into the whole Lilith connection. If she mentioned it, he'd use it as an argument for her to free him, that it was fated. And she wasn't ready to accept that fate controlled her.

"I told you, we're a magical family."

"The demon blood."

Damn. She'd forgotten she'd already mentioned the connection. She wiped away some of his blood as she pondered it.

"So you think I might actually shift if you released me."

"Not necessarily."

What she was thinking was that if she had sex with him, there would be no escaping fate. This guy had *literal* Fates messing with his life. She'd have to be crazy to do anything more with him. Not that she was going to. She'd promised Leo she wouldn't. She was going to be the responsible one. Even if she *had* torn up one of Leo's expensive leather restraints. And she sure as hell wasn't setting him loose.

"But you're not taking any chances."

Rhea shrugged. "I also made a promise."

Leo jerked his arm away as she was about to press the needles to it, his eyes dark with anger. "Fuck your promises. Fuck both of you."

"If you want to screw up this tattoo permanently, just keep doing stupid shit like that while I have a bunch of needles full of ink poised over your skin." She set the machine aside. Maybe it was time to wrap it up for tonight. She'd done just about everything she wanted to. Any sharpening she'd missed could be addressed during touch-up. Rhea peeled off the gloves and rose to wash up, but Leo grabbed her hand before she could step away.

"I'm sorry. I think. I mean, I don't have a soul, but I'm experiencing a general sense of displeasure and discomfort with myself right now thinking about the way I snapped at you, so I'm pretty sure this would be categorized as regret."

Rhea looked down, not wanting him to see her smile, but he had the advantage of being seated.

"So this is you forgiving me, right? Because now I have a pleasant, relieved feeling."

She couldn't keep from laughing. "Yes, dammit. I forgive you. I wasn't all that upset with you in the first place. You have a right to be pissed about the situation you're in, and I know I'm not making it any easier."

"That's not true. You've made it quite a bit easier." He pulled her closer to the chair. "Come make it easier some more and I'll forgive you, too. I mean, if that's a thing I can do—"

"Shut up, Leo." As Rhea straddled him and kissed him

to silence him once more, her conscience nagged at her. She'd promised Leo nothing untoward would happen. But it wasn't as if she was going to do anything she hadn't already done.

With his arm free, however, that wasn't entirely up to her. Leo slid his hand up her side, letting his fingers brush lightly against the underside of her breast. It was very middle-school, over-the-bra kind of contact, but it sent a delicious shiver through her.

He moved his fingers higher, stroking her nipple with his thumb as he cupped her breast. The nipple was already hard, but the motion tightened the flesh. Without meaning to, she was rocking into his lap.

Rhea disengaged her mouth, though he leaned forward to pursue her. "We can't get too carried away here."

Leo made a dismissive noise. "Why not? What's he going to do about it? Nothing. Just like he's been doing. Is that really what you want? Me gone and Leo the Dull being excessively cautious and polite until he bores you into frigidity?"

"Okay, that was a little harsh. And you're forgetting you won't, in fact, be gone at all. You'll be sharing the skin with him."

"How do you know? Are you an expert on Norn curses? If I can't remember ever being him, how is he me? Maybe the real curse is that he has no will except for these stolen hours once a year? No desire at all—that's me, the *munr*, absent entirely. Are you willing to take that chance? What if he's worse than dull by tomorrow morning?"

Rhea frowned. She hadn't thought of that. But he would say anything to be free, which she couldn't even blame him for. Who wouldn't?

"Leo, I—" She paused. She'd become gradually aware of a familiar scent, like someone had set a fire in the fireplace.

But the shop didn't have a fireplace. It also apparently didn't have a functioning smoke alarm, because as soon as she'd made the realization, her eyes began to water. "Shit."

Chapter 16

Leo tensed beneath her. "Is that smoke?"

"I think the building's on fire." She swung off his lap, and Leo grabbed her arm.

"You can't leave me in here."

"Leave you? Are you insane?" She pulled away from him and grabbed the fish-scaling knife.

The smoke was getting thick as she sawed frantically at the leather. Rhea coughed into her sleeve, eyes watering.

"Let me do it." Leo took the knife from her hand. "You go. Get out. I'll be right behind you."

"No, I'm not—" A coughing fit swallowed the rest of her protest.

"Get out, goddammit! Get the fuck out!" He'd switched on the rage as suddenly as before, though this time it was designed to anger her into leaving. She started to object once more, but he'd yanked the knife upward and severed the restraint. Leo grabbed her hand and ran with her for the exit.

The fire had started on the stairs. They could feel the heat through the door.

"There's no back way out?"

Rhea shook her head, coughing. "We'll have to go out the window."

Leo grabbed the stool behind the counter and threw it

through the window, shattering the pane, before she could tell him it opened easily from the inside. That was going to be expensive. The absurdity of the thought hit her. The whole building was going to be gone, if not the entire shopping center.

Leo kicked out the jagged pieces and took off his shirt, folding it up and placing it over the sharp edges still clinging to the frame, and held out his hand. "Come on, you first."

Rhea peered out dubiously. They were only one flight up, but she was going to break her shins—if she even landed on her feet, which was doubtful.

"What are you waiting for?"

"It's a little far down. I'm trying to gather my nerve." The last word was a strangled cough.

"You don't have time to gather your nerve." Leo moved her aside. "If I go first and promise to catch you, will you jump when I tell you to?"

Rhea nodded, and he climbed through the window and leaped before she could even catch her breath. "Leo?" She hurried to the edge and looked down, expecting to see him digging himself off the sidewalk covered in scrapes and cuts, but he was standing there holding up his arms. Something crashed behind her.

"Jump, Rhea. *Now.*"

She climbed onto the shirt-covered frame and flung herself out, closing her eyes in her panic, and barreled into Leo like a wrecking ball. He broke her fall, catching her firmly in his shirtless arms without even stumbling back.

Sirens were blaring when she looked up at him, fire trucks already coming up the hill.

"You must be freezing," was all she could think of to say.

"Not really." Leo shrugged. "Feeling the cold must be a thought-self kind of thing."

And he didn't have his thought-self—and if they understood the curse correctly, he never would again. Rhea looked up at the flames engulfing her shop, the Demoness Ink sign singed around the edges. She almost wished she were missing her own thought-self so she wouldn't feel this crushing heartache at realizing her dream had gone up in smoke.

After talking to the firefighters and the officers who'd arrived on the scene while the crew put out the blaze, Rhea discovered a note tucked under her windshield wiper. *"Thou shalt not suffer a witch to live,"* it informed her in a cheery font. And to make sure she got the message, they'd added, *"You're all going to burn. Keep Sedona pure."* A couple of swastikas were thrown in for good measure.

"I'm not even a witch," she muttered, sinking against the car door.

Leo stroked her arm. "I'll drive you home."

"You don't have your glasses."

"Those were his. I don't need them." He held out his hand expectantly. "Do you have the keys?"

Rhea started to laugh, and it turned into crying. Of course she didn't have the keys. Had her brain been even partly functional, she might have grabbed her bag and her tablet before jumping out the window. Even her phone was inside.

"I don't even have that damn fifty," she whimpered against him as he gathered her in his arms.

"It's okay. The important thing is that you're safe. Things can be replaced."

Rhea choked in a breath in a strangled laugh against his bare chest. "Is that sympathy? Do *munrs* have that?"

"I don't know. Is sympathy when you want to kick someone to death for hurting your girl?"

"Your *girl*?" Rhea wiped her eyes. "I don't know if I like that. And no, that sounds more like vengeance."

"Okay, well, I've got that, anyway." He reached into his back pocket as she straightened. "I've also got Leo's phone."

At least one of them had been thinking. Which was ironic, since he was missing his thought-self. Rhea accepted the phone, staring at the screen. She couldn't get into her apartment, and it was way too late to be calling the landlord. She didn't even have the landlord's number, for that matter.

Phoebe was her first choice, but Ione's number was the only one she remembered since Ione had only recently gotten her first cell phone. Everyone else had been available at the click of an icon for ages. Rhea hadn't realized how much she depended on one little metal-and-glass box.

Ione came immediately, her dark ombré hair natural instead of ironed straight, as if she'd just crawled out of bed, and she was in full mother hen mode. "Are you okay?" She looked Rhea over, still standing in the parking lot. "What's this?" She held up Rhea's right palm, caked with dried blood. A piece of glass was embedded in it that Rhea hadn't even noticed. Leo watched them with interest, leaning back against Rhea's MINI with his arms folded, dwarfing the little car.

Rhea introduced him while Ione picked out the glass. "This is Leo Ström."

Ione looked up, her eyes narrowed at the shirtless Viking beside her little sister. "And who is 'Leo Ström'?"

"He's my…" Rhea felt her face go hot. "Goddammit. I don't know." She was too tired for long-winded explanations.

Leo chuckled and stepped forward, holding out his hand. "Rhea was tattooing me when the fire broke out."

"Ione Carlisle." She shook his hand, her expression still dubious, eyes taking in the Norse tattoos and pendant. "Can I drop you somewhere?"

"He's with me," Rhea said before Leo could answer.

Ione's expression was more mistrust than dubiousness at this point, but she nodded. "Let's get you guys warmed up. You'll catch your death."

Maybe Rhea would, but she was beginning to doubt whether Leo even *could* die.

Ione's place was toasty warm despite the giant glass wall along one side, and it smelled like cinnamon. Rhea paused in the entryway to take off her boots before stepping on Ione's carpet, but Leo had taken his off before strapping in for the night.

Dev, looking like he'd stepped off the cover of *GQ*, as usual, greeted them in the kitchen with hot cocoa.

Leo looked dubiously at the mug Dev offered him. "Got anything stronger?"

Dev's golden-brown eyes twinkled. "Give it a taste."

Rhea took a sip and grinned. "Wow. Now that's what I call hot cocoa."

Dev was pleased. "I got the recipe from Rafe. It's Mexican cocoa with tequila. And a dash of cayenne pepper."

Leo drank his experimentally and looked up with a surprised nod. "I wouldn't have thought to put that together, but it's not bad." He turned with another look of surprise when Ione draped one of Dev's shirts over his shoulders.

"Let's get that hand cleaned up." Ione steered Rhea to the bathroom as if she were still in grade school.

Rhea sighed as she submitted. "Yes, Mom."

"Don't 'mom' me, young lady." She took the mug out of Rhea's other hand and set it on the counter before examining her palm. "So are you going to tell me why a half-naked man was there with you? And why you didn't tell me you'd rented a place to hang out your shingle? I could have helped you with that."

"I didn't want anyone to help me. Everyone's always trying to help me, dammit." Rhea grimaced at the sting of the rubbing alcohol and the look from Ione. "Let me rephrase that. It's wonderful having sisters who believe in me and want to help me succeed, and I adore you, but I needed to do this on my own. Of course, now everything is gone, so I guess it's Universe one, Rhea zero."

"You didn't have insurance?"

Rhea tried to set fire to Ione with her eyes, and Ione dropped the subject.

"And the naked guy?"

"He was not naked, for God's sake. He used his shirt to keep me from cutting myself on the broken glass when I jumped out the window."

"You jumped out a *window*?" The adhesive bandage Ione was trying to peel the backing from snapped in half.

"Can I have my cocoa back now?"

Finally managing to get a bandage in place, Ione picked up the cocoa but held it out of Rhea's reach. "First, tell me about Leo."

"I already told you. I was touching up his tattoo. There's nothing more to tell."

Ione shook her head and drank Rhea's cocoa.

"Oh, come *on*." She'd never been able to pull one over on Ione. It was ridiculous to try. "Fine. I hired him to help get the place ready before opening, and I'm paying him in ink. Or I was."

"And?"

"And…we kind of have…a thing…something. I don't really know. He called me his 'girl.'" Rhea stomped her foot in a mock tantrum since Ione was treating her like a child. "Give me my cocoa."

Ione passed it back, half-empty, licking whipped cream off her upper lip. "He has a snake tattoo."

Rhea drank the rest of the cocoa without stopping until it was empty. "Yep. Yes, he does. And he's…" She wasn't sure she was ready to share everything about Leo with anyone yet. Leo was hers. Well, not *hers* hers. But she finally had something all her own to keep secret and she didn't feel like giving it to the entire family just yet. "He's maybe under some kind of curse. We don't know yet." He hadn't turned into a serpent, anyway, and he'd been free for a couple of hours, so there was that.

"Okay. But you're in love with him."

"Oh my God. Stop leaping to conclusions. I just met him a week ago."

"And you are also a Carlisle who has Madeleine Marchant's Lilith blood in her veins, and he's got something serpentine going on. And…he looks like Thor, for crying out loud. If *you* don't want him, maybe I'll see if Dev minds if I get a little something on the side."

Rhea put her hands over her ears. "Please stop. You're creeping me out."

"But if you don't *want* him—"

"I want him!" Rhea's eyes widened and she covered her mouth with her hands. "Oh my God. I hate you, Di. That was so loud."

Ione pushed away from the counter with a smirk and opened the bathroom door.

Dev and Leo were in the kitchen, where Leo had discovered the bottle of tequila.

Leo sniffed the open bottle appreciatively. "As enjoyable as that was, perhaps you have a shot glass or two around here?"

"I think Ione does, yes."

"Top right cabinet," said Ione from the doorway.

Dev got down four shot glasses and started to pour.

"None for me, thanks." Rhea took her mug to the stove. "I think I'll stick with the magic cocoa." She ladled more into her mug and Dev poured two shots into the cup. Rhea laughed. "Okay, I didn't realize how much you'd put in there. But to be fair, Di drank mine." She stuck her tongue out at her sister, trying to act as if they hadn't heard her loud declaration.

"Whipped cream's in the fridge," said Dev. "And you can sprinkle some cinnamon on top if you like."

As Rhea sprayed the canned whipped cream into her mug—clearly Dev's influence, since Ione was all about the real thing when it came to pretty much anything and pre-ferred to make hers from scratch—she noticed the bottle of tequila. "Peligroso" it was called, and the embossed sym-bol on the glass was a coiled snake with rays fanning out around it that looked like they were meant to be feathers.

"Interesting bottle," she said to Ione.

"Rafe recommended it to Dev apparently. They've de-veloped a bit of a bromance."

Leo tossed back his shot and poured another. "So Rafe, he's the one who channels Quetzalcoatl?" He looked at Dev. "So you must be—"

"Okay," Rhea interrupted loudly. "That wasn't exactly meant for public consumption, Leo."

Eyes flashing, Ione dragged her aside to the living room. "You told him about Rafe and Dev? About us?"

Rhea swallowed a gulp of cocoa and burned her throat. "He wasn't supposed to remember."

"How exactly was he not supposed to remember?"

"I told you about the curse. From dusk to dawn during

the period between All Souls and Yule, he separates from his *hugr*—"

"His what?"

"It's like his soul. It goes off somewhere, and when it rejoins him in the morning, it leaves him without memory of the previous night."

"This just gets better and better. So you're telling me he doesn't have a soul right now?"

"Who needs one?" Leo entered the room behind Ione and smiled when she turned. "Bothersome things." He tucked his hands into his pockets, the crisp white shirt he'd borrowed from Dev still unbuttoned. "I should probably get going. I appreciate you coming to our rescue."

"Going?" Rhea extracted her arm from Ione's grasp. "Where are you going?"

"I have a little money. I can get a room somewhere."

"With the holiday room rates?" Ione shook her head. "Don't be ridiculous. You and Rhea are staying in our guestroom until we can get Rhea back into her place in the morning."

"It seems a bit awkward. I don't want to be any bother."

Dev leaned against the kitchen doorway behind him, his warm-copper skin a striking contrast to Leo's Nordic pallor. "You think this is awkward, mate? You don't know the Carlisle sisters. And you especially do not know Ione. When she says you're staying, you're staying. I've already set up the guestroom." He smiled. "Nice chat. We'll see you in the morning." He stepped forward and took Ione's hand, ignoring her attempt to hang back, and led her up the spiral staircase to her room on the second floor of the split-level house.

Rhea sat on the sofa to finish her cocoa, careful not to spill anything on the cream-colored cushions. "So you're staying, then."

Leo laughed. "I don't seem to have much choice." He sat beside her, manspreading both arms and legs. "Sorry about that. I didn't realize it was a secret."

"It's my fault. I had no business telling you."

"Have you told your sister about me?"

Rhea lowered her voice. "As little as possible."

"Yeah." He nodded thoughtfully. "I imagine she's not too keen on the idea of her baby sister dating someone so much older." He winked one impossibly vivid blue eye at her.

Rhea regarded him slyly. "So we're dating, then?"

"Well. You were quite insistent that you wanted me." The teasing look in his eyes was merciless.

Rhea set the mug on the coffee table and groaned into her hands.

Chapter 17

The guestroom had a somewhat narrow bed, but it beat being strapped to a chair.

As Leo started to unbutton his jeans, the expression on Rhea's face, staring him down with her hands on her hips, made him pause. "What?"

"What are you doing?"

"Taking off my clothes."

"What exactly do you think is about to happen here?"

Leo shrugged. "*Munr.* Not big on thinking."

Rhea sighed, sitting on the bed. "First of all, that's total crap. I don't know exactly what a thought-self does, but you've done plenty of thinking. You were the one who got us out of a burning building an hour ago. Second, I think we've already established that I made a promise to Leo, and there won't be any hanky-panky."

He couldn't help but smile at her quaint choice of words, even though her insistence on not crossing some imaginary sexual line was becoming tiresome. "I can sleep in my clothes—can't really recall a time when I had a choice—but I have to point out that you're the one who seems to have trouble keeping your hands off me."

"That's because you didn't have the use of *your* hands." Rhea's gray eyes darkened, a dead giveaway that just thinking about touching him had gotten her blood pumping.

"Also, my sister, who was basically my mom growing up, is directly above us right now, and there is no way in hell anything is going to happen, even if I wanted it to happen."

"Which you do."

"Leo."

"I'm merely stating the obvious, not trying to persuade you to acquiesce to your own desires. If you want to sleep side by side in this little bed like chaste siblings, that's your call. I can't remember the last time I slept at all, so it will be a novel experience for me nonetheless." He re-buttoned the jeans and started to remove the shirt. "Can I take this off, at least? It's not really my style."

"No."

"Now you're just being petty."

Rhea threw back the covers and climbed between the sheets. "Nope. Just acknowledging my own limitations. You're the one who pointed out that I couldn't control myself around you, so you have only yourself to thank. And button it," she added before rolling onto her side to face the wall.

With a shrug, Leo complied and climbed into bed beside her. He snuggled up behind her, spooning her, and she didn't resist, her arms curving around his. Her hair smelled like smoke. And violets.

"So what happens at dawn?" she asked quietly, giving voice to the question in the back of both their minds since they'd escaped the fire.

"Honestly, I don't know for certain. But I know what I want to happen. Absolutely nothing. I want to wake up beside you and remember this entire weird, wonderful and terrifying night. And when I do, perhaps you'll stop waiting for him to come back and let yourself feel what you feel without having to analyze it and berate yourself for it."

In truth, he was afraid to fall asleep. Afraid he'd wake

to find himself in another town, in another motel room, miles and months away from Rhea Carlisle and the smell of violets.

But it turned out Leo the Dull had been right about how this worked. He'd fallen asleep despite himself and despite the fact that Rhea was in his arms...and had woken up in the morning. And he was still here. Still himself. He didn't feel like he was missing anything. Maybe the curse only served to keep him from remembering his true self. And breaking the bonds had broken the curse. This was who Leo was supposed to be. He was free.

He nibbled at Rhea's earlobe, and she swatted at him in her sleep. The collar of her flannel shirt slipped down to expose her shoulder, and he kissed the warm flesh. He recalled brief flashes of memory of his daytime life over the past however many years, and he knew he'd been intimate with more than a few women, but it was like the memory of a recorded event, not the sensations. Like watching it on television. But Rhea was real.

He moved slowly up the slope of her neck, planting a chaste kiss every half inch.

Rhea shivered and stirred. "Leo?"

"The one and only." He slipped his hand beneath her shirt, teasing his fingers upward along her side.

She rolled over to face him. "One and only. Are you saying...?"

"I haven't gone anywhere. And I remember everything." He meant he'd remembered everything that had passed during his nightly confinements, but it was clear from her response she believed he'd remembered his daytime self as well. That he was whole. And he considered himself whole, so there was no reason to split hairs.

Rhea slid her arms around his neck. "That's wonderful news. No more nightly flights on the Wild Hunt." She kissed him, and he felt like Sleeping Beauty awakened. Not the most masculine of images, perhaps, but the symbolism fit. He tasted her mouth as if for the first time, explored the velvet softness of her lips and tongue, forgetting to breathe until her hand slipped down between their bodies, making him gasp.

He covered by nipping at her ear. "What about your sister-mom?"

Rhea's hand was making it hard for him to concentrate. "Not above us anymore. I hear her banging around in the kitchen. She'll be busy for a while."

Leo laughed nervously, his forehead against hers, feeling like an adolescent losing his virginity. It was absurd. He'd spent four of the last five nights doggedly trying to woo her, and now a single touch from her, knowing he was about to get what he wanted, made him nervous.

Rhea's forehead creased. "What's so funny?"

"Just that I feel this is the first time I've been myself in hundreds of years and I somehow feel like an amateur. I hope I still remember how to do this properly."

It was Rhea's turn to laugh. "I'm pretty sure you'll figure it out." She pushed him onto his back and climbed over him. "But in case you don't, I'm happy to give you a refresher." Rhea took off her top and tossed it aside before she began working through the buttons on his borrowed shirt.

He wove his fingers together behind his head and watched her with a grin. "So I don't have to keep the shirt on?"

"Only if you want to seem like a creepy businessman having a nooner with a prostitute. But the socks are going to have to go. That's just a rule I have." He pulled off his socks with his toes while she bared his chest and ran her hands over his skin, sending little ripples of anticipation through him connected directly to his groin, before pausing to examine his pendant.

"Yggdrasil," he said. "The World Tree."

"It's lovely." She moved on to the pants. Her fingers were cold, but the slight shock of it against his flesh when she tugged down his briefs and exposed him was part of the pleasure.

Rhea's eyes went a bit wide as she curled her hand around him. "Well, hello there. Aren't you a big boy?"

Leo breathed in, trying to suppress the groan that wanted out. "Not sure I care for being called a boy," he managed to say with what he felt was the right touch of amusement and arousal.

Rhea flicked her gaze up to meet his with an amused arch of her brow. "I wasn't talking to you."

It drew an unexpected laugh from him, earning one of those smiles of hers that said his laugh turned her on, which turned him on more, making his cock twitch eagerly in her hand.

"But maybe you'll remember the feeling next time you're tempted to call someone a girl." She winked, her fingers corkscrewing slightly around his shaft.

Leo closed his eyes to slow his breathing. "I will," he said after a moment, opening them again. "I will indeed remember the feeling."

"Glad to hear it."

She was still wearing her pink lace bra, and Leo nodded at it. "Are you going to keep that on?"

"Why?" She cupped one breast in her free hand. "Did you want me to take it off?"

"I would very much like it if you did, yes." He let out a slight gasp as her hand twisted once more against him. "Please," he added to cover the gasp. It was probably the sort of thing someone with a thought-self would say, anyway.

She seemed to appreciate the gesture. His cock ached when she let go, but it was worth the deprivation to watch her twist the little clasp of the front-closing bra—the best kind—and open it, freeing her petite breasts, dusky peach-colored tips hard in the cold air.

"Oh, gods." He hadn't realized he'd groaned the words aloud until she blushed. "You are utterly fantastic," he added with a grin. He unhooked his hands from behind his head and reached to touch her, but Rhea seized his wrists and pushed them down to the pillow, her breasts now out of his reach yet tantalizingly close.

"No touching. Just looking."

Leo raised an eyebrow. "Is this what we're doing now?"

"For the moment. I need my concentration. Nipple stimulation is my kryptonite."

"I will keep that in mind."

When she let him go, he tucked his hands behind his head once more, watching her shimmy out of her pants. She kept on the matching pink lace panties, rising onto her knees as she straddled him, and Leo's cock bobbed in his lap when she inched them down, slowly, maddeningly, revealing the tip of her dark, trimmed bush.

"This is some kind of torture, isn't it? That's what you're trying to do? Torture me?"

"I don't know. You're the expert. You tell me." Something sparkled between her thighs as the panties went lower, a little gold ring, nestled into her...

"Ohhhh, *fuuuuuck*." The words escaped him slowly, luxuriously, as it dawned on him. The hood of her clitoris was pierced.

She tilted her head, multicolored pastel strands falling forward into her eyes. "Something wrong?"

Leo moved one hand to his cock compulsively, choking it, his thumbnail hard against the tip to keep from having the ultimate adolescent moment. "Something," he groaned, "is exactly one hundred percent the opposite of wrong."

Rhea grinned, one hand moving up to pinch her nipple while the other slid down to tug on the ring. As she opened her mouth, presumably to tease him further, the door behind her swung open.

"Rhea, what do you and—" Her sister's face went white.

"Oh my *God*!" Rhea dove forward, ostensibly to cover herself but effectively throwing herself on top of his erection. "What the fuck, Ione? Get *out*!"

The white of her sister's face went crimson, and she backed out and pulled the door closed with a snap.

Leo put his arms around Rhea, stroking the silk of her skin as the ring decorating her pussy rubbed against his cock.

She moaned against his chest, but it wasn't a moan of pleasure. "I can't believe she did that."

"From the look on her face, I think she feels the same."

Rhea wriggled in his arms, shaking with a sound between crying and laughing. Above the pink lace, her ass cheek was tattooed with a little blue crescent moon.

"*Älskling*, if we're not going to finish, I need you to move a bit. Or *I'm* going to finish."

Rhea choked back the laugh-crying and rolled onto the mattress on her side, burying her face in his shoulder. "Sorry. This was not how I intended this to go. But there's no way I can—"

"Totally understandable. If incredibly uncomfortable." He pulled up his briefs, trying to tuck in his erection.

"I knew I shouldn't have tried to do anything here." Rhea sighed regretfully and propped herself on her elbow. Little tattoos decorated the insides of her arms. There were others between her thighs and her lower belly he'd noticed only peripherally while watching her panties come away.

He stroked one on her arm, a little sprig of pink blossoms. "Did you do this? All these?"

"Most of them. They're not my best work. I was still learning."

"No, it's beautiful. You're like a canvas, a living sketchpad. The portfolio of the artist on her own skin. You shouldn't cover them all the time."

"I figured they wouldn't be good examples to show clients."

"Nonsense. They would be stunned by the evidence of your growing talent. I don't imagine tattooing oneself is the easiest thing to do."

"No, it isn't." Rhea brushed her fingers over the fresh work on Mjölnir, visible beneath the unbuttoned cuff of the borrowed shirt he still wore. "I didn't get a chance to bandage this up at the shop, and I forgot after. But it looks good. You heal fast."

"The benefits of being charmed."

A tentative knock sounded on the door, and Rhea hitched her panties up and pulled the sheet up over them both. *"What?"*

"Sorry. Not coming in. I wasn't going to bother you, but Dev made pancakes. But we can reheat them later."

Rhea made a growling huff of frustration. "We'll be out in a minute." She glanced at Leo. "I mean, we don't have to. She's a pain in the ass. If you need to…uh…"

Leo laughed. "No, I'll be fine. And pancakes sound delicious." Everything sounded delicious. The bastard had rarely left anything within his reach to eat.

While they ate breakfast, Rhea showed Ione the note from her windshield. "I assume this was from whoever keeps vandalizing the parking lot at the shopping center. And Leo tore down a poster the other day with the same words as the graffiti." Rhea swallowed a bite of her pancake. "You're going to hate what it said."

Ione narrowed her eyes as she handed the note to Dev. "What did it say?"

"The impure shall be cast out."

"Goddammit." Ione clenched her fist around her fork. "He's like a cockroach." She looked at the note again as Dev passed it back. "I'll talk to Phoebe later and see if she can put on her PI hat and find out if anyone else is visiting Carter in prison."

"You don't think it could be Laurel again?"

Ione shook her head. "No, she's learned her lesson. I don't think she ever wants anything to do with Carter Hamilton again, let alone us."

Rhea was fine with that outcome. If only Theia would leave it alone.

It took the better part of the day to chase down the landlord for a spare set of keys and get a replacement set made for the car while also, at Ione's insistence, stopping at the bank to get her cards replaced and at the cellular store to get a new phone. With Ione chauffeuring them about, Rhea felt like she was back in high school, her "date" relegated to the back seat. Which totally didn't make the awkwardness from this morning worse.

Once Rhea had everything sorted, Ione dropped her off at the site of the fire—formerly the site of her business—to assess the damage and see if anything had survived among the ashes. She sent Leo to buy some clothes, insisting he take the car and some cash and get what he needed. Right now, she desperately needed alone time.

Her best tattoo machine was charred rubble, the electrical cord a melted piece of goo. Not to mention the water damage. She had the one she used at home, but it hardly mattered. It wasn't as if she had any clients. The ink bottles were ruined, but the packages of needles and steel tubes inside the drawers and cabinets might be salvageable. Everything else was gone.

Rhea collapsed onto the couch, bizarrely still standing largely intact among the wreckage. She tried to focus on restoring her phone from the cloud backup to avoid thinking about the money she'd sunk into this business and the fact that she was now officially unemployed.

The little bell that had once been on the door made a sad thunking noise as someone stepped on it. Rhea looked up, surprised Leo would be back so quickly. Instead, the most out-of-place person she'd ever seen stood amid the charred doorframe and warped floorboards in a long and absurdly expensive fox fur coat with the hood drawn up.

"We're not open for business," said Rhea in a stunningly stupid statement of the obvious.

The woman drew back her hood, revealing a long fall of red waves, and glared at Rhea with piercing green eyes. "What the hell have you done?"

"I... Huh?" She couldn't seem to form words. She'd seen this woman before. In Leo's vision and with the Hunt. The Valkyrie, Kára, was standing in Rhea's burned-out shop.

"You've let him loose. Your job was to protect him, not free his pettiest self and condemn him to wander as a wraith for all eternity."

"My job?"

"I came to you in good faith because you had the gift of vision. You promised to protect him."

The power of speech was coming back to her, awe giving way to irritation. "Look, lady, I've never met you before in my life, and I sure as hell never promised you anything."

A look of supreme annoyance overtook the flawless features. "I forget how small the human mind is." As the words left her mouth, the fur she wore shimmered and transformed into a living coat, her hair blending with the fur, pointed ears rising from it, and the fur covering a face that ended in a petite black snout.

"Vixen." Rhea shoved back hair in desperate need of product and a cut. She'd been played by the Valkyrie who'd enslaved Leo. God, she was stupid. "So I guess you're not my *fylgja* after all."

"Really, now. Why would *your fylgja* look like this?" Vixen smoothed her hands over her disturbingly curvaceous fox form. "You're so simple."

"Could you please *stop* looking like that? You're kind of creeping me out right now."

The fox shrugged, and with a little shake of her hair, she was a woman once more. At least, she seemed to be. Who knew what she really was.

"So what are you telling me? That Leo's lost his *hugr* permanently? He told me he remembered everything, that he was finally himself."

"He is himself. The self he believes to be central to his being. And he won't give it up without a fight."

"So it can be given up. He can be restored?"

"If he does so voluntarily before the Hunt has scattered on the wind for another year. It ought to have ended on the longest night, but I have managed to assure the Hunt will linger until Yuletide's end. You must persuade the *munr* to take back his other selves before the Hunt has ended or he will be forever broken. You have also left the Chieftain of the Hunt vulnerable to his enemies. They will seek to destroy him."

Neck aching from looking up at her, Rhea stood, though

the Valkyrie still loomed over her. "You said other 'selves.' Are you saying he's missing more than one?"

"It is only the will that remains within his skin. His *hugr*, his *fylgja*, even his *hamingja* will be lost on the wind."

"So Leo has a *fylgja*, too?"

"Of course he does. Every man does. And every woman. Except for you, that is."

Rhea breathed in too sharply and nearly choked on her own spit. "Wait, wait." She pounded on her chest, coughing until she caught her breath. "Wait a minute. Why wouldn't I have one if everyone else does? Is there something wrong with me?" She'd always suspected there must be.

The Valkyrie smiled as though Rhea had said something adorable and amusing, stepping close to her. "Because you *are* a *fylgja*." Rhea felt her face go white as the Valkyrie stroked a finger along her jaw. "And your sister is yours."

"My...my sister? You mean Theia?"

"Monozygotic twins are always each the *fylgja* of the other."

"So you're not saying I'm only half a person or something."

"Oh, goodness, no. You have all your other selves. It's only the *fylgja* that splits off in twinning. Every human has a complete set of selves otherwise."

Rhea shook her head to clear it. "Okay, let's forget about me for a moment. What was the other thing you said? The other self Leo's missing?"

"The *hamingja*. It's not so much a separate self as his personal embodiment of luck. Without it, he will be plagued with misfortune."

Becoming chilled in the open room, Rhea tucked her hands into her pockets and began to pace. "And how am I supposed to help him get them back? Especially if he doesn't want them? Where do I even find them?"

"The *hamingja* will come on its own if it chooses to, once the others have returned. The Chieftain, his *hugr*, you have seen. He leads the Hunt nightly. And his *fylgja* would have shown itself to you. It accompanies his warden spirit, watching from the shadows."

"You mean the black wolf?"

"I cannot say how it will appear to you, but if you have seen this wolf near him, it is most likely the one. You must seek its aid."

Rhea regarded her with mistrust. "And why can't you do any of this? Aren't you the one who did this to him? Shouldn't you have been protecting him? Why can't *you* round up the troops?"

The Valkyrie fluffed the collar of her fur beneath her throat. "Leo left me."

"But I've seen you riding with him in the Hunt."

"My spirit rides with the Chieftain, yes. But he has not recognized me since…"

"Since you gave the Norns his mind."

Her preternaturally green eyes went wide. "How do you know of this?"

Rhea shrugged. "I see things."

"Wyrd could simply have healed him," she said bitterly. "But she refused. And I couldn't let him die. Not after all we had been through. I let her take his mind as she had taken his will. That is when he came to know me as Faye in his waking hours. He didn't remember Kára, who saved him, who gave up everything for him. So I became what he needed me to be, and I helped him when his memory failed him. But eventually, he left. So I whispered in his *hugr*'s ear to encourage him to choose someone worthy to be his human protector."

"But why would I be worthy?"

"Because of your blood. And because of your strength.

I admit I was surprised at first to see whom he'd chosen."
She smiled again, almost fondly. "But though thou be but
little, thou art fierce."

The reference made Rhea smile despite herself. She'd
played Hermia in *A Midsummer Night's Dream* in high
school.

Faye sighed and drew up her collar, once again all business. "He cannot know I have spoken to you. You must
convince him to do what is necessary on your own. And
you must ensure no harm comes to his *hugr* in the meantime. I will ride beside him in the Hunt, as Kára, and try
to protect him as I always have. But you must stop the one
who has been seeking him before he comes too close."
Faye turned toward the door as she spoke, and Rhea took
a step after her.

"What one? How do I stop him?"

But when she followed Faye through the door, there
was no one on the other side. And Leo was coming around
the corner.

Chapter 18

Rhea pondered how to broach the subject of Leo's missing selves without mentioning Faye as they drove to her place. Had he deliberately deceived her this morning, or was it as Faye said, that he believed himself to be the self he was meant to be?

His eyes were on her as she parked the car. "Anything wrong?"

"Why would anything be wrong?"

"You're very quiet. I know it must have been hard seeing the place like that. After everything you put into it."

"Yeah, it sucks," Rhea agreed with a sigh. "But I talked to the owners of the shopping center, and they're going to refund the January rent—eventually. They're assessing the structural damage, and it might even be possible to move back in after they've made repairs in a couple of months. In the meantime, I'm going to have to borrow money from Ione to cover rent for my apartment. I'm royally screwed. Of course, I do have the check from Brock, since I deposited it electronically before it got burned up."

"Brock?"

Rhea studied his face. He didn't have a clue who Brock was. Which meant Faye was right. This wasn't the whole Leo.

"You have no idea who I'm talking about, do you? My first client. The guy you punched in the face."

Leo was obviously trying to hide his surprise. "Of course. I'd forgotten that was his name."

"No, you didn't."

Leo frowned at her. "What do you mean, I didn't? It slipped my mind for a moment. Brock Dressler, the neo-Nazi asshole I punched on the street."

That was unexpected. Maybe Faye was wrong.

He flexed his knuckles, still lightly scabbed over from the encounter, though the cuts on his fingertips had already healed. Rhea wondered if the physical evidence had jogged his memory. He'd said before he had flashes of memory from Leo the Dull's daily life.

"How are your fingers, by the way?"

Leo's expression was guarded. "Fingers?"

"The paper cuts you got when you were putting up those posters for me the other day. Looks like they healed up."

He turned his palms up and nodded as if he knew what she was talking about. "Yeah, it was nothing. I barely remember it happening."

"You don't remember it because that's not what happened, Leo. You tore down some racist propaganda and there were razor blades on the back. You sliced open the tips of your fingers pretty badly. There were bandages and everything. But you don't remember because it happened when your *hugr* was occupying the skin, and since you heal so quickly, there wasn't anything to jog your memory. And your *hugr* isn't in there, is he?"

"Rhea…"

"Why did you lie?"

"I didn't lie."

"You said you remembered everything."

Leo leaned back against the seat. "I meant that I remembered the night. That I was still me."

"But you knew that wasn't how I took it."

"Are we going to argue about his precious soul, now? About your promises to him?"

"It's your soul, too."

"Well, I don't need it. I've never felt the lack of it. I am perfectly whole, *mitt hjärta*. I promise you. We don't need him. *You* don't need him."

"What's that mean? *Meet...?*"

Leo blushed. For a man without a soul, he seemed sensitive enough. "*Mitt hjärta.* 'My heart.' It's a term of—"

"I can tell what it is." Rhea took his hand, and Leo raised her knuckles to his mouth and brushed them with his lips. Maybe he didn't need the *hugr*. But the *hugr* needed him. She couldn't just abandon it. And Faye had said he would be forever broken if the *hugr* was lost.

They got out of the car without further discussion, taking the salvaged supplies and Leo's new duffel bag of clothes up the stairs to her apartment.

When they'd stepped inside, Leo tossed his bag on the floor and took the shopping bag from Rhea's hand to set it down carefully before closing the door.

He pressed her back against it, his lips at her temple. "Let me make you forget him," he whispered. His amber-resin scent was intoxicating.

Rhea closed her eyes. Maybe just for a night. She could figure out what to do about Leo's broken pieces in the morning. Maybe just for tonight she could let him do this— let him pull her shirt over her head and toss it on the couch. Let him open her bra with one expert snap of his finger and thumb and slide the straps down her arms, making her nipples tighten in the cold air. Let him unzip her pants as he bent to suck one hard nipple into his mouth until she was moaning. Let the pants pool at her ankles while he dropped to his knees and peeled her panties down with his teeth. Maybe just for tonight she could let him open her with his tongue and—

"Oh. *God.*"

Her knees nearly buckled as he took the gold ring between his teeth and tugged while his tongue curled inside her and lapped at the wetness dripping over his cheeks. The orgasm was powerful and immediate, and she couldn't catch her breath. Rhea felt the room going gray.

"Rhea?" She came around to find Leo lightly slapping at her cheek. "You still with me?"

Rhea nodded and managed to make a vague murmur in the affirmative.

Scooping her up into his arms, he carried her to the bedroom like a bride over a threshold, letting her jeans slip to the floor, and laid her gently on the bed. "You scared the hell out of me. Has that happened to you before?"

She rubbed her bare arms in the cold air. "Can't say it has."

Leo placed the fleece throw from the end of the bed around her shoulders. "Where's your thermostat?"

"In the hallway next to the kitchen."

Leo went to switch it on and came back to wrap her in his arms. Pretty attentive for a soulless *munr*. How could Rhea even be sure Faye was telling her the truth, anyway? Maybe she just wanted him back in one piece so he'd remember her and return to her. But keeping Leo fragmented just to keep him from remembering some past love would be a pretty shitty thing to do.

"I know what you're thinking," he said, startling her.

"You do?"

"You're wondering if you can put me back together."

"Would that be so terrible?"

Leo shrugged, tightening his hold on her. "It doesn't matter. It can't be done."

"How do you know?"

"Because I remember the curse. The original one, spoken by the Norn. 'If the bonds be not broken 'ere the dawn, the wandering spirit will come anon. Should the will be loosed before the light, the spirit thought shall swift take flight; an it not return by break of day, the wandering wraith shall hie away.'"

The wandering wraith. Faye had called the *hugr* the same. But Faye had told her the *hugr* could be persuaded to return. Leo either didn't know there was a remedy to the curse or he didn't want Rhea to know. She considered revealing what she'd learned from the Valkyrie, but his reaction the other night when Rhea had mentioned the Kára of his past had been explosive. Keeping it from him felt awkward and made her uncomfortable, but if he knew about Faye, he might be the one to take flight and never return.

The real question was whether Rhea could even find any of Leo's other selves. "Second sight" notwithstanding, the Hunt only appeared to her when it wanted to. She hadn't sought it out. How could she seek out the invisible? Then the obvious hit her. She happened to know two people who possessed the ability to communicate with shades. And what was a shade but a disembodied soul?

Leo nuzzled her ear. "You're awfully quiet. Just sleepy?"

The suggestion made her yawn, and Rhea nodded. "It's been a long day." She looked over her shoulder with a grin. "And you kind of wiped me out, to be honest. Not that I'm complaining."

"So you're not avoiding me."

"Why would I be avoiding you?"

Leo sighed against her shoulder. "You realize you keep rephrasing and repeating my questions instead of answering them. It's making me feel a bit suspicious."

She sucked at keeping secrets. "I'm sorry. You're right.

I didn't realize I was doing that." She turned to face him. "But I am *not* avoiding you."

Leo stroked his hand down her arm beneath the throw. "I mean, it's perfectly fine if you want to go to sleep." The Mjölnir tattoo brushed her side, making her shiver. There was something about that ink that was like an aphrodisiac. "*I'm* perfectly fine, is what I'm saying." He drew her closer, and she could feel the hardness through his jeans against her bare thigh.

"Are you? Perfectly?"

Leo gave her a sly half smile. "I suppose I should let you be the judge."

"It's kind of hard to judge with all those clothes on."

"Maybe I should do something about that."

"Maybe you should." Rhea drew the throw around herself as Leo climbed out of the bed and stood to remove the borrowed shirt he was still wearing. He unbuttoned it slowly, teasingly, revealing his well-toned pecs, the Yggdrasil pendant lying between them, and his ungodly abs. She nodded approval. "So far, so good."

"So far, eh?" He tossed the shirt at her, and Rhea dropped the throw to slip it on. He nodded appreciatively. "Looks good on you. You should dress like that all the time."

"I'll consider it. Quit stalling."

Leo laughed. "There's not much else you haven't seen, if you recall what we almost did this morning."

"I do recall, yes. And the initial inspection was very satisfactory. But I haven't seen your ass."

"I didn't realize that was a deal-breaker."

"Oh God, yes. Have you never read a women's magazine?"

"Not that I recall. I'll have to defer to your expertise." He unbuttoned the jeans and stepped out of them, the white cotton of his briefs straining, clearly at capacity. "You'll want to see the ass first, I take it."

Rhea nodded. "Naturally."

Leo turned away, legs planted firmly apart, giving her a glimpse of his well-shaped glutes within the briefs before drawing the garment down.

Rhea put her fist in her mouth to muffle a groan. From the glimpses she'd gotten of his ass in jeans, she'd already known it would be spectacular, but it was completely unfair that any man should have an ass like that, rock hard yet lightly rounded at the top. She wanted to bite it.

Leo looked over his shoulder, the briefs still at his thighs. "Does it meet with your approval?"

"I'm afraid I'm going to have to do a tactile inspection before I can make a final determination." Her voice was amusingly gruff with desire, when she was trying to be nonchalant.

Leo stepped out of the briefs and turned to climb back onto the bed, his expression amused at the involuntary high-pitched humming noise that escaped her at the sight of that glorious cock.

He lay on his stomach and turned his head toward her, resting his cheek on his folded arms. "All yours." She could get used to those words.

Rhea climbed over him and sat on his thighs, smoothing her hands over the tight curves of his ass. "Yes, this will do nicely." She gave one cheek a little slap, and Leo lifted his head with a noise of protest. "That's what you have to do," she explained. "To test the firmness. Like with a mattress."

"I think you'll find the other side much firmer." Leo rolled beneath her, and Rhea came up on all fours over him, their bodies tantalizingly close.

"You are," she murmured, "indeed, perfectly fine."

"Would I lie to you?" He pulled her down, their bodies skin to skin, and wrapped his arms around her as he brought his mouth to hers.

Rhea moaned softly into him, her eyes closing, every inch of her skin where it touched his tingling with arousal. This morning, she'd thought he was fully Leo. Now that she knew only the *munr* was in the skin, she shouldn't be doing this. She'd promised him. But what if the Leo she'd made that promise to was gone forever?

Leo's hand slid down her back to her ass, caressing it before sliding farther into the cleft, his fingers teasing at the edges of her pussy. She reached back and took hold of his hand, pushing it lower as she opened her legs to encourage him, and Leo drew back from her mouth with a deep laugh.

"Am I going too slowly for you, *älskling*?"

Rhea grinned. "Just a bit."

He pressed two fingers between her thighs and entered her, eyes locked on hers. "Better?" When Rhea nodded, biting her lip, Leo went deeper, stroking slowly inside her. "Do you want me to fuck you?"

"God *yes*." The second word came out in a long moan.

He pumped his fingers into her a few more times until she was squirming. Just as she was ready to beg for it, he moved his fingers away and brought the head of his cock against her.

Rhea grabbed his hand. "What are you doing?"

Leo blinked. "I thought... Didn't you say—?"

"Where's the condom? You have a condom, don't you?"

His winter sky blues looked blank.

Rhea groaned and rolled onto her side. "This is one of those things you have no memory of, isn't it?"

Leo gave her an amused smirk. "A lesson once learned in the body remains in the flesh. I'm quite certain I can find my way without any trouble."

"Oh, I have no doubt of that." After the expert way he'd

used his tongue, she was sure it would be fantastic. "But we can't do it without a condom. A prophylactic," she explained. "A rubber." He kept shrugging. Why the hell didn't she keep any herself?

Rhea rolled out of bed and started digging through the dresser for something to throw on.

Leo propped himself up on his elbows, watching her, his impressive cock like an absurd flagpole in his lap. "What are you doing?"

"I'm going to drive to the convenience store and buy some condoms." She pulled on a pair of black paisley leggings without bothering with underwear, hopping as she pulled them up, and dragged an old sweatshirt on over her head before shoving her feet into a pair of furry boots. "I'll only be a few minutes, so…" She glanced at his erection. "Hold that thought."

"You're not serious."

"I mean, you can hold it or not hold it, but we can work on that when I get back."

Rhea came to the bed to give him a kiss, and he nearly succeeded in distracting her once more into throwing caution to the wind, but she managed to tear herself away.

"Ten minutes," she promised and hurried out the door before her body could persuade her to forget the condoms. He was over a thousand years old. He was going to wear a condom whether he remembered what it was or not.

Stepping back out into the cold was brutal after having his body warm her. Rhea dashed to the car and ran the windshield wipers with some wiper fluid, with the heat on full blast until the window defogged enough to drive.

The trip to the store was uneventful. She managed to get the condoms, ignoring the clerk's look at the evidence of her hasty dress. It was obvious why she was out looking like this and making this purchase. Let him snicker.

But as she got back into the car, she saw a dark shape in the rearview mirror. The black wolf-dog sat directly behind her in the path of her vehicle.

Chapter 19

Starting the engine and turning on the lights did nothing to persuade the wolfish dog to move. If she started backing out, maybe it would get the hint. Rhea put the car in Reverse and let it roll back an inch or two, but the dog just sat there panting idly.

"Goddammit, dog. *Move*." She growled in frustration while staring at it in the rearview mirror. "You don't get it, dog. I *really* need to have sex."

The literally mind-numbing orgasm that had resulted in her fainting from the sudden dearth of blood to her brain had marked the beginning of the end of an epic dry spell she'd been denying to herself. Ever since the visions started, in fact. She hadn't even had sexy time with *herself* in weeks. Listening to Phoebe go on and on about Rafe's quetzal stamina for months now—then finding out uptight, reserved Ione had picked up a crazy-hot stranger in a bar and screwed him so hard he'd turned into a dragon—had driven her right to the edge of the cliff she hadn't even known she was perched on.

Rhea laid on the horn, startling a kid walking out of the store with beer he'd obviously bought with a fake ID, but the dog didn't budge.

Fists clenched against the steering wheel, she closed her eyes. "I hate you, wolf-dog." Of course, wolf-dog, if

Faye could be trusted—and who wouldn't trust a Valkyrie-turned-sexy dominatrix-turned-talking fox?—was Leo's *fylgja*. Maybe, like Vixen, he was capable of human speech. "All right, dammit. You win."

She shut off the engine and opened the door, cautiously stepping out with one furry boot to peer around the car. It could be a wild animal for all she knew. It might not be a *fylgja* at all. No sense taking chances.

The dog stood beside her bumper, watching her expectantly.

"Okay. You've got my attention. What do you want?" This had to look awesome on the store's security camera.

As soon as she stepped out of the car completely, the dog took off running across the parking lot and out onto the road.

"God*dam*mit!" Rhea jumped back into the car and re-started the engine.

The dog was no longer blocking her way. She could forget about this and go home, climb into that warm bed with Leo, and get her brains screwed out. But Faye's exhortation to help Leo find his way back to himself nagged at her conscience. She was Leo's only hope. Faye had said Rhea would have to seek the *fylgja*'s aid, and the *fylgja* was currently trotting down the highway.

With a sigh, she pulled out of the lot and turned in the direction the dog had gone. There had still been a little twilight left when she'd gotten in the car, but it was already pitch-black out here away from the city limits, especially on a moonless night. But her headlights illuminated the dog's shadowy form a hundred yards away—in the opposite direction from where Leo and her warm bed were waiting. Rhea followed, slowing when she caught up with the animal. The dog kept to the side of the road but continued trotting along at a good clip.

The box of condoms sat forlornly on the seat beside her. Magnum. Because *goddammit*.

She followed the stupid dog for at least a mile before it turned off onto a path that barely qualified as a road. If she'd thought it was dark before, this was like driving into a cave. Rhea switched on the high beams, illuminating the rocky twists and turns in the road, and after several minutes, the dog abruptly disappeared.

Rhea slowed the car. Fantastic. She could be in bed with Leo finding out if those magnums even fit, and instead she was out driving around in the middle of nowhere. In lazy-bitch pajamas. And it was starting to snow again.

She was about to stop and turn around when the circle of her headlights fell on a wooden paddock a few yards ahead. She'd reached the end of the road.

Rhea sighed and pulled over. She drew up her hood and stuffed her hands into her pockets as she got out. Why hadn't she grabbed a coat? Oh, right—because she was just going to get some damn condoms so she could get laid.

As she approached the paddock, something moved in the darkness beyond the fence. Fear seized her, and she clutched the pepper spray canister on her keys—a stocking stuffer from Theia. Something snorted and pawed at the ground. She was going to be eaten by wolves. Wait, did wolves snort?

As her eyes adjusted to the darkness, the large head of the beast turned toward her, eyes glowing white, and Rhea realized with relief that it was a horse. What was a horse doing in a paddock at night? But it wasn't alone. Shapes began to define from the darkness. There were half a dozen horses here. Maybe more. What kind of asshole would leave horses out in the snow?

She stepped up on the bottom rung of the fence, arms hooked over the top, and reached out to pet one of the muzzles, but her hand stopped halfway. Their eyes weren't just glowing from the reflected light. In fact, there was no reflected light; her car's headlights were pointing the other way. These were the specters of the Hunt, their hides stretched tight over their skeletons as if there were no muscle beneath. Certainly no fat. They were like the horses of the Apocalypse, except they were all Famine.

The closest of the horses had lifted its muzzle as if hoping for a treat, and her hand passed right through it. Rhea snatched her arm back with a shudder. It hadn't felt like passing through air but like putting her hand through gummy spider webs.

The message chime on her phone sounded from her pocket, and Rhea nearly jumped out of her skin and joined the specters. A message from Leo was on the screen.

Having spent many a night staring at the red glowing digits of a hotel alarm clock, I have a very keen sense of time. Also, I am staring at the red glowing digits of the clock by your (now rather cold) bed. It has been more than ten minutes. Where are you? I "Googled" condoms, and I must say I'm rather offended.

Rhea typed back a quick note.

They didn't have any. Taking a quick run into town to find some. Nothing to be offended about. Google "safer sex."

Before she dropped the phone back into her pocket, she noticed it was just after eight. That was about when she'd seen the Hunt the first time. These horses were awaiting their riders.

Her phone chimed once more, unnerving her as much as the first time.

Do you have chlamydia?

"Oh my God." She muted the phone.

Pockets of air shimmered around her in rainbow colors like the membrane of a soap bubble, and when the "bubble" popped, noise burst out of it—raucous, excited voices, as though a window had opened onto a party—seconds before the images of the hunters coalesced from the smoky shadows.

The riders took to their mounts as soon as they materialized. The others didn't notice her, but the Chieftain—Leo's *hugr*—doffed his cowboy hat in her direction as he mounted his horse.

He looked more substantial, less spectral than he had before, more closely resembling the vision she'd first had of the Hunt. His eyes were clear, blue as the Sedona winter sky at high noon. How she could see that, she wasn't sure. They did seem to be glowing a bit.

The other riders were heading out, the horses leaping straight over the fence, but the Chieftain lingered.

Rhea took a step toward him. "Leo?"

"That name did once belong to me, but no more." He held the hat to his chest and bowed over the horse's mane. "You may call me Gunnar."

Rhea's lips parted in disbelief. "Gunnar?"

"I must extend my gratitude to you."

"To me?"

"You have freed me to pursue my sacred calling, fair Rhea of Carlisle. I am no longer bound to the base appetites of the flesh to which the spineless Leo Ström returned me each morning through his foolish and slavish devotion."

"Leo is not spineless. He's a decent, responsible person trying to do the right thing."

"What has he done to earn your admiration? What valiant deeds has this giant of bravery done that you defend him so?"

Rhea folded her arms, half in umbrage and half to keep warm. "He punched a Nazi douchebag in the face the other day."

"Oh, yes. That takes courage. Saving humanity from a sad little braggart by assaulting him with a surprise right hook."

He set his hat on his head and urged the horse forward, leaping from the paddock and over Rhea's head while she ducked.

After she'd spun about, "Gunnar" turned back. "Careful rolling about in the mud with that mindless animal you've trapped in the skin. He knows nothing but his urges." The horse took off after the rest of the hunters at a gallop as the Chieftain let out an exuberant battle cry that echoed off the snow-covered rocks.

Rhea's eyes narrowed as disbelief gave way to aggravation. Leo's *hugr* was a pompous ass.

Teeth chattering, she hurried back to the car and huddled behind the wheel, holding her hands up to the heating vents. Good thing she'd left the engine running.

The condom box judged her silently from the passenger seat. Rhea pulled out her phone to find Leo had left another message. *Jesus.* It was accompanied by the most impressive dick pic she'd ever seen, his hand wrapped around the base.

You told me to hold the thought. The fact that I have no thought-self notwithstanding, I have been holding this for nearly an hour. I am fairly certain it's going to fall off if I hold it any longer. Difficult to Google left-handed,

but several articles of dubious authorship seem to support this claim.

Rhea dashed off a quick response. So sorry. Found
some. Heading back now. She put the car in Drive but
paused and picked up the phone again to add VERY photo-
genic before tearing up the unmarked dirt road to get back
to the highway as fast as she could.

She'd driven farther than she'd thought. The lights were
out when she entered the apartment. *Please let him be setting the mood.*
But Leo was sprawled on the bed with his phone still
in his hand, naked and sound asleep. Rhea slid the phone
from his fingers and set it aside. He didn't stir. With a sigh
of regret, she picked up the throw where she'd tossed it on
the floor in her haste to get condoms and laid it over him.
It barely covered the magnificent physique. The physique
she could be riding right now like a Brahma bull if she
hadn't followed Leo's *fylgja.*
And speaking of *fylgjas*—or not—she hadn't seen the
Valkyrie with the Hunt tonight. What did that mean? And
what dictated when she appeared as Vixen? Rhea hated to
think of the fox woman appearing in her bedroom if she
and Leo ever did manage to close the deal.
While she contemplated the idea, someone pounded on
her front door. Would Vixen knock?
But when Rhea opened it, Phoebe stood on her doorstep
looking slightly manic, like she'd had too much caffeine
after waking up in the middle of the night.
"Rhea Iris Carlisle!" Her sister swept in and closed the
door. "Why didn't you tell me you were nearly killed in a
fire?" Phoebe hugged her and shook her simultaneously.
"And why did I have to hear it from Ione?"

"My phone was torched and she said she'd call you. And I wasn't nearly killed. There was a small fire, but I'm fine—"

"A *small* fire? I saw it on the news, and it was not small. Not to mention they think it was arson. And Ione said you had to jump out a two-story window!"

"Barely one story."

"But your shop. Honey, are you going to be okay? Do the police have any idea who did it?" As Phoebe let go of Rhea, her gaze fixed on the box of condoms still in Rhea's hand.

Cheeks flaming, Rhea tossed the condoms onto the coffee table.

Phoebe's eyebrows lifted with amusement. "Am I... interrupting something? Cowgirl?"

Rhea rolled her eyes and flopped onto the couch. "Not exactly."

"Uh-oh." Phoebe joined her after taking off her coat and tossing it over the armrest. "Did you guys have a fight?"

"No. I just took too long getting condoms. He fell asleep."

"Oh, boy. Amateur. You're supposed to keep those in stock."

"You don't say." Rhea put her fur-clad feet up on the coffee table and crossed one boot over the other.

"Damn, those are cute." Phoebe tugged on one of the pompons dangling from the decorative ties. "When did you get those?"

"Theia gave them to me for our birthday last year." Rhea frowned, remembering their last gift exchange. Theia had bought them so Rhea would have something to wear in the winter when she moved up to Flag with her, which had been the plan at the time.

"She's over at my place, by the way."

Rhea glanced up. "What's she doing there?"

"She had a dream you were in trouble. She knew you wouldn't talk to her, so she came to me." Phoebe nudged Rhea's foot with her own on the coffee table. "And it's officially Christmas Eve as of twenty minutes ago."

Rhea blinked at her. "No, it's not. It was just…" The winter solstice had been on the twenty-second this year. And that had been yesterday. Or, rather, the day before, since it was now after midnight on the twenty-fourth. "When does Yuletide end?"

"Yuletide?"

"The original Germanic Yuletide. How long is it?"

"Why would I know?"

Rhea reached for the bag that held her tablet before remembering she didn't have one anymore. "Dammit." She grabbed her phone instead and looked up Yuletide, but scanning the first few links yielded several answers. "Damn the stupid internet."

"Rhea, *what* are you looking for?"

"I need to know how long it lasts. How long he has left."

"Who?"

Rhea stopped thumbing through links. "Leo. There are some things I didn't tell you the other day. And then I found out some more things."

Phoebe leaned in with interest. "What kinds of things?"

There had never been secrets between the Carlisle sisters. At least not before Theia had started keeping them. But this wasn't her story to tell. She supposed she could tell her as much as she'd told Ione, though.

"Leo's under some kind of spell. His will—his id—is separated from his ego during Yuletide."

"Are you talking about his other selves? Like the *fylgja*?"

"That's exactly what I'm talking about. His are fragmented, and because his ritual confinement was interrupted the other night by the fire, he can't naturally reintegrate.

I have to convince him—all of his selves—to come back together before Yuletide ends or his soul and his ego will be lost forever. He'll be nothing but id. Broken. So I need to figure out when Yuletide ends officially, but it doesn't look like there's anything official." She tossed the phone down, gesturing at the search results. "Could be a couple of days, could be twelve."

Phoebe looked thoughtful. "Does this have anything to do with the serpent energy we were talking about?"

"Maybe. The other Leo—the whole Leo, the one you met the other day—said he thought his *munr*—his id—would unleash the negative energy of the Midgard Serpent if the ritual was interrupted." She was so *not* telling Phoebe about the restraints. She'd never hear the end of it after all her teasing about the sex tape.

Phoebe caught Rhea's little hesitation, and her eyes narrowed, but she didn't press. "Maybe Rafe can figure out the dates for you. He has a Covent Compendium from his father containing a lot of obscure ritual information. Come to think of it, Dev should know if Rafe doesn't. He was a Covent assayer for years before Ione—"

"Boned the dragon out of him and got him fired?"

"She didn't get him fired. He quit voluntarily."

"However she wants to spin it. Anyway, that's promising. I still have to figure out how to get the soul and the id back together, whenever the deadline is. I had a chance to talk to his *hugr* tonight, and this is not going to be easy."

"Wait, how did you talk to a disembodied soul? That's my area."

"Remember that Wild Hunt I kept seeing?"

Phoebe's eyes widened. "You're kidding. He's a Hunt wraith?"

"He's *the* Hunt wraith. The Chieftain. Leader of the Hunt."

Phoebe's phone chimed. After glancing at the message, she got up and put her coat back on.

"That's Rafe. He's all by his lonesome in front of the fire." She grinned. "I just wanted to make sure you were all right. You brat." She flicked Rhea's arm as she turned to go, and her gaze fell on the box of condoms. "Hope you get a chance to use those before dinner tomorrow. Today. You know what I mean." Phoebe paused on her way out the door. "And your bucking bronco is totally invited, in case that wasn't clear."

"Brahma bull." Rhea groaned as she realized she'd walked right into that one.

Leo didn't stir when she climbed into bed beside him. She folded the bedspread over him from the other side, even if he didn't feel the cold, and got under the covers on her side, snuggling up to him. She left a condom on the nightstand just in case.

Leo opened his eyes and stared at the ceiling once he was sure Rhea was asleep. He should have known something was up when she was gone so long. She'd been with that insufferable *hugr*, conspiring against him with the bastard who'd chained him up nightly over a thousand Yuletides.

He rolled over and observed her, silvery pastel strands of hair sticking to cheeks flushed pink with the heat of sleep. He'd believed she'd fallen for him at last, that she wanted *him* and not that passionless milquetoast who cared about nothing but his uptight morality.

Leo let his hand hover over her, wanting to pluck the sweat-damp strands from her cheek. The other Leo could never have given her so much pleasure that she fainted in his arms. Wouldn't have bothered. But the other Leo was the one she wanted: the one too timid to act on his desires, even if they burned inside him as they must if he, the *munr*, embodied them.

She had called him broken. The word twisted in his heart like a shard of glass as he'd lain listening to their voices, awakened by the sound of their affectionate banter. The way she was with her sisters made him love her more—*desire* her more, he amended. A stupid, brutish *munr* couldn't love. Rhea had the sort of familial bond he'd never experienced. He barely remembered his life before Kára, but he knew there had been nothing like that.

The idea of spending a holiday with Rhea and her family, playing at being an ordinary man for a day, was tempting. But Kára had owned him, the *hugr* had enslaved him for her, and now he was free. There was no way in Hel he was going to be made anyone's captive again. And certainly not by someone who thought of him as broken.

He couldn't stay till morning. If he did, he'd end up making love to her, and then he'd never be able to leave. Just the smell of her skin beside him made him want to give up his freedom just to touch it and taste it again. He still smelled of her himself. She was imprinted on his senses. Leo slid quietly off the other side of the bed and gathered his clothes, taking them to the living room to dress.

On the table in front of the couch was the box of condoms she'd purchased. He'd done enough Googling to know that if he happened to meet someone else to take his mind off Rhea, she'd expect him to have some of these. Leo slid the box into his pocket before slipping quietly out the door.

Chapter 20

Leo had gotten up early, apparently, maybe to take a shower. But he wasn't in the house. Maybe he'd gone out to get breakfast for the two of them. It would be just like him. It was ironic that the *munr* with no thought-self was more thoughtful than anyone she'd ever dated.

Then she discovered the box of condoms missing from the table.

Son of a bitch. He'd really had her fooled, making her think his relentless expression of desire was specific to her, when it was simply that he *was* desire. She'd left him at home for one night with the internet at his disposal, and he'd gone off to find someone else who maybe wasn't so difficult.

It hurt even more that he'd gone off without leaving a note. Not that she had notepaper lying around. But he could have sent her a text. Well, screw him. Now she didn't have to worry about fixing him, convincing his stupid *hugr* to make nice and step back inside the skin.

Rhea stalked to the kitchen and opened the fridge, looking for something to eat. She'd been trying to live on the bare minimum until she got a few clients, and her grocery reserves were dwindling. She had oatmeal, but there wasn't even enough milk for a bowl of cereal. She supposed she could eat it without.

As she closed the refrigerator door, Rhea let out a yelp. "Dammit, Vixen. Have you ever considered knocking?"

The Valkyrie pulled her fur coat tight around her. "It's dreadfully cold in here. And there is no Vixen, darling. I made her up." She sniffed and looked offended. "Now, then. Care to tell me what the hell you've done to Leo?"

"Who says I've done something to him?"

"He was your responsibility. And now he's gone. Do you think I wouldn't be able to tell? I took him from the battlefield. I am attuned to the rhythm of his breathing and his heart. I know where the body is and what he's doing with it at all times."

Rhea rubbed at her neck. "All times?"

Faye smiled knowingly. "He's quite talented, isn't he? Sadly, I have never had the pleasure of experiencing his talents when the *munr* alone embodied the skin, but I did teach the skin itself."

"Okay. Too much information." Rhea leaned back against the fridge with her arms folded. "So what's he doing with it? Shouldn't you know where he is?"

"I know *where* he is. It's why he's there instead of here with you that I wish to know. How do you intend to bring his selves together if you've driven him off? And how on earth did you manage to do so after the pleasure he'd given you?"

"Okay, look. We are *not* doing this. You are way too interested in my sexual intimacy with Leo." And it was weird how Faye wasn't the least bit bothered by it. "I don't know why he left. I woke up and he was gone. He fell asleep last night while I was out getting condoms."

An expression of pure surprise lit Faye's features before her entire being seemed to explode into delighted laughter. "You thought you were going to get a mindless *munr* to wear a condom. No wonder he left. A *munr* does not care to have its pleasure compromised."

"Oh, really? Then why did he take the box of condoms with him while I was sleeping?"

Faye's eyebrows rose comically. "Did he really? How peculiar. He also took your car."

"What?" Rhea ran to the window and looked out. Her spot was empty. Tears of frustration burned behind her eyes. She had four years of car payments left.

"There's a simple remedy," said Faye when Rhea let the curtain fall. "Report the car stolen. When he's apprehended, you can collect him."

"Collect him? He's not a piece of property."

"But he is your responsibility."

"Why the hell is he my responsibility? You're the one who did this to him. Why don't *you* go 'collect' him?"

Faye looked wounded. "That is part of the price I paid to spare his life. I cannot affect his will. I ride with the wraith, though he does not know me. But I cannot be with him when only the *munr* inhabits the skin. Only when he is whole can I interact with him and have him see me for who I am."

"So that's what this is about. You want me to put him back together so you can be with him."

Faye shrugged, though the gesture seemed to belie some deeper emotion. "See it how you will. The fact remains that you are the one who released him—"

"My shop was on fire. Should I have let him burn with it?"

Faye fluffed her collar. "He cannot burn. He would have felt it, but it would not have damaged him."

"Oh, well, that would have been just fine, then. Let him *experience* burning to death."

"The greater issue is that you've left his *hugr* vulnerable to attack."

"So you've said. You know, I spoke to his *hugr* last night. And he was an insufferable bore."

A half smile lifted the corner of her mouth. "He is... single-minded."

"You keep saying his *hugr* is vulnerable to attack. From whom? The Norns?"

"Oh, no. Wyrd and her sisters prefer to stay far above the fray, maintaining their fiction of blamelessness, all the while weaving and cutting capriciously." Faye's eyes flashed with anger. "His enemies are those who seek to undermine the Hunt itself. Many have come through the ages, intent on overthrowing him as Chieftain, but while his body and his *munr* remained bound to him, they could not harm him. Now, thanks to you, he is fair game." Faye gave her a reproachful look. "And now you've lost his body. I suggest you make that report and get back what belongs to both of us."

Rhea opened her mouth to object, but Faye had apparently said all she intended to and was simply gone.

Despite the Valkyrie's insistence, she couldn't bring herself to get Leo arrested. She'd have to report the car stolen eventually, but it seemed like a betrayal of trust to use the police to track him down. Maybe she was being a fool. He'd betrayed her trust first. But she wasn't going to have Leo thrown in jail—shackled again—on Christmas Eve.

Anyway, how did she know Faye was even telling her the truth? She'd revealed her true motive for reuniting Leo's selves. She wanted him for her own selfish purposes, just as she had when she'd interfered with the course of his life a thousand years ago. These "enemies" she claimed were after him didn't sound all that credible.

When she called Phoebe later to tell her she couldn't

make it to Christmas Eve dinner, Phoebe wouldn't have it. Rhea had made up a story about her car being in the shop, and before she knew it, Phoebe was at her door to pick her up.

"Don't think I don't know what this is about," she said when Rhea answered the door. "You're avoiding Theia. But it's Christmas Eve and this has gone far enough. Get Leo and let's go."

Rhea hugged her arms. "He's not here."

"What do you mean, he's not here? Where is he?"

"He left."

"That's all you're going to tell me?"

"I don't want to talk about it."

"Okay, well, you have two choices—tell me and you can stay here and sulk, or get your butt in the car. And tell me later."

"You're really going to let me stay here if I tell you?"

Phoebe rolled her eyes. "Are you high? It's Christmas." She pointed to her Jeep in the parking lot. "March."

After exchanging the sweatshirt for a more festive chartreuse and fuchsia vintage sweater set from the '80s and running some sculpting cream through her hair, Rhea reluctantly got into the Jeep, rubbing her arms through her coat sleeves. "Who drives a Jeep in the snow?"

"It's not snowing at the moment. And it's not like the top is open."

"It's a lot like the top is open. Your windows are made out of vinyl."

"Stop stalling. What happened to Leo?"

"Oh, so this is 'later,' is it?"

Phoebe grinned as she pulled the Jeep out onto the highway. "Yep. And now you're my captive, so we're driving around until you tell me."

Rhea sighed. "There's nothing to tell. I woke up this morning and he was gone."

"That's it?" Phoebe glanced at her. "You didn't have a fight or anything?"

"Nope. Just gone. I have no idea when he left. Woke up about nine o'clock and there was no Leo, no note and no condoms."

"No." Phoebe nearly pulled the Jeep over. Rhea could only imagine what her sister would have done if she'd mentioned the car. "That is just evil."

Phoebe's house was a winter wonderland. In addition to a plethora of lights and a nine-foot tree, luminarias lit the walkway, and a host of marvelous smells struck Rhea as Phoebe opened the door. Cinnamon and cloves from the mulled cider mixed with the scent of fresh pine and the mesquite wood burning in the fireplace, while scented candles in peppermint and caramel apple and pumpkin pie perched on every surface.

Rhea was the last to arrive. Dev's and Rafe's impressive forms dominated the kitchen, where they were busy adding their family specialties to the feast—in matching Hello Kitty aprons that had to be Phoebe's doing. Ione and Theia sat cross-legged by the fire taking turns petting Puddleglum, stretched on the hearth between them like feline royalty. And Phoebe, true to form, had the classic Christmas carols from their childhood playing on her sound system.

Rhea tried studiously not to look in Theia's direction, but the ranch house was too small to accommodate acting like a child. She sat in the coveted papasan chair, temporarily empty, as Ione got up to help Dev with something in the kitchen.

Theia looked up at her with a hesitant smile. Her eyes looked a little puffy. Maybe it was all the perfumey candles.

All four of them were a bit allergic to perfume, and all of them suffered through it, because they loved scented things.

"Hey," said Theia. "I'm glad you came."

"Who would want to miss Rafe and Dev in Hello Kitty aprons?"

Theia grinned, pulling her knees up and wrapping her arms around them as she glanced into the kitchen over the breakfast bar at the pair of khaki-clad muscular behinds topped by the pink bows of the apron strings. "Yeah, the view is pret-ty nice from here."

"Of course, it would be better if they weren't wearing pants."

Theia covered her mouth to stifle a loud burst of laughter. "Dammit, Rhe, now I'll never get that image out of my head."

"It's a good one, isn't it?" Rhea rested one ankle on her knee, and Puddleglum came unglued as the pompons from the furry boot swung from the end of the tie. Without Rhea having to do a thing to entertain him, he was batting and flipping the furry balls wildly, hanging on with both paws as he twisted around.

"Those are the boots I got you."

"Yeah. They're perfect for this weather. It's kind of crazy, huh?"

Theia leaned back with her arms behind her, palms braced against the stone hearth. "We don't even have this much snow in Flag yet. Guess you're learning to drive in the white stuff, now, huh?"

"A bit, yeah."

"So what happened to your car? It's still under warranty, isn't it?"

Rhea jiggled her foot to swing Puddleglum, now attached by both feet and his jaws. "It's just the alternator or something. I'm sure it's covered."

"Listen, whatever I did——"

"We don't have to talk about it."

Theia's face fell. "We do, though. I want to make it right."

"You can't."

"Rhe——"

To Rhea's relief, Phoebe swept into the room with a tray full of tapas, ending the conversation. "Okay, we've got puris from Dev and empanaditas from Rafe, and of course Yiayia's spanakopita."

Ione followed, setting out little plates decorated with holly, and Rhea got up to load her plate.

Phoebe set the tray on the coffee table amid the candles. "And the vegetarian options are on the left for you weirdos who are tormenting yourselves in that fashion. Luckily, everything's delicious."

Rhea slapped Phoebe's hand as she reached for one of the options she'd pointed out. "If they're all so great, stick to the carnivore side, meat monger."

"*Meat* monger?"

Rhea popped a curry puff into her mouth. "If they're all so delicious, you can leave the vegetarian stuff to Ione and me."

Ione reached for one of the beef empanaditas as the words left Rhea's mouth. "Oh, I'm not doing that anymore. We have to keep meat in the house all the time for Kur, and Dev has to eat a fair amount of it himself because of his metabolism, so I kind of gave up on it."

"Gone to the dark side because of a man. Typical."

After dinner, they all struggled to make room for Phoebe's pumpkin pie accompanied by eggnog spiked with tequila and whiskey—another of Rafe's specialties. Being the heir to the

Diamante Construction fortune had its perks, one of which was apparently having a massive wet bar of the finest liquors.

Rhea had just sat down with a second piece of pie when they heard a car on the drive. She tensed and threw an accusatory glance at Theia, thinking she'd gotten Laurel to come after all, but from her spot by the window, she saw the car was a MINI. She paused in midbite. Leo was driving it.

Chapter 21

Sitting across from her on the faux leather chair, Phoebe followed Rhea's glance. "Isn't that your car?"

Rhea nodded dumbly, watching as Leo's large frame somehow managed to exit the vehicle with grace. He stood beside the car, looking around as though he wasn't quite sure how he'd gotten there. Neither was Rhea.

She set down her plate and went outside. "Leo. What...?" She couldn't think of a reasonable question.

He stuck his hands in his pockets and swayed back on his heels. "I was halfway to Tucson when I just...felt wrong and had to turn back. And something led me here."

"Felt wrong? You stole my car."

Leo's eyes were defiant. "I didn't come back because I was sorry."

"So you're a jackass and you decided to come tell me that on Christmas Eve."

"No, I—I don't know why, but I had to come back."

Rhea hugged her bare arms, the cardigan abandoned inside by the warmth of the fire. "Why did you leave?"

"You want me to give up my life. For *him*."

Her stomach knotted. "You heard me talking to Phoebe. Leo, it's not that I want you to give anything up. I'm trying to help you. You need your *hugr*. And it needs you."

"Says who?" He paced away from the car, his expression pained. "I came back because the farther I drove away from you, the more the sense of wrongness overwhelmed me. Not emotionally or physically but in everything around me, as though the fabric of the world was unraveling. I've felt this before." He took a breath. "It's magical."

"Magical?" She smiled quizzically, thinking he was talking about the two of them together, but he didn't return the smile, and hers faded.

"I'm bound to you. I don't know if you did it consciously—"

"Leo, I would never—"

"Then it's her. It's Kára. She's behind this." He stepped close to her finally, and the defiant look was gone. "But if she had to bind me to someone, I'm glad it's you." He stroked Rhea's cheek with the back of his hand, making her shiver. "I won't go back, you understand. I will fight you. I will fight *him*. But I didn't like being away from you, magic or no."

She didn't know how to respond to that. Parts of it made her feet feel floaty beneath her, and parts of it felt like a threat.

But Leo didn't wait for a response. "You're freezing." He rubbed her arms and pulled her into the circle of his own. "Should we go inside? Or do you want to be alone with your family?"

Rhea shook her head, looking up into eyes as bright and blue as tumbled sea glass. She'd felt wrong too with him gone. She couldn't bear the thought of him leaving again.

"Are you guys coming in or what?" Phoebe was at the screen door. "We're about to open presents."

Rhea turned, biting her lip. "I didn't bring mine." She hadn't brought them because she hadn't bought them. Because she was flat broke.

"Sweetie, Rafe has so much money he doesn't know

what to do with it. The only present we need from you is you."

After bringing Leo inside, Rhea introduced him to Rafe, who was standing just inside the living room. It was the first time she'd ever seen Rafe look shorter than anyone, which she assumed was an illusion of the sunken floor until Leo stepped down to shake his hand. Somehow, it was irrationally pleasing that Leo was taller.

"Ione and Dev you've already met," said Rhea. "And this is my..." She glanced awkwardly from Leo to Theia, remembering belatedly that they knew each other all too well.

Theia rose and held out her hand. "As you know, I'm her evil twin. Nice to see you again."

Leo studied her quizzically as he shook her hand. "Have we...?" He paused, still holding her hand as she tried to pull it back, looking embarrassed. "Ah! Theia Dawn. The one who 'swiped right.'" He pulled her hand to his lips and kissed it. "Delighted to make your acquaintance in the flesh."

Theia frowned as she withdrew her hand. She probably thought he was messing with her.

"Leo has some short-term memory problems," said Rhea. It was the easiest explanation for now.

Theia still looked suspicious, like maybe Rhea was in on whatever game Leo was playing. "You don't remember meeting me?"

Leo smiled and shrugged. "Not specifically. I am aware of who you are, though. Of how we met."

Theia glanced at Rhea, trying to gauge the situation.

"It's complicated," said Rhea. "He retains certain details, like a narrative, even if he doesn't consciously recall them as having happened to himself."

Theia nodded, clearly not convinced.

Leo put his hands in his pockets. "I'm afraid I've interrupted your gift giving." He looked around for Phoebe.

Phoebe smiled. "You didn't interrupt. We were just about to get started."

Dev offered Leo his seat on the couch as Ione brought an extra slice of pie and a glass of eggnog from the kitchen. Leo examined the glass as he sat. "What's this?"

"It's nog." Rhea grabbed her own and took her seat in the papasan, not wanting to appear like lovestruck teens who needed to sit in each other's laps and couldn't keep their hands off each other. Like certain sisters she could name.

"Nog?" Leo's eyes crinkled. "Is that like glögg?"

Rhea shook her head, taking a sip of hers. "Eggnog. It's cream and eggs with tequila and whiskey."

Leo looked askance at the glass. "Eggs?"

"Just try it. It's good. What's glögg?"

"Mulled wine," said Theia.

Leo tasted the beverage hesitantly. "Interesting." He looked up at Rafe. "This has your Peligroso in it, doesn't it?"

Rafe smiled quizzically. "How did you know?"

Dev grinned. "I made your Mexican chocolate for them the other night."

Phoebe was hauling presents out from under the tree. "Okay, enough about alcohol. Present time. Theia, this one's for you. And one for Rhea."

Rhea's was weighty...and felt like some kind of metal case. "No. No, you *didn't*." She ripped the paper off to find a full professional tattoo kit, complete with more than a dozen bottles of ink, ink cups, needles and the works. "Oh my God. You guys..." She was too choked up to thank them properly. Theia smiled at her, acknowledging the unspoken gratitude. Only Theia would have known exactly what brand Rhea preferred.

"And this one's for Leo."

Leo's expression of surprise was almost comical as Phoebe set the package in his lap. "You got me a gift?"

"Of course we did. It's Christmas. It's from all of us."

He turned the package about as though it were a foreign object. "I don't really do Christmas. I'm not a Christian."

Phoebe snorted. "Neither are we."

"Speak for yourself." Ione's tone was reproachful.

"Right. Sorry," said Phoebe. "With the exception of Ione, the high priestess of her local coven of witches, neither are we."

"Nice," said Ione. "And...not wrong." She admired the candleholder she'd unwrapped.

"So call it a Yule present," Phoebe said to Leo. "Go ahead. Open it."

Leo unwrapped the paper carefully, setting it aside before opening the plain white box. Nestled in tissue paper inside was a leather-bound book with a fancy pen.

"It's a blank book," said Phoebe. "For writing down things you want to remember. They say doing it physically with a pen and paper helps memory."

Leo smoothed his hand over the leather cover. "That's very...thoughtful." He glanced around at the others, seemingly overcome. "I don't remember ever receiving such a nice gift."

One thing Rhea had come to realize since Leo's *munr* had been freed was that he had no use for casual lying to make someone feel good. The *munr* was motivated strictly by his desires. He didn't do flattery.

Pretending to examine one of the bottles of ink, she looked down at her lap to suppress the sudden rush of feeling for him, that he was so moved by such a simple gift. And that he'd never received anything thoughtful before was a testament not to his lack of memory but to what his existence had been since the curse. His memories through Leo's experiences would have yielded that sort of detail. And his personal memories were of nothing but confinement. It made her heart ache.

Dev, standing by the breakfast bar, picked up a small gift bag from the floor. "Ione and I got you a little something else as well."

Bemused, Leo took the bag and folded back the tissue paper, pulling out a knitted scarf and a matching cap in a pale grayish-blue. He put the scarf around his neck and tugged the cap onto his head with an amused smile directed at Rhea. The cap he'd worn before had belonged to Leo the Dull. The color made the blue of his eyes pop like aquamarine gemstones.

"Rhea mentioned you'd lost a few things in the fire," said Ione. "We thought you could use a little something to keep you warm."

"But that's really just the wrapping," said Dev. "Dig deeper."

Eyebrows knitting with curiosity, Leo fished in the tissue in the bottom of the bag and pulled out a bottle of Peligroso with a red bow tied around the neck. His laugh as he held it up was the sort that made Rhea tingly.

"Thank you. Sincerely." He gripped the bottle like he'd won an Oscar. "This will indeed keep me warm."

Rhea's imbibing, meanwhile, had made her more than warm. She got up to use the bathroom, and when she came out, Theia was waiting in the hallway.

Before she could step aside, Theia steered her back in and shut the door, blocking it with her body. "Okay, *who* is that?"

"What are you talking about?"

"That is not Leo Ström. Not the Leo Ström I met. When Phoebe told me you were seeing him, I thought, 'Well, that's nice for Rhea. He's a little indecisive and aimless

but very cute, and very sweet. She'll have fun with him.'
But that guy…" Theia jerked her thumb over her shoulder
toward the door. "He's like something out of a sexy pirate
movie. He talks different, and he exudes—" Theia's cheeks
colored. "He's like walking man candy."

Rhea blinked at her, stunned. "Are you actually jealous of me?"

"No, I'm not j—" Theia stopped and looked at the ceiling. "Okay, yes, in the pure abstract, I'm seething with jealousy. Not because I wish it had worked out between him and
me but because I've never had anybody look at me the way
he looks at you—like he worships the ground you walk on."

Rhea laughed. "Yeah, sure you haven't."

"What's that supposed to mean?"

"Oh my God, Thei. *Every* guy looked at you like that
in school. You were the one they wanted to ask out. I'm
the one they came to when they wanted to know whether
you'd say yes if they did."

"That's not true."

"Jesus, what alternate reality were you living in?"

"That doesn't even make sense. We're identical."

"Really? You're trying to play the 'identical' card with
me? Look, I'm not upset about it. I mean, sometimes I am,
because it sucks being the one guys want to be friends with
so they can get close to my sister who looks just like me.
But it is what it is. I've never blamed you for it. We're different people. Just…own it, for Christ's sake."

Theia's arms dropped to her sides. "I had no idea you
felt this way. Honestly, I never knew that was happening
when we were in school. I guess maybe I was a little self-
absorbed."

"Well…wake up, Cupcake." Rhea flicked Theia's forehead with her thumb and forefinger, like she would a ripe
melon.

"Ow!" Theia rubbed her forehead ruefully. "My apparent superiority aside—" she jumped to the side with a grin to avoid another head flick "—quit avoiding the question. Who is that guy?"

"He's Leo Ström. Mostly."

"What do you mean, mostly?"

"He's..." Rhea lifted her shoulders with a sigh. "He's a thousand-year-old Viking living under a Norn curse that separates his essential selves every Yuletide while his soul goes off to lead the Wild Hunt. His soul is AWOL at the moment. That's why he can't remember anything. The Norns exacted a price for his life—his mind and his will. Leo—the Leo in Phoebe's living room—is his will, and he's been trapped in a sort of limbo until I helped free him the night of the fire."

Theia leaned back against the door abruptly, her head striking it with a thud. "Wow. I—did not pick up on that on our handful of awkward dates."

"Well, you know...you're self-absorbed." Rhea grinned. "So you really think he worships the ground I walk on?"

Theia laughed. "Yeah, I really do." She shook her head, still looking a little dazed. "What are you going to do about his soul?"

"Honestly, I don't know. Neither of them seem particularly keen on reintegrating. But if he doesn't do it before Yuletide officially ends, he won't be able to do it at all."

"So the soul-Leo—"

"The *hugr*. This one's the *munr*."

"The *hugr*. Is that who I met in Flagstaff?"

"Oh, I doubt it. The *hugr*'s kind of an asshole. I assume you met the same one I did, the fully integrated Leo, except with his mind and will suppressed."

A loud knock sounded on the door. "Other people have to pee, you know." Phoebe rattled the handle.

Theia opened the door. "Don't you have another bathroom?"

"Yeah. That's why I said *people*, as in more than one peeing person. Ione's using it." She moved Theia aside. "You two are welcome to stay in here and watch me do my thing if that's what floats your boat, but I'm not waiting any longer."

Theia grabbed Rhea by the hand and headed out the door. "No, thanks. You can float your own boat...and that metaphor is really gross, Phoebes." She paused in the hallway after Phoebe shut the door. "So we're... Are we good, Rhe? I've really missed you."

Rhea shrugged, pulling her hand out of Theia's and hugging her arms. "I've missed you, too. But you're the one who shut me out."

"What?" Theia looked genuinely confused. "Rhe—"

"We never kept things from each other before. But you knew about Dad, and you knew about our other sisters, and you kept it from me. We shared everything. And now I feel like I don't even know you."

The hurt in Theia's eyes was palpable. "Rhea—"

"You can't make things right by giving me sad eyes, Theia. I'm sorry if that hurts you. But you hurt me, and you're just going to have to live with the way that makes you feel." Rhea started down the hallway but turned back before she reached the living room. "And also? I don't know who you went to for that Lilith tattoo, but they messed up the lines."

Belatedly, Theia covered the inside of her forearm with her palm, and Rhea turned and rejoined the gathering.

Chapter 22

Leo glanced over at Rhea as he drove her home after the gathering wound down. Though she'd argued the point briefly, she'd been in no condition to drive, amply demonstrated by nodding off as soon as they hit the road. He'd wanted to talk to her about the other Leo, but that would have to wait.

He chafed against the idea of being bound once again, but he had to believe her when she swore she hadn't done it herself. He had to believe her, because if she would lie to him—this beautiful contradiction of soft and hard, fierce and vulnerable, sarcastic and sensual presently slumped in the seat beside him with a bit of drool on her cheek— if she could lie to him, there was nothing worth desiring in the universe. Everything was pointless rot and decay, and he was nothing but a revenant reanimated by Kára to no purpose.

And as he'd said to her earlier, if he had to be bound to someone, he would want it to be Rhea. The new ink in Mjölnir on his right arm tingled with that sense of rightness he'd felt as she'd tattooed his skin. Skin that might have been the other Leo's by morning if not for the fire. He couldn't bear the thought of that insufferable version of him being with Rhea in his place, bound to *his* Rhea by the Valkyrie's magic. But *he* had the skin now. And he had

Rhea. And even if he was a stupid, besotted fool without a soul, he wanted to be hers. The question was whether he was enough for her, or whether she would always be seeking the other. But he wasn't about to give up the skin now that he had it.

He tried to rouse her when they arrived at her apartment, managing to get her out of the car and briefly onto her feet before she went boneless and floppy and he had to pick her up and carry her inside. Leo set her on the bed, and she murmured something and curled into a ball like a cat. With a little nudging, he was able to tug the sheet from the unmade bed from beneath her. He took off her fluffy boots and covered her before removing his own boots and climbing in beside her.

Something poked his hip at his back pocket, and it wasn't his phone. Leo worked the item out of his pants—the box of condoms. He set it on the bedside table with a sigh. Eventually, he hoped, they'd actually have a chance to use them.

Rhea's sleep was uneasy. A shadowy presence followed her through dark corridors and curtained, labyrinthine places out into the night, where the streets were unlit and empty and led to an endless succession of parking lots on which the ground tilted and swayed. The unpopulated landscape eventually morphed into a macabre carnival that remained in total darkness while the presence pursued her onto carousels and Tilt-A-Whirls, always one seat behind her, no one else on the rides. The shadow seemed to have been always there, always in the background, waiting for its moment.

She woke around three to find herself in bed at home, with Leo asleep beside her. Her phone had buzzed in her pocket. Rhea got up to use the bathroom and opened the message as she sat on the toilet, yawning.

This is important. Don't delete.

What was Theia up to now?

Come to the Chapel of the Holy Cross.

What in the world? She sure as hell wasn't going to drive up to the Chapel of the Holy Cross at three in the morning.

Another message popped up before she could fire off her terse refusal. I have your fylgja.

Rhea stared at the text. What was she talking about? Had Phoebe told Theia Rafe's theory about Vixen being her *fylgja*? And how could Theia "have" Vixen? There was no way Theia could capture a Valkyrie. More to the point, why would she?

Something about the wording, beyond the oddness of the request, was off. A feeling of dread settled in her stomach. Theia? Is this you?

The screen showed a message in progress for several interminable seconds. Perhaps I should have said, "I have your doppelgänger." It's remarkable how genes dictate biological destiny, isn't it? But I suppose you have your own fingerprints. Nature is not fooled.

Rhea's thumbs were shaking as she typed. Who is this?

Let's just call me Skuld for now. A laughing emoji followed. That was an unintentional play on words. But think of me as your destiny: that which is happening. And her destiny. I see you share a tattoo.

Rhea began typing a furious reply, as if words could somehow bridge the physical distance to intimidate whoever this was, but another message interrupted.

No more talk. Do not contact anyone. Do not wake the soulless munr. Come alone.

Rhea sat trembling before getting up to pad carefully into the bedroom and grab her boots from beside the bed. Leo didn't stir. For a few panicked minutes after searching the top of the bureau she thought he must have the car keys in his pocket, but she discovered them in the living room lying on the coffee table. She let herself out quietly and descended the stairs to the parking lot to start the car, sick with anxiety while she waited for the window to defog enough to drive.

As she pulled out of her space, she saw something dark in the shadows, and her heart leaped into her throat. The presence from her dream had somehow emerged from it with her. But in the dim light of the parking lot lamps, she saw it was the wolf-dog.

Rhea hesitated. The person who'd texted her hadn't said anything about not bringing a dog. She opened the passenger door, and the animal trotted over with purpose and jumped in, making itself comfortable on the seat as though it rode with her all the time.

"Okay, dog. I don't know if you're part of Leo or what, but we're going to get my sister Theia, and I need you to be on board with this, got it?"

The dog regarded her with a patient gaze. She supposed that was all the answer she was going to get.

The darkness was almost total as she wound through the hills toward the highway, as if the dream had followed her into reality. At least the snow had stopped, though it left a chilly, damp air and a slick of ice on the road, forcing her to drive more carefully than usual, when she wanted to be reckless and fast.

"So, you're not like Vixen, are you? I mean, you don't

talk, do you?" She glanced at the dog. "Then again, you look like an actual, normal wolf-dog, not a creepy, upright, oversexed fox, so I'm guessing you don't."

No response.

"I still don't know what a *fylgja* does, exactly. They say if you see your own, it's a portent of death, but you're not mine, so I'm hoping we're cool. Anyway, mine is apparently my own twin, and I've been seeing her my entire life, so I don't think that necessarily bears out."

The only sound was the soft hum of the heater and the quiet whir of the wheels against the highway.

"Maybe you have some of Leo's consciousness. I don't really get how this whole thing works. But you led me to the *hugr*, so he certainly doesn't share your consciousness while you're separate or he'd know you had. Not that I'm trying to keep it from him. You. I mean, I guess Leo knows now anyway because he heard me talking to Phoebe."

She was possibly losing it a little bit. What if this was some random stray that happened to be hanging around her car? Rhea gripped the wheel as she turned onto the winding road leading toward the hillside into which the cross-shaped chapel was built. Wherever the dog had come from, she needed to keep talking to stave off the fear of what was happening to Theia. Who cared whether it was really Leo's *fylgja*?

"I hope you can understand that I only want what's best for you. I don't want you to be lost or broken. And Kára... who knows what she wants? I mean, she wants you, obviously. Or him. Whatever."

She'd passed through Sedona proper already and had reached the turnoff onto the twisting drive up to the hilltop where the chapel perched between red buttes that appeared gray and flat in the darkness. A gate blocked the road, apparently intended to discourage visitors after hours. Except whoever had taken Theia had obviously gotten through. Unless he'd walked all the way up the hill. Maybe that's what she should do. There weren't any other cars parked here, but Theia's kidnapper could have parked on a side road.

Rhea stopped on the shoulder and turned to the dog. "I guess this is where I get out." But as she spoke, the gate creaked in the silence and swung open. "Or not." She started through slowly, afraid someone was going to come running out to stop her, afraid something terrible was waiting on the other side. Nothing was, and no one did. Rhea continued up the hill, her high beams illuminating only the two hundred or so feet ahead of her. It was like her dreamscape.

After she'd parked at the top, Rhea sat in the car trying to breathe, trying not to be terrified. She had to be able to face this, whatever it was, for Theia.

The dog growled softly, staring at nothing.

"That's not helping, dog."

Rhea turned off the engine and clutched the pepper spray in her hand, heart battering her chest as she opened the door. The dog leaped over her, nearly giving her a heart attack, and landed on the tarmac, where it paced as if keeping guard, still softly growling. She got out. The dog flanked her. She felt a little braver with the wolf-dog beside her.

Another metal guard on a hinged post was positioned across the walkway before the chapel. The dog went over it, and Rhea went around it. The chapel was dark. What if somebody was just yanking her chain? The place was locked up tight. She turned to ask the dog its opinion, but it was gone. *Great. Abandon me now, weird* fylgja *wolf-dog.*

As she pondered the darkened chapel, one of the glass doors swung slowly open.

Rhea swallowed, her palms sweating. "Hello?"

Flickering candlelight she hadn't noticed through the tinted door illuminated the altar beneath the towering cross that formed the four panes of the far window. Someone with a familiar silhouette was seated on the front row of benches, facing the altar.

"Theia?"

A figure moved in the shadows beside the cross. "Thank you for following instructions." The figure emerged before the altar.

Rhea blinked, confused. "Mr. Dressler?"

"Please. Call me Brock. Come have a seat with your lovely doppelgänger and let's have a chat."

How could he have hidden this intent from her when she'd read him?

"The thing about second sight," said Dressler as if he'd read her mind, "is that it's painfully obvious when it's being used on someone else who also possesses it." He gestured to the pew. "Please sit. This won't take long, and I'm not interested in harming you. I just need something you have."

Rhea walked slowly up the aisle, the pepper spray cap still flipped up.

Dressler nodded toward it. "You won't need that. I promise. But keep it if it makes you more comfortable."

"If it makes *you* uncomfortable, I'm keeping it." She'd reached the front. On the pew, Theia stared ahead with a vacant expression, not bound or gagged, just...empty. "What did you do to her?"

"She's in a trance state. She'll be fine. Once I say so."

Rhea sat beside her and took Theia's hand, to no reaction. She glared daggers at Dressler. "What the hell do you want?"

"First of all, let me say how pleased I am with the tattoo." He folded back his sleeve, showing her the healing ink: *I am. I think. I will.* "You do excellent work. I wouldn't be surprised if the fire turns out to have been only a momentary blip in your budding career."

"Great. You can give me five stars on Yelp."

He smiled, somehow managing to seem genuinely nice despite having abducted her sister to use as bait. Rhea fiddled with the pepper spray lid as Dressler turned to the altar and picked up some kind of short-handled blade. Maybe it was an athame, although this was the wrong kind of altar.

"What I want is very little. Just a drop of your blood."

Rhea laughed, though her skin had gone clammy. "Is that all?"

"The key is to take it with this." He held up the blade in the candlelight. The handle was a broken stick, and the hammered metal tip gleamed like gold. "It took me many years to track this down. This is the Holy Lance that pierced Christ's side on the cross. Adolf Hitler had it during the war, and afterward, it was supposed to have been returned to its reliquary in Vienna's Hofburg Palace. But I went there to acquire it shortly after the war, and I knew immediately it was a fake."

"Shortly after what war?"

"World War II, of course."

"I see. And you're...?"

"Very well preserved." Dressler grinned. "You see, I used the lance myself while it was in the Führer's possession. It was said to bestow immortality. Which may be true, since here I am. Unfortunately, a prick with it also results in an unhealable wound. And more than a prick, well... let's say Adolf wasn't long for this world anyway when he shot himself in the head." He rolled his sleeve higher, revealing a gauze bandage taped above his elbow, and pulled the tape away. The smell that emanated from what looked like a necrotic sore nearly made Rhea vomit. Dressler grimaced. "Not pretty, is it?" He covered it again, somehow masking the smell, to her relief.

"So you gave yourself a little prick and now you're rotting. What does that have to do with me?"

"You have the magic ingredient to heal the wound for good—the blood of the first demon."

"I'm pretty sure it's extremely diluted by now."

"Doesn't matter. As evidenced by the gifts you and your sisters possess, its power is still quite strong." He stepped toward her.

Rhea raised the pepper spray. "I thought you said that thing was a fake."

"This? No." Dressler turned the relic in his hand. "This I recovered several months ago with the help of a friend." He smiled. "A necromancer."

No. Effing. Way. Would that asshole never go away? "Let me guess. His name is Carter Hamilton."

"The very same. He's the one who told me about you and your six lovely sisters full of demon blood. He'd hoped to have two or three of you in his thrall by now, but he's greedy. And a bit uncouth in his magical methods. Frankly, he's nuts." He wasn't going to get any argument from her there. "Like I said, all I need is a drop."

"And you think I'm going to give you one."

"You forget I have second sight myself. I know you are."

"Why did you choose me? I mean, I'd rather you didn't choose any of us, but you already had Theia. Why didn't you take a drop from her?"

"Your twin was my first target. We ruled out the three half siblings. They have a different strain, unpredictable. And Phoebe and Ione, Carter felt, would give me too much of a fight, particularly with their dragon consorts. You two, on the other hand—you're very easy to manipulate. I don't mean that as an insult. You're just more trusting.

Perhaps your older sisters have shielded you from the ugly realities of the world. Or perhaps they had it harder losing your parents in their teens. And then there was one more crucial element."

Rhea's hand was getting stiff gripping the spray can. "And what would that be?"

"The Viking."

"So you *were* stalking him."

"I wouldn't call it stalking. I learned of his existence before the war, when I was a leader in the Hitlerjugend. He was a legend. The warrior who couldn't die, cursed to lead Odin's Hunt. I saw it once, you know. Those wild horses whinnying like banshees, the ghostly riders. Their appearance changes with the time and the place. When I saw them, they looked like SS officers. They'd come for the Führer, in fact. They smelled the stench of dark magic on him. The funny thing is, Hitler didn't even believe in the relic. He'd cut himself to show it was nonsense. But as these things often go, before they could get close enough to him, he did the job himself."

Rhea's hand was cramping. "That's a lovely story. I still don't see what Leo has to do with my blood."

"It's not that he has anything to do with your blood, per se. It's that, together, his blood and your blood will give me what I need—the chance at true immortality. And I already have his. But the most important thing you did for me where Leo is concerned was separating him from his *hugr*, which is crucial to my future aims. I have plans for the *hugr*."

Rhea finally connected the dots. "*You* set that fire."

"It was a little desperate, I admit, but I was out of time. I would have had to wait yet another year for an opportunity, and this damn wound is becoming unbearable." He took another step toward her.

Rhea stood and aimed. "If you think I'm going to let you stab me with that thing and take on an unhealable wound, you're out of your goddamned mind."

"Oh, but that's the beauty of it. Your blood mitigates the effects of the physical corruption. And I'm not going to stab you. I only need a finger prick. Which you *are* going to give me."

Rhea opened her mouth to tell him where he could shove his Holy Lance, but a smell far worse than his rotting wound suddenly filled the air, making her stomach convulse and her head swim. She grabbed for the pew to steady herself, but it was too low, and she dropped onto the seat beside Theia, who seemed unaffected by the stench.

Gagging, Rhea threw her arm over her mouth and nose. Her vision blurred and doubled as something—*shambled* was the only word for it—up the stairs from below. The hair rose on the back of her neck. She wanted to turn around, desperate not to have some hulking thing behind her she couldn't see, but the dizziness was too intense.

"He's a bit unpleasant, I admit," said Dressler. *A bit?* "But he's intensely loyal. Kurt served under me in the war, and he died doing it. But I learned how to use the Old Ways to bring him back."

"Kurt" shambled into view, a bloated, gray obscenity in the shape of a man, with putrescent flesh that looked as though it might slough off at any moment. From the dizziness and the sensation of cold in her bones, she recognized the dark presence from her dream. Rhea's stomach rebelled, and she lurched forward over the pew and vomited up her lovely Christmas Eve dinner. Which somehow managed not to smell anywhere near as awful as Kurt.

As she huddled, dry heaving, with her head between her legs, something sharp pricked her finger. She couldn't remember when the pepper spray canister had fallen out of her hand. Let him have the damn blood. She was going to die of vomiting if that nasty thing came any closer.

Dressler's blurry image wavered before Rhea, wrapping the Holy Lance carefully in a scarlet cloth. "Kurt will stay here and keep you company for a bit."

Rhea gagged out the word *no*, but he ignored her.

"I need to take care of some things, and I don't want to have to worry about where you are while I'm doing them. But once my business is handled, I'll use the spell to send Kurt back to his grave. And your sister should be back to her eternally optimistic self by daybreak. She really is charming, isn't she?" Dressler's blurry face smiled— probably. "Thank you so much for your little gift. It means the world to me." His footsteps sounded on the floor as he headed for the door. "Oh, and keep in mind, Kurt can be rather irritable. Try not to provoke him."

Rhea tried to swear at him, but she only got as far as "fuh." She had to get some distance between this thing and herself. She swayed to her feet, and Theia rose with her automatically. Rhea grabbed her hand and lurched toward the door, but the thing moved faster than it looked like it ought to be able to—hell, it didn't look like it ought to be able to move at all—and stood between them and the doorway.

"Look, Kurgh—" Rhea put her hand over her mouth and swallowed bile, focusing on the floor to try to keep it down. Against the leg of the pew across from her, the keychain with her pepper spray canister lay just two feet away. It must have slid across the aisle when she dropped it. She let go of Theia's hand and took a wavering step toward it. The creature didn't move. Rhea dove for the canister and caught herself against the pew before aiming the pepper spray at Kurt and squeezing the trigger.

The thing let out a bellow of outrage that Rhea could only describe as the sound of decaying flesh trying to swear. It lunged for her, and its clammy, putrid hand went around her throat.

The ground swayed beneath her, the chapel floor tilting like the tarmac in her dreams, and the candles lighting the altar seemed to go out. She was no longer in the chapel but in some nightmare-scape. Blighted, misshapen trees loomed and swayed around her in a foul wind, something scrabbling through their branches. And something was crawling in the creature's mouth. The dead maw opened, and roaches swarmed from it, down Kurt's cheeks and along his arms toward her.

She tried to scream, but no sound came out. And then the hand dropped from her throat, and she was back in the chapel, stumbling backward. The creature had turned toward the doorway. Someone stood in it. She couldn't focus on the figure, but something bright and metallic flashed in the figure's hand as the dead thing charged forward with that same inhuman, pulpy growl. The shiny metal swung and went clean through its neck. Kurt's rotten head tumbled onto the floor and rolled under a pew, one of the eyes sliding out of the socket with a wet sound.

Chapter 23

Rhea's vision cleared. "Leo?"

He stood holding the axe that had decapitated the thing, dressed in leather and furs and homespun flax, his hair long, two plaits braided at his temples, like Leo in Viking cosplay. "I am his *vördr*."

Damn, how many of him were there? "What's a... vorther?"

"The warden of his soul," said Leo. "The guardian. You and the other damsel are not harmed?"

"Damsel?" Rhea gave him a dubious look. "No, we're fine. At least, I think she's fine." Theia still stood motionless in the aisle. Rhea took her hand and sat her on the pew by the door.

The stench had lessened considerably, and Rhea was no longer gagging. Kurt's body was dissolving into some kind of nasty sludge.

"Thanks for stepping in when you did, though. I'm not sure what that thing was doing to me."

"Rotting your brain, I should think." Leo's *vördr* wiped the blade of the axe on his sleeve and set it in the loop on his belt. The long hair and those little braids were kind of sexy. As was the thick kohl lining his eyes. "A *draugr*'s purpose is to drive one mad."

"Well, thanks for not letting it rot my brain." She gri-

maced at the now gelatinous pile of goo that was left of the
draugr. "I suppose we'd better clean this up somehow. And
I kind of made a mess in front of the altar." She wasn't a
practicing Catholic, but she wasn't feeling too good about
desecrating a church.

"You must get your sister home. I will see to this."

Rhea was in no mood to argue. "Whatever you say."
She prodded Theia up once more and stepped around the
draugr goo but paused outside the door. "If you're the *hugr*'s guardian, why are you here? Is the Hunt nearby?"

Leo's *vördr* regarded her, a sort of hidden smile behind the crystalline blue gaze, though his expression didn't
change. "It was not the *hugr* I said I watched over. I am the
warden of his soul. And what is dear to it."

"Oh." The word made her unreasonably warm. She
couldn't meet those intense eyes of his any longer. Rhea
mumbled her thanks again and hurried Theia out. "I don't
know how much of this you're going to remember tomorrow," Rhea murmured as they walked down the drive, "but
you can keep that 'dear' comment to yourself, if you know
what's good for you."

Once they reached the car, she guzzled a bottle of water
she'd left in the pocket behind the seat, gargling and spitting out the last of it onto the roadside to get the nasty taste
out of her mouth.

Theia's silence was unnerving as Rhea drove toward
home, and Rhea rambled to fill in the awkwardness and
keep herself awake. When she pulled into the parking lot,
Leo stood on the landing in the open door of her apartment.

He scowled as she got out of the car. "Where did you
go?" He paused when he saw Theia in the passenger seat
and his accusatory expression turned puzzled. "Is that your
sister?"

"She's in a trance," said Rhea. "Help me get her inside."

Leo moved quickly down the stairs to open the car door and scoop Theia up.

Rhea swallowed an irrational twinge of jealousy at the sight of Theia in Leo's arms. "She can walk, actually, but sure, that'll work."

He took Theia inside and set her on the couch. At least he hadn't put her in Rhea's bed. Rhea groaned inwardly, immediately feeling guilty about begrudging Theia anything. There was no telling what that creep had done to her.

"What happened?" Leo lifted one of Theia's eyelids to peer at her. "Who put her in a trance?"

"Well, you're not going to believe this. Or maybe you will. Maybe you'll say 'I told you so.' But Brock Dressler kidnapped her to get me to meet him. It turns out he's a full-on Nazi, as in actual World War II German Nazi—or at least he claims to be—and he wanted my blood. He says the trance is supposed to wear off by daybreak."

Leo looked baffled. "Who the hell is Brock Dressler?"

"Jesus. Are we doing this again? We went through this the other night. The Nazi you punched. Sorry—that Leo the Dull punched."

"Oh. No, I remember him. I remember punching him, anyway. Or I remember *him* punching him." Leo slumped onto the couch next to Theia and brushed his hand through his unkempt hair in a way that seemed to belong wholly to the other Leo. "It's exhausting trying to keep this straight. Thank the gods I won't have to try to figure out if I'm remembering my own life anymore." He didn't seem to notice her frown. "So why would this Nazi want your blood? And how did you manage to get away from him without giving it to him?"

"He said it would make him immortal. Or heal the consequences of the relic he used to try to make himself immortal. I'm not sure whether it was supposed to add to the immortality part. But I didn't get away. He stabbed my finger." The adrenaline that had been keeping her going abruptly deserted her as she held out the insulted finger, and she wobbled on her feet.

Leo leaped up. "*Älskling*, I'm sorry. *You* should be sitting down." He led her to the couch, and Rhea sank onto it gratefully. Leo examined her finger prick. "That's it? He abducted your sister and put her in a trance just to poke your fingertip?"

"Maybe he was testing my blood sugar level." Rhea laughed at the absurdity, and the tiredness made the laugh sound a little hysterical.

Leo frowned. "Why didn't you wake me? Why would you go off on your own to face some lunatic?"

"He said he'd hurt Theia if I didn't come alone." Rhea jumped up again. "Dammit, I forgot. I have to warn your *hugr*. I think Dressler's going to do something to him."

Leo's face was stony. "He's not *my hugr*. Why is it your responsibility what happens to him? Can't he take care of himself?"

"He needs to know what he's up against. It's my fault Dressler has some kind of power over him." Rhea headed for the door, but Leo stepped in front of her with his arms folded. "Get out of my way, Leo."

"You're not going anywhere except back to bed. You can barely keep your eyes open."

"Don't tell me what I'm going to do."

"You would rather be with *him*, is that it?"

Rhea growled in frustration. "When are you going to stop being so damned competitive with your own freaking soul?"

After staring her down for a moment longer, Leo sighed and stepped aside. "Do what you want, then, but you're on your own. Somebody needs to stay here to watch over your sister."

Even though the intent was to be spiteful and sabotage her efforts to save his *hugr*, she couldn't help but be touched by his concern for Theia. "No, you're right. Thank you, Leo. I'll be back as soon as I find him and give him the message."

Leo stared openmouthed as she went out. He obviously hadn't expected her to call his bluff.

Getting back into the car right now was the last thing she wanted to do, but whether he wanted to acknowledge his *hugr* or not, Leo's life hung in the balance. And Rhea was the reason he was vulnerable.

Rhea waited after starting the engine, hoping to see the wolf-dog nearby. No such luck. She figured she'd drive the same stretch of highway where she'd seen the Hunt before, and if she didn't find it there, she'd go back to the paddock.

But after driving for almost an hour, her plan seemed a little less certain. She was bone tired, and there was no sign of the Hunt and no sign of that stupid road she was sure she'd turned down last night—or two nights ago, technically, since it was now Christmas morning. She was about to give up when her phone rang. Thank the goddess for psychic sisters. It was exactly the person she needed.

"Phoebe. I was just about to call you."

"Is Theia with you?" Phoebe's voice was raspy with sleep and worry. "I got up to get some water, and she wasn't in her room, and her car is gone—"

"She's fine, just got into a tiny fender bender. She's asleep at my place."

"Your place? Where are you?"

"I'm on Dry Creek near Boynton Pass, and I could use some magical help from you and Rafe."

"Magical? Right now?"

"The deadline for saving Leo's soul got moved up, and I need to know how to find a wraith."

"What do you mean you need to find Rafe?" Phoebe was still half-asleep.

"Not Rafe, a *wraith*." A shuffling noise followed before Rafe apparently took over the phone.

"Hey, Rhea. What's up?"

"I need to find the Wild Hunt. I thought maybe you'd know how to seek out a wraith since you can command shades."

"I *can* command them, but I don't, generally. I prefer to respect their autonomy. But a wraith is different. They're something between living and dead. Cursed souls. I assume it would require a special ritual to summon one, and I'm afraid it's not one I'm familiar with."

But Rhea had accidentally summoned one before.

"I think I might know how to do that, actually. Do you have any idea where I would find pristine snow?"

"Pristine snow? I guess it would have to be somewhere no one's been since the snow fell. Probably just about any hiking trail, since it's not light out yet and the last snowfall was just a few hours ago."

"Perfect, thanks."

"Do you need any help?"

"No, I think I've got this. Tell Phoebe not to worry about Theia. I'll bring her back in the morning."

Boynton Canyon Trail was just up the road. Rhea parked at the trailhead and grabbed the fish-scaling knife out of the glove compartment—rescued from the wreckage of her shop—and gave it a scrub with her hand sanitizer. It would have to do.

The snow-covered trail was as pristine as she could have hoped for. Rhea chose a spot where the snow was thick enough to qualify as a "bank" and crouched to pull up her legging, steeling herself for the cut. She watched her breath fog in the air. Damn, it was cold out here. And absolutely beautiful. Snow blanketed the surrounding scrub brush and the branches of the cottonwood trees in a lacy rime that made her feel like she was in a fairy realm.

She took a deep breath and put the edge of the blade to the tattoo. Here went nothing. Rhea made a shallow nick, just enough to get the blood dripping.

The first drop struck the snow, and then a second, but nothing happened. She wasn't sure exactly what she was expecting. Maybe she needed to be touching the— Rhea swallowed. Something was watching her.

She clutched her keys, standing slowly. A pair of eyes glowed at her through the snow-laced trees, low to the ground. Maybe it was a coyote. She didn't want to have to pepper spray a coyote. It moved between the low branches, and Rhea held her breath, but as it emerged from the brush onto the trail some yards ahead of her, she saw the curled-over tail. Rhea heaved a sigh of relief and hurried after the *fylgja*.

Snow clouds hung low around the sandstone formations up ahead, wispy forms moving like mist, increasing the otherworldly aura of the place—as well as the chill. Rhea had forgotten to wear gloves. She put her hands in her pockets and hurried on. The wolf-dog had disappeared around a turn of the trail.

"If you've come to persuade me to return to the skin, you have wasted your time."

Rhea nearly jumped out of hers. Not two feet in front of her, "Gunnar" sat mounted on his spectral horse.

She shivered and found her voice. "I came to warn you. That 'sad little braggart' you thought was so inconsequential? He's coming after you with a piece of the Holy Lance."

"No weapon can harm me. I am made of spirit, not flesh."

"Apparently, this one can. It's imbued with your *líkamr*'s blood—and mine—and he means to use it to steal your immortality."

Gunnar smiled. "I appreciate the warning, but I have things well in hand." Gunnar held his hand down to her as a distant hunting horn sounded. "Would you like to see?"

"Would I like to—?" Rhea let out a squeal of surprise when he clasped her arm and hoisted her in the air to toss her onto the horse behind him.

"Hold fast to me" was the only warning she got before the phantom mare thundered into the frigid air.

Rhea shrieked, throwing her arms around Gunnar and clinging tight as they galloped over nothing but currents, charging into the mist. The clouds shifted and swirled into the roiling, surf-like thunderheads she'd seen the Hunt ride in on before, and the ghostly horde appeared before them, cowboy-Viking wraiths shouting war cries and spectral hounds baying eagerly, on the scent of their prey.

Gunnar spurred his horse onward to take the lead, and in the pale, predawn light, Rhea saw the object of their pursuit. As they thundered onto the desert floor, the hunting party had effectively herded him into the box canyon—a human rider on an ordinary horse. Gunnar's horse touched ground and galloped toward him, and the hunted man turned his mount to face them.

Brock Dressler's pretentious smile greeted them as if he were out for a morning ride.

Rhea grabbed Gunnar's arm. "It's a trap."

He ignored her warning and dismounted, drawing his sword as he advanced. "Pray to your gods, mortal, for today you meet them."

"I'm well prepared." Dressler dismounted and drew his

own weapon, the gold gleaming in the soft ruby glow of imminent dawn. "Though I'm not so certain you are."

Rhea leaned forward, clinging to the phantom's mane. "Don't let him touch you with it!"

Dressler glanced in her direction, evidently surprised to see her there. "I suppose I might have saved myself the time and trouble of luring you if I'd factored in the intensity of your devotion. Could have just collected what I needed from you here, eh?"

"You will collect nothing but your just reward." Gunnar raised his sword, powerful arm drawn back, but Dressler dodged as he swung, darting forward before Gunnar's arm could change course.

"No!" The word burst out of her as the relic made contact with Gunnar's side, the blade cutting deep. Rhea made an awkward, fumbling dismount from the horse, landing on her ass, and picked herself up to run to him.

But he'd caught Dressler by the ear and was lifting him off the ground with one hand, apparently unaffected. "Your crude talisman is useless against me." Slapping Dressler on the side of his head with the flat of his sword, Gunnar dazed him and swung the smaller man like a shot put. Dressler landed with a startled grunt on Gunnar's horse, scrambling for a hold on the mane. With a smooth, running leap, Gunnar swung back into his saddle behind him and raised his sword in the air. "For Odin and Freyja!"

A victory cry rang out from the spectral horde, an unearthly whooping and howling that made the hairs rise on the back of Rhea's neck.

Gunnar tipped his hat to her with a wink of one glowing blue eye. "Many thanks for your help." He raised his sword once more. "To Náströnd!"

"Wait! What about your *munr*? Your *líkamr*? You can't

just leave!" But the wraiths were galloping into the air, their ghostly edges gilded by the dawn as the thunderheads closed around them.

Chapter 24

The trance state had rendered Rhea's sister highly suggestible. When Leo asked if she might want to lie down, she'd gotten up and gone into the bedroom, where he'd covered her with a blanket, leaving the door open a wedge so he could see in from the living room in case her condition changed.

A knock on the door woke him sometime later, and he realized he'd dozed on the couch. He jumped up to open it, thinking it was Rhea and not stopping to wonder why Rhea would be knocking on her own front door.

An unremarkable fellow with brown hair buzzed short at the sides smiled at him when he opened the door. "Leo Ström. Just the man I wanted to see."

Leo tilted his head. Had he met this man while Leo the Dull held the reins?

The visitor held out his hand. "We met at the genetics in biotech conference. Brock Dressler."

Leo took the hand automatically before the significance of the name struck him, and something passed from Dressler's palm to his. Something invisible. And magical. Leo stumbled back, staring at his palm, his reflexes slowing along with his thought processes.

"What did you…?"

"It's a simple spell, designed to give you temporary mild

euphoria." Dressler stepped inside. "There's something I need from you."

Leo's tongue felt heavy. "You took…Rhea's blood."

"That's right."

"Now you want mine."

"Not precisely. I already took your blood. Remember when we ran into each other the other day? I provoked you on the street." Dressler smiled. "You don't really think I'd have stood there and let you punch me in the face if it wasn't my plan?"

Leo looked down at his knuckles. He remembered that punch. It was very satisfying. And he remembered something else.

"You put up those posters. With the…sharp blades."

"A fail-safe measure in case the first plan didn't pan out." He was full of shit. The punch had been lucky happenstance.

Leo tried to stay focused. "What do you want?"

"Something you don't even want." Dressler took an object wrapped in red silk cloth from inside his coat. "Your soul."

Leo laughed. "The *hugr*? You can have the damn thing. But it's not here."

Dressler slowly unwrapped the cloth. "As it turns out, it *is* here. It's your *hamr* that currently rides in Odin's Hunt, an astral projection of your physical form. The *hugr* has remained within the skin. The Norns' curse suppresses the mind and the will by default. It's only during the dark hours of Yuletide that they awaken."

Leo shook his head. "How do you know any of… You know the curse?"

"I've been studying you for many years." He unfolded the last corner of the cloth, revealing a jagged piece of ancient wood topped with a gold-plated spear tip. "The Holy Lance would have given me what I needed long ago, but your blood was insufficient. It needed a catalyst. And then a friend of mine turned me on to the Carlisle sisters' stash of original demon blood. Theia's, it turned out, was inert. I put her in your path to see if it would spark something, but you didn't respond to her. There was something special, however, about her twin's magic. Something intimately tied into her art. So I sold her the ink I'd blended, which already had some of your blood in it along with the ash of Eyjafjallajökull from the land where you were meant to die."

"Iceland?" Leo shook his head. "I was wounded in the Battle of Sulcoit on the island of Éire."

"That's all the Valkyrie told you, no doubt. I suppose she failed to mention the second mortal wound you received in the Battle of Haugsnes that sealed your fate. She seems to have left out a great many things for her own convenience." Dressler moved without warning, and Leo's reflexes were too slow to respond. The artifact plunged into his gut, and he stumbled against Dressler with a grunt of surprise. "Such as the fact that the *hugr* remains within your skin."

"You—son of a whore." Leo gripped Dressler's forearm, too late to stop the blade but determined not to let him yank it out. But there was something beyond pain here, some sense of wrongness spreading inside him—like the wrongness that made him turn back when he'd tried to leave Rhea, but far worse. "What are you doing?"

"Relieving you of your burden." Dressler shoved him off the blade, and blood seeped from the open wound. Leo fell to his knees. "Your soul is mine now. And Odin's Hunt will ride to do my bidding."

The icy first light of dawn spilled in through the open doorway as Leo slumped to the floor, illuminating the blood soaking into the carpet. Rhea was going to lose her deposit. *Dammit.* He'd really wanted to stay with Rhea. Now he couldn't even say goodbye.

"Leo?"

She was standing over him, soft gray eyes wide.

"You're here." He smiled, holding his hand up to her. "I thought you'd gone."

"Oh God! Leo, what happened?" She knelt beside him, hands pressed against the hole in his gut, the pain making him abruptly alert. It wasn't Rhea after all but her dark-haired twin.

She had to hike back out of the canyon on her own, leading the abandoned horse as far as she could, and ended up calling Phoebe again to have Rafe come take the animal to his stables. Rhea drove home, exhausted and resigned—and feeling guilty because a part of her was relieved. The thought of losing the *munr*, even though it meant having Leo whole, had begun to make her increasingly unhappy. It wasn't just that she'd miss his unfettered desire, it was the way he said what he was thinking without trying to hide his feelings or his thoughts, the way he experienced things so deeply and purely—the way he laughed. Not having a soul somehow made him more human than anyone she'd ever known.

When she pulled into the parking lot to find Theia waiting on the landing looking fully alert, Rhea jumped out and hurried up the stairs. "Thei! I'm so glad you're okay. And I'm so sorry I've been such a bitch..." Her voice trailed off at the look on Theia's face as she drew closer. There were tearstains on her cheeks. "Theia?"

"Did you find his soul?"

"I talked to him, but he wouldn't... Theia, what's going on?"

Fresh tears streamed down Theia's cheeks. "You'd better go in."

A sick feeling settled over her as she opened the door. The carpet was stained with blood.

"Leo?" Rhea felt her own blood drain from her cheeks as she ran to the bedroom. "Leo, are you here?"

It took her a moment to understand. Faye sat on the side of the bed, lengths of blue silk draping the floor and flowing red locks draping the recumbent figure whom Rhea's mind refused to recognize. He lay with a sheet covering the lower half of his body, his hair dark with sweat and his skin gray and clammy. Bloody bandages were taped over his abdomen, and his hands were at his sides, covered by the sheet. It was only the tattoo of the serpent around his upper arm that demanded she acknowledge his identity.

"Leo?"

Faye raised her head, her cheeks damp and her eyes sorrowful. "With his *hugr* gone, I can finally be with him. And yet still he does not know me."

Rhea stood paralyzed in the doorway. "His *hugr*... I tried to convince him to come back, but—"

"You tried to convince the *hamr*. A projection of the physical self. Like a *fylgja*, but with more agency. I tried to keep him safe from the Norns by hiding the *hugr* within him, even from himself. Even though it meant I must be banished from him whenever he *was* himself. Rejoining his other selves would have returned him to the curse but would have protected him."

"Protected him? From what? What happened?"

"There have been many who have sought his power of immortality over the centuries. Men like that vile little worm, Brock Dressler. But I have no dominion over living men. Only through the Hunt can we rid the world of them and only through the power of the Chieftain. And this man—this *worm*—has stolen his *hugr*. I felt it as soon as it happened. I knew immediately the one we were hunting was like the Chieftain, a projection acting as a decoy while his true self attacked my Leo. I left the Hunt to come to his side, but I was too late. Unless I take him to Valhalla, the wound will fester and corrupt, killing him without killing him. He will eventually become *draugr*."

Rhea's skin went cold. "No. No, we have to do something. What can we do? Can't the Norns heal the wound?"

"And what price would they exact this time? They have taken his will and his mind. In punishing me, they have punished him for more than a thousand years. To save him from death yet again, in defiance of the laws I've broken, they would have nothing less than his heart." Faye began to sob. "And I would give it to them. I would give them anything, but it is not mine to give."

The words delivered a hollow victory: *because it's mine*. Leo's heart belonged to Rhea—and she was losing him. And yet it was obvious the Valkyrie's love for him was genuine. Rhea put her hand on Faye's shoulder, and Faye gripped it, lowering her head. As her weeping grew silent, Leo's labored breathing seemed frighteningly loud.

A soft knock on the doorframe broke the silence. Rhea turned to see Theia beckoning to her.

"What is it?" She slipped her hand out of Faye's and came to the door.

"There's someone outside you need to see."

Rhea followed her, puzzled by the odd phrasing, until she saw who was waiting for her in the parking lot. An extremely healthy version of Leo in traditional Viking attire leaned against her car, dwarfing it. Though she knew it wasn't her Leo, the sight of him, whole and hale, made her heart skip a beat.

"I have made a grave error." He pushed away from the car, and the little MINI rocked under the easing of his weight. "Though it is one I would make again if given the choice between your sanity and my existence."

"I'm not sure what you…" She seemed to lose her train of thought when looking at this Leo.

"I left the soul unguarded to protect you. I walked right into the trap that had been set for me."

"I think we all did."

"There is a recourse, however. If you are willing."

Rhea leaped upon the little ray of hope. "Of course I'm willing. What is it? What do I need to do?"

"You must convince the *hamr* of its true nature. The one known as the Chieftain who leads the Hunt. Once it recognizes itself for what it is, the *hamr* can seek his enemy to retrieve the soul and return with it to rejoin the *líkamr*."

The fleeting ray of hope dimmed. "I couldn't even convince the *hamr* to return when we both believed it was the *hugr*."

"That is why you could not convince it. The *hamr* perceives itself as the essence of the being that is Leo Ström. It believes you have freed it to dwell in its purest form. But the longer it remains apart from the physical body, the weaker it will become, until it simply fades away."

"Wouldn't it be more likely to believe this coming from you?"

"The guardian can only be seen by someone other than the self. All I can do is watch out for the *hugr*. And I have failed at that."

"What about Faye? Kára, I mean. She knows him best. She rides beside him in the Hunt."

"The Valkyrie is the one who convinced the *hamr* of its own authenticity. Her magic prevents him from seeing otherwise." Warden-Leo took her hand. His form, though it appeared physical, turned out to be not quite solid after all. His touch felt like an electrical field buzzing across her flesh. "What I ask of you, dear one, is great, but you are our only hope."

Rhea nodded, not trusting her voice to ask the question she needed to ask, but the *vördr* seemed to know it already.

"You need not seek the *hamr* on your own. I can lend you the *hamingja*, the embodiment of the soul's luck. It will reside within you. The *hamingja* will take you to the *hamr*. And it will tell you what to do when the time is right."

Rhea swallowed. "Okay. So how do we...?"

Still holding her hand, he stepped in close and slid his other not-quite-corporeal palm against her nape and kissed her. As with the vision of the climax she'd had with Leo's *munr* that time in the chair, the *vördr*'s kiss nearly knocked her off her feet. It was like kissing a live wire—not a painful sensation but unbearably wild with energy—her mouth felt as though it were having an orgasm all on its own.

When he let go of her, a sense of relief warred with a longing for it not to have ended. She opened her eyes to discover the *vördr* had disappeared.

Behind her, Theia coughed politely. "So...who was that, exactly?"

Rhea's first attempt to answer resulted in nothing but a raspy, high-pitched squeak. She cleared her throat and tried again. "Leo's warden spirit. He was at the chapel with us. I take it you don't remember any of that."

"Not a bit, no."

"It's probably better that you don't." Inside her head, she sensed a thought that wasn't her own. *Go back to the paddock.* "I have to go."

"Go? Go where? Don't you want to...to be with Leo when...?"

"He's not dying. Or he is, sort of, but his bodily functions won't stop. It's part of the curse. I have to get his soul back."

Chapter 25

A light snow fell on mostly empty streets. The few other drivers, probably on their way to celebrate with family, smiled at Rhea as they passed. Instinctively—though it was the *hamingja*'s instinct and not her own—she knew Gunnar would be keeping close to the paddock. It was only his second day as an independent being, and with the vanishing of the rest of the Hunt at daybreak, he would be on his own without a plan or a place to sleep.

Sure enough, when she arrived at the paddock, he was there. Leaning against the fence in his Western attire, he had his arms crossed over the top rail as though watching invisible livestock. Which maybe he was.

Gunnar turned at the sound of her car door opening and gave her a pleased but quizzical smile as she approached. "Fair Rhea. How did you know I would be here?"

"Just had a feeling."

"Your company is welcome, but you must understand there is nothing you can say to persuade me to return."

"I'm not here to persuade you."

Gunnar looked skeptical. "You are not?"

Rhea stepped up to the fence beside him and hooked her arms over it, gazing at the nonexistent herd. "I was hoping to engage your services."

"My services?" Gunnar returned to his earlier pose,

mimicking her stance, and watched her with amusement. "And how can I be of assistance?"

"I need to track down an immortal Nazi."

"If you mean the one who sought my power, he is hardly immortal. He is presently a denizen of the underworld. He cannot escape it."

"I hate to tell you this, but the guy you took this morning was a decoy. The real Dressler is still at large. And now he's immortal."

"Impossible." Gunnar rested one booted foot on the bottom rail of the fence. "He needed my life force to achieve immortality, and he failed in trying to acquire it."

"Did he really seem like he was trying all that hard?"

"He was a weak, ineffectual man."

"That may be true, but he had a plan. He managed to finagle blood out of your *líkamr*, kidnap my sister to lure me to him so he could steal my blood, use a *draugr* to keep me there while he went off to steal your *hugr*...and then just let you corner him and box his ears and take him to hell?"

Gunnar's frown said he was troubled by her logic, but he wasn't persuaded yet. "He commanded a *draugr*?"

"A real nasty one. I mean, I suppose they're all nasty..." She let her words trail off, trying not to think of Leo's body rotting away.

"But I remain free. How can he have become immortal without my life force?"

Rhea turned to look him in the eye. "You don't have any life force. You're a decoy. Just like the man you defeated this morning."

Gunnar shoved away from the railing, his eyes glowing with offense. "Nonsense. I am the Chieftain, leader of the Hunt. Every night during Yuletide for ten centuries I have left the skin of Leo Ström to lead it. I am the *hugr*. I am no decoy."

"So you're made of spirit, not of flesh."

"Of course I am."

"Take off your shirt."

"I beg your pardon?"

"I want to see if you have Leo's tattoos on your spirit skin."

"What difference does that make?"

"Don't be a pussy. Just take off your shirt." It wasn't her favorite insult—as someone who happened to own a pussy, she thought they were pretty great, actually—but it seemed to be effective on thousand-year-old Viking pride.

Eyes flashing with anger instead of the preternatural glow, Gunnar took off his coat and hung it on one of the fence posts before unbuttoning the shirt and tossing it at Rhea.

Jesus. Those abs. She almost forgot why she'd wanted him to take off the shirt.

The ink was replicated as thoroughly as every other delicious part of Leo's skin. Rhea traced her fingers over the lines of the snake, and Gunnar shivered. Not very spirit-like. She pressed her palm to the ink and held the question in her mind: *Is this spirit or is this flesh?*

The snake began to uncoil. It was all she could do not to yank her hand away. Rhea had never experienced a vision like this. As it writhed beneath her hand, the ink became bumpy—*scaly*—a tactile, 3-D tattoo. Suddenly, she understood. The mark Faye had placed on Leo's skin was meant to keep not just the *munr* but the *hugr* bound to the skin. It was how she'd fooled the Norns. But it was also the home of the curse itself, the Jörmungandr energy Leo had so feared. Just as it would have on Leo's flesh, the mark was becoming manifest in the *hamr* through her—her connection to Leo through ink and blood. She was calling it forth, summoning the snake more surely than she had summoned the first vision of the Hunt.

Gunnar stepped back, breaking the connection. "What are you doing?" His eyes had gone from blue to a vivid aquamarine, the irises variegated with dark lines like fissures in marble, pupils elongated into vertical slits. Was it wrong that she was finding a bare-chested, cowboy-hat-wearing version of Leo with snake eyes super hot?

"Shifting your shape, apparently. Because you're *hamr*, not *hugr*. You're a projection of Leo's flesh. You are *not* spirit."

The *hamingja* gave her a mental fist bump.

Gunnar paced away from her, blinking his eyes, blinking away the shift. "If I am not spirit...where in the Allfather's name is the *hugr*?"

"Dressler stabbed Leo with the Holy Lance and took it. Leo's body is dying. Without it, Faye says he'll become *draugr*."

Gunnar's brow furrowed. "Faye?"

"It's the name Kára goes by now. She's at Leo's bedside."

"Kára. So that is where she went. Yesterday, we spent the day together. I thought we might today, but she never returned."

Rhea tried to shake off the little sting of unexpected jealousy. This wasn't Leo. It was only the physical projection of his form. He could spend his time with whomever he pleased.

"Leo's *vördr* said you'd know where to find Dressler—the real one."

He looked at her sharply. "You say he has acquired the blood of Leo Ström. If this man has also stolen the *hugr* of the rightful Chieftain, he will have rejoined his *hamr* in Náströnd, the Shore of Corpses, where the souls of those taken by the Hunt are relegated. He means to trap the *hugr* there to seal his immortality." Gunnar's eyes darkened. "It will also make him the leader of the Hunt."

"Shore of Corpses?" Rhea shuddered. "He can go there?"

"As an immortal, he can."

"And can you follow him?"

"Until the *hugr* is bound and I become nothing but the echo of a dying mortal man, yes." Gunnar took off the cowboy hat, looking defeated, and dropped it in the snow. Rhea watched, puzzled, as he braced one hand against the fence and removed his boots and socks. When he unzipped his pants, she cleared her throat.

"Uh...what exactly are you doing?"

"Preparing to follow the whoreson." Without the slightest bit of self-consciousness, he stepped out of his pants and his briefs and laid them over the rest of his clothes on the fence. "I will need your assistance."

Rhea tried to keep her eyes on his face. "With...what?"

"Releasing the snake."

"Excuse me?"

"To go below, I must take on the form of one who moves among the dead. Your touch upon the mark of the snake seemed to spark the change. If you would...?" He turned his tattooed shoulder toward her.

"Oh. Right." Rhea laid her hand over the ink once more, and the 3-D sensation of movement began immediately.

His eyes were changing, and as he stepped back, a transformation had definitely come over him, but for the moment, he still had the appearance of a man. And his expression was sad.

"I'm sorry."

He tilted his head. "For what?" It was becoming difficult to look at him as the perception shifted, like a lenticular print being tilted in the light.

"That you had to find out you weren't *hugr*."

Gunnar shrugged, resigned. "One cannot fight destiny." In the next instant, he coiled to the ground, no longer a man, but a massive serpentine reptile as thick as the man's waist, with a spiked head and short, lizard-like limbs— the Jörmungandr tattoo come to life, a sea serpent on land with a dragon's legs.

The aquamarine eyes blinked one last time as if to say goodbye before it slithered away into a crevice in the rocks.

Rhea turned to head back to her car with a feeling of vague unease. If Gunnar couldn't get the *hugr* back, what then? How would she even know what had happened in the underworld? An insistent thought reminded her that the *hamingja* was still with her: *Perhaps you know of some-one else who moves among the dead.* Of course she did.

Ione answered her call with a cheerful, "Merry Christmas!" Apparently, Phoebe hadn't told her about Theia yet. Or any of this.

"Okay, don't freak out, but—"

"Rhea Iris Carlisle." She'd done an instant switch into mom-voice. "How many times have I told you not to lead with that if you don't want me to freak out?"

"Sorry. But you're going to freak out. And...just don't."

"Rhea—"

She delivered the words in a single, rapid breath before Ione could interrupt her. "Theia was kidnapped and put in a trance by a Nazi dickweed, but she's fine now, and I need to borrow Kur to get my boyfriend's soul back."

"Theia was...? What... Nazi? Rhea!"

"I told you, she's fine now. He just wanted to lure me to his altar so he could swipe some of my blood to help make himself immortal."

"This is Christmas, not April Fool's." Ione's voice said she was about to hang up.

"I'm not joking. Any more than Phoebe was joking that night when she tried to tell you that you were dating a necromancer."

That got her attention. "Where is Theia now?"

"She's at my place with Leo. The Nazi who burned down my shop stabbed him and took his soul, and now Leo's shape-shifting astral projection is seeking him in the Viking underworld, and I need someone who can move among the dead."

A button clicked on Ione's phone. "I'm putting you on speaker. Dev's here. Tell him what you need."

"Hello, Rhea. Happy Christmas."

"You know you're not Christian, right?" She couldn't resist teasing him even in the middle of this. Or maybe teasing made her feel less like freaking out herself.

"Ione likes Christmas, so it's Christmas. What do you need me to do?"

"I need Kur. When he's inside his cage, he's in the underworld, right? And he can go anywhere in it?"

"In essence, yes."

"Can you communicate with him?"

"To some degree, but mostly it's a shared sense of emotion."

"Oh." Maybe this wasn't going to work after all.

"But Rafe can command him. We've discovered Ione can call his shade from the cage without releasing him physically into our world. And once he's shade-walking, he's in Rafe's domain."

Awesome. Might as well make it a family affair.

When they'd gathered at Ione's place, Rafe stripped down to his briefs to conjure the quetzal power, spreading his gorgeous wings that stretched the width of the living room, the tattoo of Quetzalcoatl on his back expanding with them, becoming a second skin. Ione had to coax Kur's shade from Dev before Rafe could see it, and Rhea was afraid he wouldn't come, until Rafe began to talk to the invisible dragon.

"Sorry to disturb you, my friend, but I have a favor to ask of you. I need you to find someone in Mictlan—in the Realm of the Dead."

"Gunnar called it the Shore of Corpses," Rhea put in.

Rafe nodded patiently. "Shore of Corpses or Mictlan from my own tradition, the demon will perceive it as equivalent to his own underworld." He turned his focus back to the dragon's shade. "I need you to seek another dragon. A serpent. One projected by a living man who is of this realm." Silence followed as Rafe listened intently, frowning, before he spoke again, addressing Rhea. "He says he already knows of this man and that there are two dragons."

"Two?"

"'The dragon who gnaws is loose,' he says. I don't know what that means, but it sounds like the two are fighting."

Nidhöggr. The name came to her with certainty. *Malice Striker. The dragon that gnaws at the roots of Yggdrasil and feeds on the bones of the dead. Náströnd is his domain.*

"I need to go to him." This was what she had to do. The *hamingja* was insistent. "I need to go to the Shore of Corpses."

Ione rose from the couch. "We are *not* putting you into a magical coma so you can leave your body to go to the underworld." It was how Dev had gone below to release Phoebe's soul when Carter had sent it there, a risky move that had almost cost them both Phoebe and Dev.

"But I can help him."

Rafe rolled his shoulders, and the wings disappeared. "I'm sorry, Rhea. I can't be a party to that."

Dev inhaled sharply, as if breathing in the shade, and shook his head. "Neither can we."

Beside Dev, Ione took his hand, her expression sympathetic but firm. They were a united front against her.

"I can help you."

The others turned swiftly, startled by the sudden appearance of the redhead inside Ione's foyer, but Rhea was becoming used to her pop-up entrances.

Dev took a step toward her, his golden-brown eyes going a little dragony. "Who the devil are you?"

"She's the Valkyrie." Rhea regarded her with skepticism. "How can you help? Leo's *vördr* says you're the one who kept the *hamr* from understanding his nature."

"Of course I did. How else would I have kept his *hugr* from Wyrd?" Faye smoothed a plait of hair over her shoulder. "Be that as it may, I can escort you into Náströnd. But there is a price." Naturally. There was always a price.

"And what would that be?"

"It must be negotiated there."

Ione folded her arms. "You tell her the price now or she's not going."

Rhea gave her a warning look. "Back off, Di."

Ione's eyes widened with surprise. She was used to being the final authority in the Carlisle family.

"As long as it doesn't mean giving up my soul or staying forever on the Shore of Corpses," said Rhea, "I'm in."

Faye gave her a slight smile, the first since she'd seen her at Leo's bedside. "It will be within your power to give. No souls or lives will be asked of you."

Rhea nodded. "All right. Let's go."

Ione stepped toward her. "Rhea—"

But whatever she was going to say, Rhea never heard. Faye touched her hand and the room winked out.

Chapter 26

They stood on the shore of a dark subterranean lake.

"Watch your step."

Rhea glanced down and leaped backward from the writhing snakes covering the ground, nearly sliding into another coil of them on the rocks behind her.

She steadied herself against Faye, swallowing the urge to scream. "This was not in the brochure."

Faye pulled up her fur hood, glancing up. "And watch your head."

Globs of something black and snotty-looking dangled from the stone ceiling, slowly dripping to the ground like thick molasses. Where it struck the snakes, they hissed and writhed as if the stuff burned.

"Nidhöggr's poison."

Rhea hunched her shoulders. "How am I supposed to avoid that? I don't have a hood."

Faye sighed and removed the coat, giving it to Rhea. In its place, a more Valkyrie-like horned helmet appeared on Faye's head, leather body armor and gauntlets replacing her flowing dress. Girl was looking badass.

Rhea shrugged the coat on quickly, narrowly missing a drop of poison that slid off the fur as though deflected by it. "So how do we find Gunnar?"

"Ask the corpses."

"What cor—?" Rhea swallowed. The waves on the churning lake had grown more defined. That wasn't water. It was, as the name should have warned her, a lake of decomposing bodies.

Those still in one piece rose up from the churn, and some climbed onto the shore, slouching closer. "Whom do you seek?" They spoke as one, and the sound from the decaying mouths reminded her of the *draugr*'s roar. These, at least, were well beyond the bloating stage of decomposition and smelled more of dank, rotting plant matter than rotting flesh.

Rhea glanced at Faye. "Gunnar?"

"Nidhöggr," said the Valkyrie. "We seek the Malice Striker."

The corpses creaked and shuffled as they raised their arms together and pointed into the darkness toward a passage thick with snakes.

Faye pressed a weapon into Rhea's hand—a battle-axe that had appeared at her side, the sharp curve of the blade carved with intricate runes. "You must go alone from here."

"*What?* Wait—"

"I have brought you as far as I can. This is not my realm."

"Well, what am I supposed to do?"

"That you must figure out for yourself."

"What about the price? You said we had to negotiate."

The Valkyrie answered without any of her usual sly smiles and affectations. "Leo is the price."

Angry heat rushed to Rhea's face. "You said no souls and no lives."

"Not his life. Him. The Norns have taken him from me piece by piece—his will, his mind, his soul that I cannot touch though he lives because of me—and now you have taken his heart."

"Look, you're the one who encouraged him to seek me out as his protector. I didn't ask for him to fall in love with me. I was perfectly content on my own." She hadn't been, though. She'd thought she had, but now the idea of being without Leo was crushing.

"If you succeed here, if you bring his selves back together, if he lives…he lives with me."

Before Rhea could object, the Valkyrie was gone.

She gripped the handle of the axe and took a deep breath. There was nothing else to do but go into the tunnel. She wasn't about to stay here and hang out with the corpses, who were looking unsettlingly interested in her life force. She stepped carefully, dodging snakes, hoping none of them were poisonous, which they probably were. There was almost no light in the tunnel, just the glow of something at the other end, and there was no getting through that carpet of snakes by simply walking. Rhea's fingers closed tight around the axe. She hated the idea of killing a defenseless creature just trying to survive, but she had the feeling these weren't exactly living. And it was them or her.

She took a step and swung at anything that came toward her or wouldn't move out of her way, wielding the axe like a machete clearing brush in a jungle or a scythe cutting down wheat. There was more of the drippy goo inside the tunnel, which actually helped, since it got rid of more snakes she wouldn't have to step on or kill. The whole environment seemed fairly impractical, but it was the underworld after all. *Swing. Step. Now dodge. Swing right.* The *hamingja* was guiding her. She'd forgotten it was there. Its presence was comforting, a bit of Leo with her in the darkness.

The gloomy light at the other end grew larger, and the snakes grew fewer until at last she emerged into a sort of smoggy mist.

"Fancy meeting you here."

Rhea jumped, the axe held in both hands in front of her. "Who's there?"

A figure distinguished from the mist, short-cropped hair at the sides visible before the features of his face became clear. "I suppose the Valkyrie let you in," said Dressler. "You're too late, though. I've delivered your Leo's soul to the ruler of this realm and released Nidhöggr from the fetters that keep him here. I've just been waiting around to see the dragon emerge into the living world. Shake things up a bit." So that was his deal. Typical "embrace disruption" chaos-loving-bro bullshit.

"Don't get too excited." Rhea clutched the axe. "You're the one who's going to get shaken up." She said it with more confidence than she felt.

Dressler laughed. "What are you going to do? Swing that at me? I'm immortal, thanks to you."

Rhea swung as he spoke and the blade of the axe sliced across his thigh, cutting his laughter short. "Probably still hurts, though, huh?"

Dressler swore and stepped back, looking ready to swing his fist, but the ground beneath them rumbled with a heavy impact, and a dark, leathery beast the size of a tank barreled into view within the mist—which turned out to be smoke after all, coming from the thing's nostrils.

"Ah, here he comes now," said Dressler. "Behold— Malice Striker." There was no sign of Gunnar yet.

Rhea had to keep Dressler talking until she figured out where Gunnar was or thought of something to do. "How did you set him free?"

"With the lance, naturally. I offered him Leo's soul as tribute, an immortal warrior kept from Valhalla through a bargain with Destiny. The lance contained the *hugr*, so the dragon consumed it whole. I was a bit surprised, but it had served its purpose. And that's when he broke free."

Consumed? Rhea's heart lurched. Leo's *hugr* was gone. She really was too late.

Look to the ground. Rhea scanned the cavern floor, expecting to see more writhing snakes, but out of the corner of her eye, she saw the movement of something much larger: the Jörmungandr-Gunnar. Or Jörmungunnar. Whatever. It coiled around the larger dragon's legs, striking at the underbelly while Malice Striker thrashed its tail and roared outrage at what amounted to a pest.

She wondered if Gunnar knew the *hugr* was gone. Perhaps he'd been here in the shadows watching as Malice Striker swallowed it. How long would it be before he faded from the world? Leo might be lost, but she still owed Gunnar something.

Step in to the right and aim for the breast.

Without second-guessing the *hamingja*, Rhea followed its instructions and leaped, swinging, into the fight.

"You're wasting your time," Dressler called out. "The creature is invulnerable."

Her axe sank into the flesh between the dragon's front legs, and the dragon reared back with a roar of pain, contradicting Dressler's claim. Unfortunately, the blade stuck, and the dragon's movement yanked the handle from her hands.

Jörmungunnar went for the creature's flank, distracting it long enough for Rhea to dash in and grab hold of the handle again. She hung on tight while the dragon swung about and did the work of twisting out the blade for her. When it came loose, she dropped and rolled, her body instinctively moving at the *hamingja*'s direction. Rhea came up on her feet, the axe still gripped in front of her, to find the dragon charging her, hot smoke billowing out of its snout. Rhea screwed her eyes shut, feeling the heat of its breath, waiting for the teeth to close over her head, but instead the dragon made a yelp of pain.

She opened one eye to see Jörmungunnar at the larger dragon's throat. The serpentine body of the shifter coiled around the dragon's torso, tightening against the rib cage as the jaws clamped down. Malice Striker's wings extended with a jolt as the dragon twisted in the serpent's grasp, and they both took to the air, though the cavern ceiling was less than twenty feet high.

The smaller but more lithe creature spun the larger onto its back, and the dragon fell to the cavern floor with a ground-quaking thud. Malice Striker's claws raked the air as it struggled to breathe, and Rhea realized it was preparing to blast its foe with dragon fire.

Climb the shoulder. Between the eyes. Rhea obeyed the thought without hesitating, practically running up the side of the wheezing dragon, and swung the axe as hard as she could into the fleshy bump between its red, rage-filled eyes. Something cracked beneath the impact, and the blade sank deep. There was no way she was getting it out again. Rhea tumbled off, coming out of the roll standing once more, ready to run. But the dragon's eyes had gone dull, and a gurgling sound came from its throat—the life leaving it.

At some point during the combat, she realized, Dressler had slipped away.

Jörmungunnar hadn't moved, its jaws clamped tight to the dead dragon's throat, the aquamarine eyes blazing and wild.

"Gunnar. Let go." Rhea stroked the scaly, serpentine body. "You won. It's dead."

His eyes blinked as he tracked Rhea's movement, and the horizontal slits flattened into circular pupils, the opposite of the serpent eyes in the man's face. Beneath her hand, the scales rippled, and the serpent uncoiled while the jaws slowly loosened.

Rising onto its hindquarters, like a cobra being charmed, the serpent shuddered and shifted. And then Gunnar was standing naked before her. He'd taken some vicious swipes of the dragon's claws to his torso. He was lucky it hadn't gutted him.

Rhea stepped toward him. "You're bleeding."

Gunnar shivered as Rhea's hand touched the gashes. "It matters not. I am not real."

"Oh, bullshit." Rising on tiptoe, she slid her arms around his neck and kissed him, and Gunnar kissed her back gently, surprised. "Did that feel real?"

"But I am only the *hamr*—"

"*Hamr*, schmamr. Every single one of your selves is infuriating with this 'but I'm not a real boy' crap. You're Leo Ström. Whether you prefer to call yourself Gunnar or not. Whether you're joined with the *líkamr* or not. Whether you're solid flesh or ghostly spirit or an astral body projected in dragon form. You're Leo. So quit whining."

The surprise on Gunnar's features morphed into amusement.

Rhea glanced at the dragon's corpse. "I just wish we'd been able to save the *hugr*."

"Nidhöggr swallowed it."

"I know."

Gunnar turned toward the dragon, his gaze focused on the axe embedded in its skull. "Where did you come by that?"

"Kára lent it to me. And your *vördr* lent me your *hamingja*, so I was able to wield it."

Gunnar continued to stare at it. "It is Valkyrie-forged?"

"I guess so."

He took hold of the handle of the axe, bracing one foot

against the dragon's neck, and yanked back and forth on the weapon until he'd worked it free. Rhea watched as he approached the dragon's massive torso with the axe raised above his head in both hands and swung it in an arc, slicing the belly open.

Rhea covered her mouth and nose at the smell and backed up as Gunnar plunged his fist into the cavity. After wriggling his arm around, he drew it out, the Holy Lance clutched in his bile-covered fist.

Rhea spoke behind her hand, trying not to throw up in her mouth. "Jesus, that's gross."

"But precious." Gunnar smiled. "It still holds the *hugr* within it."

Her hand slipped away from her mouth. "It's still alive?"

"It's immortal," said Dressler behind her.

Rhea whirled. Where the hell had he been hiding?

"And you're not leaving here with it." He stepped out of the smoky haze and murmured something in Old Norse, holding his hand out toward Gunnar. The *hamr* turned pale.

"Gunnar?" Rhea took a step toward him. "What's he saying? What's the matter?"

Gunnar tried to speak, but something was happening to him, fissures forming along his cheekbones and spreading across his face.

Rhea jerked on Dressler's arm. "What are you doing to him?"

He smiled and said nothing, and Rhea watched in horror as the lance and the battle-axe fell from Gunnar's grasp, and the *hamr* crackled into a thousand gossamer filaments that fell apart and blew away.

Dressler scooped up the Holy Lance and headed for the passageway before Rhea could react.

"You son of a bitch!" She grabbed the axe and ran after him, remembering to pull up her hood as she plunged blindly through the darkness, flinging away snakes on the edges of her blade. She broke into the outer cavern upon the Shore of Corpses to find Dressler hauling back his arm with the lance in his hand as if to pitch it into the lake with the dead.

Throw it now. At the *hamingja*'s urging, she hurled the axe toward Dressler. It tumbled through the air and came down on his forearm as he brought it forward for the throw. The blade sliced clean through flesh and bone, and the Holy Lance, still in his hand, dropped with it to the ground among the snakes.

Dressler wheeled to face her, his expression furious, as though he hadn't yet felt the loss of his hand, and grabbed her with the other. "I told you, I'm immortal!"

A thick glop of black poison dropped onto his cheek, and Dressler shrieked, stumbling backward toward the lake. His flesh was sizzling away, revealing muscle and bone.

Rhea scrambled for the lance, taking it from the severed hand. "Guess not without this." She held up the relic, and Dressler made one more lunge toward her, nearly catching her off guard, but she swung her fist with the instinct of the *hamingja* and popped him right in the kisser. As Dressler tumbled back onto the shore, the bodies rose up around him and drew him into the lake.

The dead were not looking friendly. Rhea turned to flee and realized she had no way out without Faye or Gunnar.

Climb. Her eyes went toward the rocks on the far end of the cavern wall. *To the crevice.* Rhea shoved the handle of the lance into the deep inside pocket of the fur coat and scrambled up the wall toward the narrow opening in the rocks like a pro, climbing through it into a cavern of frozen mud bounded by what appeared to be the roots of a massive tree. She remembered Rafe saying the underworld was less a physical place and more of a metaphysical one, its attributes perceived as the soul expected it. So she just had to "perceive" herself once more in the realm of the living. If only it were that simple to craft one's perception.

The Lilith bond. Call upon your blood. Of course. Theia had been the one to propose it, that the power of their blood was strengthened exponentially by combining their energy. And Theia was her *fylgja*, as she was Theia's. She placed her palm over her Black Moon Lilith tattoo and pictured the one on Theia's arm, concentrating on her twin's location while sending out a psychic "broadcast" of her own. *Theia, can you hear me? I need a hand.*

At first, nothing seemed to happen, but when she sent the thought again, the frozen mud in the roots above began to crumble, revealing a fissure of light. Rhea began to dig, trying to ignore the panic of claustrophobia setting in as the crumbling earth tumbled down on her. And then her fingers met someone else's reaching into the earth from above. She clutched the hand and scrambled out into the winter air and sunlight—and tumbled into Theia.

Rhea rolled onto her back, grinning as she caught her breath. "Thanks for the hand. You just had to go literal."

Eyes wide, Theia helped Rhea to her feet, brushing the snow and dirt from her clothes. "And just where the hell have you been?"

Rhea laughed shakily. Where the hell, indeed? "Oh, just slaying dragons and punching Nazis."

They stood beneath the snow-brushed trees surrounding Rhea's apartment complex. Leo had spoken of the World Tree, in whose roots Náströnd was buried. She'd crawled up through the symbolic representation of Leo's conception of the underworld. Of Gunnar's.

Gunnar. He was gone, faded away as surely as he'd feared. She reached inside the coat and clutched the ancient piece of wood in her hand. But she had Leo's soul.

Chapter 27

Leo looked like grim death.

Rhea stood in the doorway of her bedroom, afraid she might be too late somehow, that Gunnar had been wrong and the *hugr* hadn't survived Nidhöggr's stomach. Faye, head bowed over Leo's body, still wore the armor of the Valkyrie.

Rhea closed the door and held up the lance when Faye turned at the sound. "I have it." Faye reached for it, but Rhea held the relic away. "First, we talk about your price."

Faye's eyes darkened. "You would prolong his suffering out of jealousy?"

"No, but you obviously would. You say you're banished from his side when the *hugr* isn't dormant. How do you intend to keep him bound to you with his *hugr* returned to him?"

"His *hugr* will be suppressed as it always has been, except during the hours of the Hunt. I can be with him as I was before—if you are not in his heart."

"And how do you plan to make that happen?"

"The *munr* will remain suppressed as well. When he wakes, he will already have forgotten you."

Rhea's chest felt like lead. "So you win by cheating. You can't make him love you, but you can take his love for me away with magic. That's pretty pathetic."

Faye rose, tall and menacing in her Valkyrie attire. "His

'love' for you is nothing but your own spell cast upon him, the result of your demon blood and the magical ink you used on him."

"Magical ink?"

"The ink made from the ash of Eyjafjallajökull." Faye traced the Mjölnir tattoo on Leo's wrist. "That pathetic little rodent sold it to you so you could bewitch my Leo."

The ink. *Bloodbath.* Dressler had sold it to her?

Rhea looked at Leo, wasting, unnaturally pale. It was when she'd tattooed him with the ink that they'd both felt that tingling sense of rightness. The bond that had made him come back to her when he'd meant to leave. And it had been a lie.

"Can you remove it?" she asked quietly. "The ink... I don't want it in me. Or him."

Faye narrowed her eyes. "You would break the spell that binds him to you?"

Tears blurred her vision. "I don't want him that way. I want him to have his own will, his own mind. His own heart."

Faye's demeanor softened. "I can neutralize the ink, if that is your wish. But I will need your blood."

"Just a drop, I suppose?"

"Slightly more than a drop, I'm afraid, but not enough to do you harm."

Rhea glanced down at the lance. "And not with this. It's done nothing but harm." She opened the door, nearly stumbling over Theia, who'd been standing with her ear pressed to the wood.

Theia started guiltily, hanging back while Rhea went to the kitchen to get a sharp knife.

She squeezed Rhea's hand when Rhea returned with it. "I'm sorry, Rhe. But I think you're doing the right thing."

Rhea nodded, unable to trust her voice, and closed the

door again. She handed the knife to Faye. "Do what you need to do."

"I must take the blood from the tattoo."

Rhea set her foot on the end of the bed and pushed up her legging to reveal the Black Moon Lilith. Faye sliced across the tattoo without giving her any warning, which was just as well, because Rhea hadn't expected it to go that deep, and now it was too late to object. She hissed in air through her gritted teeth in a belated reaction.

"Let the blood drip." Faye turned to Leo and made the same slash across Mjölnir. Placing one hand against his wrist and the other against Rhea's calf, she intoned, "Let the blood of influence drain into the Well of Wyrd. Let the bond between these two be broken." The red pigment of the ink began to fade as if the ink itself were bleeding out.

Rhea could feel the magic leaving her. Leo wasn't hers anymore.

As she took the lance from inside the coat, she remembered the coat wasn't hers either and took it off, handing both of them to the Valkyrie. "Give him back his soul."

Faye untaped Leo's bandage, revealing an ugly wound that was already beginning to fester, and held the point of the relic above it.

Rhea couldn't watch. She opened the bedroom door and went out, closing it behind her, and headed for the front door.

"Rhea?" Theia jumped up from the couch. "What happened? Is he okay? Rhea?"

Rhea's hand was on the doorknob when she felt a tremor inside her—the *hamingja* leaving her. She turned and sank to the carpet.

Theia grabbed a towel from the kitchen and came to blot at the blood at Rhea's calf, but Rhea shook her head.

"It has to stop flowing on its own."

Theia stared at the tattoo. "When did you do that?"

"A couple of weeks ago. I didn't know about yours. I guess great minds think alike."

Theia pushed up her sleeve and looked at her forearm. "I got this one because I had a dream. That's why I didn't come to you to have it done. I didn't want you to ask where I'd gotten the idea."

"What dream?"

"The moon was swallowed up by a snake that ate its own tail, and then the snake became a bull that you were riding, and then a wolf...and the wolf devoured you. I saw the tattoo on your skin, and the words *Black Moon Lilith* came to me, so I looked it up when I woke up. I knew it was you in the dream, but it was kind of the generic, mental you and we still looked the same. I thought if I had the tattoo, whatever it was—it would happen to me instead."

Despite her aching heart, Rhea couldn't help a little smile tugging at the corner of her mouth. She looked down to try to hide it.

Theia nudged her with her foot. "What is that look? Why are you smiling?"

"That was really sweet of you, Thei, but...you're not going to be devoured by the wolf." She met Theia's eyes. "That happened the other night, right here up against this door. And it was a-*ma*-zing."

Theia looked puzzled before understanding dawned on her. "Oh geez." She smacked Rhea's arm. "You minx."

"I had my one brief, shining moment with him, anyway. I guess that'll have to be enough."

Theia's grin faded, and she sat beside Rhea and put her arm around her. As it had always been between them, no words were necessary.

He couldn't remember where he'd gone to sleep. Leo stretched his arms, feeling incredibly rested, and opened his eyes.

Kára sat on the edge of the bed beside him. "Hello, beautiful one."

Leo sat up swiftly. There was no fog of missing memory, no sense of fragmentation. His entire long life stretched out behind him in a cohesive narrative.

"What did you do? Where's Rhea?"

"I have returned what belongs to you. That which was yours is yours again."

Leo touched his bare chest as though he could feel the pieces of himself physically inside him. "My will...my soul?"

"All there. I have bargained a final time. That Which Became is past. That Which is Happening shall not happen again. That Which Must Become...will become. Your life is yours once more, your destiny unwritten, your future finite as any mortal man's. You are free to choose with whom you will spend it." Kára's smile was sad. "You will still be the Chieftain, but you will lead the Hunt on your own terms. There will be no curse separating you from yourself."

Leo took her hand and turned it in his, stroking it. Though resentment had turned it to hate, there had been affection between them not so long ago. She had bound him to her for her own selfish reasons, but they'd been through a great deal together. Not all of it had been unpleasant.

"Why? Why now, when you have owned me for so long?"

"It seems I have been beaten at my own game. The one I accepted as your human protector stole your heart. And I see now it was not through magic as I'd thought. You gave it to her willingly. So I must do the same." Tears sparkled in her eyes in a rare display of genuine emotion. "I thought you were dead, my love. It gave me some perspective."

A tear escaped, and Leo wiped it from her cheek with his thumb and kissed the spot to say goodbye.

As swiftly and as life-alteringly as she'd first come to him on the battlefield to take him to Valhalla before choosing to spare him instead—she was gone.

Leo threaded his fingers through his hair and took his first breath of freedom. He realized he was cold—a sensation he hadn't fully experienced in a thousand years. As Leo the Dull, he'd responded to such stimuli as a mortal man should, but he hadn't really felt it.

Leo laughed aloud. *Leo the Dull.* He supposed he had been a bit. He could blame it on the suppression of his memory, but there were choices he'd made that had been his own foolish doing. Like not taking Rhea right then and there in the tattoo shop when she'd wanted it, jealous of his own unfettered desire. A mistake he intended to remedy right now.

The bedroom door opened, and Rhea lifted her head from Theia's shoulder. Leo was beautiful and whole. And wearing nothing but her lavender faux-fur robe.

"Leo." With a surreptitious swipe at her eyes, she got to her feet as he approached. "Is Faye...?"

"She's gone. For good."

Rhea stared up at him, confused. "But aren't you...? She said..."

"She's dissolved her bargain with the Norns. I'm mortal. Mostly. I'll still lead Odin's Hunt, but not as a wraith and without the associated curse."

"So you'll ride with her."

"With her?" Leo stepped in closer and rested his large hands on her hips. "*Mitt hjärta.* You are my wild, ecstatic goddess. My Freyja. I will ride with *you*, if you will come." He put his mouth below her ear, lips brushing her jaw and making every hair follicle on her skin tingle and stand erect—not to mention other parts. "I will ride with you right here, right now, if you like." The sexy growl made the meaning unmistakable.

Theia was on her feet in a flash. "Okay. So, I'm gonna go." She grabbed Rhea's keys and coat. Rhea was in no position—or condition—to complain. "See you both at Phoebe's later?"

Rhea was sure she'd made some kind of noise of assent, but she couldn't pinpoint exactly when Theia had slipped out the door. Leo's lips were against hers, nipping and sucking at them, his hands roaming over her, in her hair, at her nape, on her waist, under her shirt.

"I thought—" She tried to form sentences between his kisses. "The ink—was responsible—magic—our bond—"

Leo paused with his hands at the small of her back after unhooking her bra. "What's that, *älskling*?"

"She said you didn't really love me."

"She's out of her mind. If I loved you any more, I'd go mad and wander the earth a blithering idiot instead of a wraith. I need this off." He tugged at her shirt, and Rhea let him pull the garment over her head. The bra slipped off when she lowered her arms, and Leo cupped her breasts in his hands, completely covering them. "By the Allfather, these are fantastic. I almost can't look at them. No, I can."

She giggled involuntarily at the feathery touch of his fingers stroking the outline of her breasts as if sizing them up for a drawing. "You're different."

"No, I'm not. You're just not used to me all in one piece. Gang's all here. Though there's one particular piece..." He let out a soft groan as her hand found it. "I have your condoms," he blurted. "We could use many."

Rhea laughed, and he laughed with her, the deep, delighted abandon that made her want to climb him. She did, threading her arms around his neck and wrapping her legs around his hips as he drew her up against him, hands beneath her ass. His cock ground against her.

"You're wearing my robe."

"I know. I'm freezing."

"Maybe we should go to my room so I can warm you up."

"Good idea." Leo spun around and carried her into the bedroom, flopping backward onto the bed with her on top of him. He grinned up at her. "Condoms, yes?" He produced one from the pocket of the robe.

"Condoms, *yes*." Rhea shuffled backward, peeling off her leggings while he opened the condom and rolled it on like a pro. He was still wearing the robe, which was oddly sexy. "You're still cold," she noted as she crawled over him.

Leo smirked. "I understand most heat is lost from the top of one's…head."

"I have just the thing for that."

He reached to pull her into his lap, but Rhea slid backward off the bed and grabbed his knit hat from the top of the dresser, the gift from Phoebe and Rafe. He laughed when she shoved it onto his head.

She straddled him, perched on her knees as she stroked his cock. "Merry Christmas, Leo."

With his hands on her hips, he drew her down until she was positioned just above him. Rhea sank onto the rock-hard heat of his erection with decadent slowness, moaning as he filled her, her arousal heightened by his unabashed groan of pleasure and relief.

Leo wrapped his arms around her and hugged her against his chest, rocking her into his hips. *"God Jul, mitt hjärta,"* he murmured and kissed her hair as he drove himself deliciously deeper. *"God Jul."*

* * * * *